The Philomel Foundation

The Philomel Foundation

JAMES GOLLIN

St. Martin's Press/New York

Library of Congress Cataloging in Publication Data

Gollin, James.
  The Philomel Foundation.

  I. Title.
PZ4.G6464Ph   [PS3557.0445]   813'.5'4   79-22868
ISBN 0-312-60428-9

To the memory of my mother

The Philomel Foundation

Should the student in listening to other music
acquire more discriminating taste, he is thence-
forth revolted by the pieces he must practice. . . .

> KARL PHILIPP EMANUEL BACH, *The True Art of Playing Keyboard
> Instruments*, p. 31.

CHAPTER ONE

ONCE UPON A TIME in New York City, four young men and one young
woman got themselves together to perform old music upon old musical
instruments. Instruments like recorders and viols and lutes and krummhorns and harpsichords. All five members of this enterprise were
mildly insane: first, because playing such instruments beautifully is
hard, specialized work even for trained professional musicians, which
we are; second, because even the most remarkable performances of
early music, though they may make critics happy and audiences ec-
static, enrich no one, least of all the performers. So, as well as being the
members of the Antiqua Players, all five of us—as you'll see—do
whatever else we can on the fringes of the music industry.

My name is Alan French. I'm one of the five eccentrics just mentioned. And what I've just said helps explain what I'm doing in front of
a small group of would-be recorder players at ten o'clock in the
morning, with last night's coffee warming on the stove and a February
sun promising nothing to Amsterdam Avenue outside my studio windows. I'm one of the lucky ones, because I can play instruments other
than the recorder. In fact, thanks to a persistent mother, I learned both
flute and violin when I was small enough not to rebel. And I can fool
around on a couple of other modern instruments and on almost every
one of the ancient instruments I've come across except the lute. This
makes me a good candidate for the classical gigs that are always turning
up around town: the one-day recording sessions with name soloists and

pickup orchestras ($121 for fifteen minutes of product), the fill-ins in theater orchestras ($53.12 a night), the low-budget live performances for student audiences ($79). And to keep the income steady, I teach. Counting group classes and private pupils, I've got about forty students. They pay the rent and buy the wine. They even learn music. And besides giving me the time I need to do what I want to do, they give me a long look at the strange side of life. Believe me, they do.

By ten-thirty, I had demonstrated to my newest songsters that most of what they were doing was wrong and had shown them what to do to make it right. By eleven, they were struggling through a simple piece—a pavane by Anthony Holborn—and you could begin to hear who was a potential musician and who wasn't. Sylvia's talents clearly lay in some other area. Apollo, however, had good fingers and good ears. Get him off of whatever he was on (amphetamines, probably), and he would learn. As for Nancy, I couldn't be sure. Her playing was ladylike, as neat as her brown hair and her Provincetown sandals. But something about her tone on the recorder and her phrasing hinted that she might be holding back. I hoped so, because in music you can't be a lady; you have to be a woman. On Nancy, I reserved judgment.

By eleven-fifteen, I had collected my ten dollars from each of them and shooed them out. In this trade, it's cash or nothing. Either you're mean-fisted or you starve. So when Apollo said, "Man, can I lay twenty on you next time?" I just shook my head. He looked pathetic, but he dug down in his jeans and came up with a crumpled five and five singles. I guess he'll be back.

There was time for a cup of coffee and a shave before my noon lesson. This one was with Judy Pepper, a private pupil who had the money for the most expensive recorders on the market, but neither the time nor the taste to learn how to play them well. Still, I was her *Kapellmeister*, and I had to shave. To put off the moment, I went downstairs for the mail. Concert notices, a bill for the telephone, a blurb for a credit card that they'd never give me even if I asked for the privilege of paying twenty-four percent a year. A letter in a creamy off-white envelope.

It could have been a notice telling when your sister's baby was born, except that my sister's baby played bass with the San Francisco Symphony. Or an announcement telling you when to be at the chapel and what to do after the ceremony. But no one I knew would be planning a church wedding. Nor did any drum tap or horn blow to tell me to hold back. Life doesn't work that way, does it? In fact, I opened that letter so quickly that I didn't even notice the foreign stamp.

In chaste blue, the letterhead admitted that my correspondent was "The Philomel Foundation." The name was totally unfamiliar, but that in turn signified nothing. There must be thousands of foundations that I've never heard of. What mattered was that this one had heard of me. "Through your writings and disks," its letter said, "your outstanding work in the field of preclassical music performance has become well known to us." Whoever they were, the Philomel people must subscribe to some of the choicest little arts magazines ever to be peddled in SoHo. My writings, including a current essay on the parallels between the early Beatles and the music of Guillame de Machaut (1300–1372), appear nowhere else. As for disks, we've made exactly three records. One of Elizabethan dances, one of Burgundian court music, and the third—the one that was going to be a huge hit and make us all rich—of medieval Christmas music. But this had been several years ago. The record company had long since collapsed gently into a snowdrift of unpaid bills. As far as I knew, the records were slowly crumbling into vinyl dust in a Long Island City warehouse.

However, on with the letter. "The Philomel Foundation is known in Europe for its interest in subsidizing promising music research and performance. By our Festival Exchange Program, we hope to succeed in furthering the spread of interest in the music among many countries."

Now, the payoff. "Yours is one of the performing groups we are desirous of sponsoring in a series of performances of ancient music. The schedule would include concerts in possibly two or three cities and also free periods in which you could conduct research. We would be prepared to offer, in addition to all travel expenses, the amount of twelve thousand dollars ($12,000 U.S.) as an honorarium for your participation in our program. Your engagement would begin April 1 and would continue for a period of approximately four weeks. If you are interested in participating, we suggest that you contact immediately our American representative, Mr. Walter Mundel. He will be most pleased to disclose further information and to assist you in making all necessary arrangements."

The final paragraph gave the address and telephone number of Mr. Walter Mundel and begged me to accept its author's most distinguished salutations. Under a neat signature in green ink was typed "Dr. Hugo Flachsmann, *Programdirektor.*"

It may be that the mark of the true professional in music is mild paranoia. At least, my first reaction to the Philomel Foundation and to

Herr Doktor Flachsmann was to go into the kitchen, pour myself a cup of tepid coffee, and sit down to figure out exactly what was wrong with the entire proposition. Strange, but the first thing that popped into my mind was another unlikely episode in my career. Once, after a concert, the trustees of whatever-it-was that was sponsoring us threw a party for the musicians. It was a noble effort, with all the daughters and daughters-in-law of the biggies brought in to enliven things. I was just pouring myself a cup of punch when I brushed knuckles with one of the daughters-in-law. She looked at me. Five minutes later, we were upstairs in one of the bedrooms making love. When it was all over, she stepped into her skirt, ran a comb through her hair, and said, "Don't you think you better join the others?" Somehow, I caught the same flat sound in the voice of the Philomel Foundation.

Their price was right, but the way the letter quoted it was all wrong. I've done some business with foundations and other charities, and every time they mention money, they start by saying, "Of course, our funds are necessarily limited," or words to that effect. Then the bargaining can begin. But the Philomel Foundation didn't bargain. First, a little bit of flattery. Then a price. As if they really didn't care what fee they promised. Which could mean that they'd be equally careless about actually paying what they said they'd pay.

That was one thing to worry about. Another thing was the buttery but faintly peremptory tone of the letter. So many patrons love to talk to artists in this special way: a little massaging of the ego, a generous offer, and the assumption that of course the poor sod will accept. Ever since the Esterhazys—hell, ever since the pharaohs—that's been the accepted routine of communication between people of property and the others whom such people call creative. The ritual works as well in the days of foundations and federal grants as it ever did in Haydn's day. Except for geniuses like Mozart and suspicious bastards like me.

I'll say in my own favor that for several minutes that morning, I was ready to throw away the letter and forget about twelve thousand dollars and a month in Europe in the spring. But, in the end, reason prevailed. While I was trying to decide what to do next about the Philomel Foundation, the downstairs buzzer rang. It was Judy Pepper, with a case full of beautiful recorders and no talent. And I hadn't shaved, after all.

If the accompanist does not look ahead as he should,
error will be avoided only by good fortune.

K.P.E. BACH, p. 219.

CHAPTER TWO

BY SIX O'CLOCK THAT EVENING, I still hadn't shaved, but I had done
some other things. First, I had given Judy Pepper her lesson. This
always takes longer than an hour. Judy had the luggage-maker line her
pigskin attaché case with green velvet fittings, so she could nestle her
recorders inside like rare antiques. By the time Judy gets out her
instruments and puts them together, the lesson is half over. I don't
really mind, because Judy makes no real demands on me for music. Her
husband approves her dresses, her cooking instructor coos over her
copper pots, and her music teacher's job is to admire her taste in the
utensils of music.

This time, Judy had acquired a treble viol. "Isn't it elegant?" she
said as she unlocked its case, "I just couldn't resist it." I couldn't tell
whether she meant the case, a little rosewood coffin with red velvet
upholstery, or the viol itself, which had a little carved head instead of a
scroll at its top. Judy wanted me to stop teaching her the recorder and
teach her the viol instead. It took me nearly three-quarters of an hour to
convince her that to struggle with a stringed instrument would only
frustrate her and waste her talent. Then, when I tuned up the viol and
played it for her, it took another ten minutes to persuade her not to *give*
it to me. That would have been her supreme sacrifice.

By the time I bundled Judy and her treasures out the door, it was three
o'clock. Time for my house call on Riverside Drive. I give guitar
lessons to the two little daughters of a psychiatrist. They also paint and
do ballet, and their mother is deep into soft sculpture. I hope the

doctor's practice is flourishing. It takes end-to-end sessions to support the arts on this scale.

The Philomel letter was still burning a hole in my pocket at six, when I got back to the studio and settled down to do some serious telephoning. *Doktor* Flachsmann, remember, wanted not just a soloist but the whole consort. I could supply the consort, all right, but it would take more than a notice on a rehearsal-hall bulletin board. First, I had to get us together. Next, I had to outline the possibilities. Then would come the question of who was available and who wasn't. Finally, we had to agree on the terms of the deal and check on my new friends at the Philomel Foundation. Only if we could work out the preliminaries was there any sense in holding even one rehearsal. And in some ways Step One, convening the Antiqua Players, was the hardest.

"Hello. Is David there?"

"Who?"

"David Brodkey. This is—"

"Naw. David isn't here. He moved out last week."

"Do you know a phone number where I can reach him?"

"Naw. Try his mother's out in Atlantic Beach."

David's mother hadn't heard from David in six months, not since his father came home from the hospital. If I got in touch with David, could I please ask him to call home? Not that that horrible girl would be any more welcome today than she was when David brought her home six months ago. Carol something or Sue something. But would I please ask David to call his mother?

I called the first number again. "Tell David it's Alan French." There was a pause while this message was relayed to some scabrous corner of the cold-water flat. How did I know it was a cold-water flat? I know David Brodkey, that's how.

"H'lo," he said mournfully.

"David," I said, "it's time you vonce again learned how to laugh." My Slavic accent has improved very little over the years.

"Ha, ha," David said. "What's new?"

"Maybe there's a concert deal you'd be interested in," I told him cautiously.

"So when do rehearsals start?" Usually, David pawns his instruments after a concert and only buys them back when a new concert seems imminent. He rehearses on any instrument he can borrow, but he likes to use his own in front of an audience.

"Don't worry," I said, "you don't have to see Jake for a couple of weeks." Jake was the *luthier*, the violin maker, who repossessed David's lute between concerts. He also held on to David's wooden flute and recorders. Sometimes David did repair work in his shop.

"Sounds good," David said. "I'll be over later, about eleven. And I'll bring my new chick. She's class like you, Alan. You'll really like her a lot."

"Later," I said. "This is business." The last time David brought a girl to rehearsal, he spent the whole time showing off to her. *She* spent the whole time getting stoned.

All told, it took fourteen telephone calls and two hours. But in the end, all four of the other members of the Antiqua Players had pledged themselves to show up at the studio of their peerless leader for a meeting and rehearsal. By this time, I didn't feel like a leader of any description. My ear was itching from the telephone, my throat was dry from all that conversation, and my morale was low. So I made one more call, to the delicatessen. I ordered six liverwurst sandwiches on plain rye, six ham and swiss on seeded rye, two six packs of beer and one of cream soda. As an afterthought, I ordered a dozen plain Danish pastries. One thing preclassical musicians are is hungry.

As always, Jackie was the first to arrive. Jackie is a tall girl, five-seven or thereabouts, who really does look like Jacqueline Kennedy Onassis; the same squarish face, the same bright eyes. Only this Jackie, whose last name is Craine, has a specialty even more rarefied than that of Mrs. Onassis. She is, with the possible exception of an elderly gentleman in Basel, Switzerland, the finest viola da gamba player in the world. The gamba is the biggest and clumsiest of the viols, almost as big as a cello. But the gamba has no floor spike to hold it up; you prop it between your knees. To play a gamba, or even to lug one around, calls for a certain amount of stamina. To play it well, and to look elegant in the process, you almost *have* to be a tall, leggy girl with beautiful hands and arms and a hank of blue-black hair falling forward to frame your sensitive face.

Well, that's our Jackie. She's never late for a rehearsal, she never forgets her music, she never misses an entrance, and I've never heard her put anyone down. She can interpret timetables, sew on buttons, and make excellent coffee. Jackie sustains us all, and music sustains her, that and nothing more. Just once, when she was washing up the coffee cups after a rehearsal break, I came up behind Jackie and put my arms around that fine body. She didn't stiffen, squeak, or grow indignant. She just said, "no," with the same unhurried timing and the same unemphatic force she'd use to bow an upbeat. That was all for Alan. When she came in, Jackie looked pale and a little thinner. But she stood her gamba up in its usual corner and made her usual face at the empty coffee cups and the full ashtrays. She had been teaching in a girls' school on Long Island, and we hadn't seen each other for six months. But that made no difference.

"Alan, how can you *live* like this?" she asked me as she began shuttling between the studio and the kitchen. "I couldn't stand it." She can't, either. Jackie lives in a one-room apartment in the Village. It's packed with books, music, a huge stereo, and even a tiny harpsichord. The kitchen is in a closet. But when you go up there for dinner— Jackie's curries and pilafs have conned reviews out of critics who've snubbed our kind of music for decades—the place is as uncluttered as a Mondrian.

"It's a sex difference," I said. She snorted, but she kept on emptying ashtrays and poking at the pillows on my couch until, as she put it, the place looked decent. Then she subsided into a chair, pushed her hair back behind her ears and looked expectant. "What's the story?"

With Jackie, you don't fool around. I handed her the Philomel letter. Like many musicians, Jackie reads slowly. "Oh, wow!" she said when she finished it. Jackie was ten years too old to use teenage expressions, but she used them anyway, and with her ear for sound they come out just right. "Alan in the big time," she said. I winced, and she burst out laughing. "The trouble with you," she said, "is that you're *too* damn paranoid. You won't take yes for an answer."

Coming from Jackie, who turns down concerts right and left because she can't stand the ego trips and the childishness of most musicians, this was laughable. I was telling her so when the doorbell rang. It was the delicatessen, with the sandwiches and drinks. I dug out the money, and Jackie disappeared into the kitchen to put the stuff on a platter in the refrigerator. This took her five minutes, four of them spent washing a perfectly clean platter. When she came out, she said, "Seriously, Alan, you're going to take it, aren't you?"

"Only if the right people come along," I said. "You, for instance."

She looked worried. "I don't know if I should."

"What's the matter, performance neurosis?"

She laughed. "You know me better than that. No, it's just that I've got this teaching thing—"

"Look, Jackie. If this Philomel is for real, it's for one month, April. You've got a dozen pupils who'd be thrilled to fill in for you. Besides, we need you." Meaning in particular, I need you. To back us all up with that silvery bass sound no one else ever gets out of a gamba. And to keep us sane. What Jackie was really saying was, the music is fine but I'm not sure I can stand being house mother to Alan French and three other idiot musicians for a month. I didn't blame her a bit. But if Jackie turned down the tour, it was a lost cause. So, snaky Alan would have to convince her.

"When's the last time you made it to Europe?"

"Four years ago, on that summer fellowship."

"Well, this is your chance to go back not as a starving music student."

Jackie looked at me reproachfully. "It's so tempting. Don't make me make up my mind right this minute."

"Relax," I said, "the others don't even know about the letter yet. And even if everybody wants to go, we still don't make a move without checking out the Philomel Foundation. It could be a phony proposition. And if we do go, we go in style. *They* do the bookings, *they* get the hotels, *they* supply the transportation. It won't be anything like the college circuit."

Jackie giggled. "Remember the Cornell bus?" None of us would ever forget that ride. On the bus with us was our competition, an acid-rock quartet, complete with its equipment and its harem of groupies. It was the dead of winter, and there was no heat in the bus except what the passengers could generate. By the time we got halfway to Ithaca, the front of the bus looked like a scene from Hogarth. We had protected Jackie's virtue only by capturing and holding as a hostage the lead guitarist's four-thousand-dollar amplifier.

"Well, this is going to be different, and let's not talk about it until the others get here." While we were waiting, we set up the stands and Jackie warmed up. She'd gotten even better in the six months since we'd last played together.

Just as she was working her way through one of Thomas Simpson's sets of variations, Ralph Mitchell signaled his arrival by whistling four bars along with her in imperfect harmony. "God, it's been a long time since I've heard anything like that," Ralph said. He was wearing a suede pullover with fringed sleeves and tight, tight leather pants. "I've been *repetiting* Respighi for *weeks* over at the barn." The barn is one of the city's most respected schools of ballet. A professional company trains there, and through a friend Ralph had gotten a job as an assistant *repetiteur*, playing the piano for the dancers at rehearsals.

Ordinarily, Ralph stays away from such routine musical chores. His father, a textile millionaire from Georgia, can't abide Ralph's homosexuality and blames music for leading his boy astray. But he bit down hard on his pride and eventually set up a trust fund. It keeps Ralph in a Fifth Avenue apartment, a small one, and it would finance any normal musical career. The trouble is, Ralph is into harpsichords, which is like being into vintage Rolls Royces. A good modern harpsichord can cost eight or nine thousand dollars. One that dates from the Golden Age of harpsichord building—about 1650 to 1780—is at least as expensive to acquire. To restore an old harpsichord properly once you've bought it, you'll pay perhaps another five thousand.

Over the past few years, Ralph has been trading up. He turned in his brand-new Neupert Model Vivaldi for a sensational instrument, also modern, built to order by John Dowd in Boston. The swap set him back about seven thousand dollars. Then, on a trip to England, he found a genuine Kirkmann, dated 1742, in the back room of a junk shop. When the unsuspecting proprietor accepted one hundred pounds for it, Ralph was delirious. He spent eighteen hundred dollars to have it crated and shipped to New York by air, and two years and another four thousand making it playable. When you're this kind of a maniac, you *need* a trust fund. And sometimes even a trust fund isn't enough. Whenever Ralph takes a job—unlike most dilettantish musical types, he's a fine and industrious performer—you know he has his eye on another expensive harpsichord.

"What is it this time?" Jackie asked him.

"Oh, God, don't even ask. It's this friend of mine in Amsterdam. He's found an old Ruckers spinet for me, and, like a fool, I cleaned out my bank account and cabled him a deposit. If father finds out, he'll disown me. But I have to finish paying for it and go over and get it ready for shipment. The whole thing really is ghastly. But a Ruckers would be marvelous, so I've got to go through with it somehow."

Aha! I thought, welcome to the Philomel Foundation spring tour. Jackie was eyeing me to see what I was going to say to Ralph. But I kept well away from the real object of the meeting. David and Terry Monza, Terry being our fifth distinguished young American artist, might as well be there when I made my speech. If there were going to be problems, maybe group solidarity would help me solve them.

As it turned out, there were no problems. First Terry showed up, then David. Terry was thinking of giving up music and going straight. His uncle runs one of the fanciest Italian restaurants in Queens. If Terry would promise to cut his hair, he could be an assistant manager; on the job five evenings a week, sleep until noon and earn twelve thousand honest dollars a year.

David would never go straight. But his high-class new girl, Rhoda from Woodmere, had big plans for him. She wanted to set him up as the owner of a boutique in the East Village where all her friends from Woodmere could go to buy clothes and make the youth scene. "You could still play your music," she told him, "like I mean the kids would go wild." Luckily for me, plans like that always made David a little nervous.

And so, when I read the letter aloud, everybody except Jackie said the equivalent of "oh, wow!" The consensus was that the Antiqua Players should be, and thereupon was, reconstituted; that all members should redeem, procure, or otherwise obtain their musical instruments and accessories; and that Alan French, who had once again proven his expertise in the musical marketplace, should take the next step of investigating the Philomel Foundation and arranging the contract. The arrangement should please include a free stopover in Amsterdam for Ralph. Terry would postpone his redemption. David would try cryogenics on Rhoda from Woodmere. And Jackie? "You think you're so damn charismatic, Alan," she said.

"Me, charismatic?"

"Yes, you. Christus Jesu," she said. "Of course I'll come."

And we all sat around eating up the delicatessen sandwiches and drinking cream soda and planning the music until three-thirty in the morning. Like a bunch of kids from Juilliard.

Many instruments do not produce a perfect, pure tone
unless a strong touch is employed.

K.P.E. BACH, p. 149.

CHAPTER THREE

THE BUILDING ITSELF was pleasantly nondescript. As a creaky elevator
hauled me up to the sixth floor, I felt reassured. No fake foundation
would ever house itself in surroundings this shabby. So the Philomel
Foundation must be real. And Mr. Walter Mundel must be real, too.

But when I opened the door to Mundel's office, I began to worry all
over again. There must be patrons of renaissance and baroque music
who can afford two-inch-thick white carpets and crystal ashtrays in
their reception rooms. Not to mention Klee paintings. But I'd never met
any before. I told myself that the carpet was Acrilon and the Klee a
reproduction, props meant to inspire proper awe in peasants like me.
But the receptionist was no reproduction. From her pale blonde hair
right down to her Gucci shoes, she was one of a kind. Even though my
suit was pressed, my tie neat, and my hair trimmed, I still felt exactly
like one of the peasantry.

"Oh, Mr. French," she said when I gave her my name, "we've
been looking forward to meeting you." Her English was faintly accented, and she wore the accent like a delicately costly perfume.
"Please wait," she entreated me. "Let me tell Mr. Mundel that you've
arrived." She pushed an ivory button on her rosewood desk. "*Ici
Monsieur French*," she cooed to somebody. "*Oui. Oui. C'est com-
pris.*" She stopped pushing the button and gave me a delicious smile.
"Mr. Mundel is coming out himself in just one moment."

Mundel himself, when he appeared, hardly seemed to justify the
carpet or the Klee, or the receptionist. He was a tired-looking little
man, with thinning gray hair combed straight back and rimless eyeglas-

13

ses. On the other hand, he didn't look like any of the booking agents or artists' representatives I'd even done business with before. And his office was as elaborately simple as the reception area. He had a plain modern table instead of a desk, stainless steel and leather to sit on, and a single rose in a crystal vase to please the eye. On his table, he had piled the modest heap of scores, phonograph records, and other landmarks in the musical life of Alan French and the Antiqua Players, plus a surprisingly thick dossier. Obviously, Mundel had done some homework. And he came right to business.

"We assume that the terms of the arrangement are acceptable to you and your associates, Mr. French." It wasn't a question. I'd only just begun to ask my own question when Mundel continued smoothly, "Very good. Here is the schedule we have prepared for you." He slid a sheet of paper across the table. "You will leave the evening of March thirty-first. First-class reservations on Swissair flight #344 have already been booked for five. You will arrive in Geneva at 10:20 A.M. Hotel accommodations at the International Plaza are arranged. A reception is being scheduled that evening. Rehearsal facilities will be made available at the University. Your first concert is tentatively booked for the evening of April 5, if that will be convenient, at the Festspielhaus. Alternative dates are the sixth and ninth. Your tour begins the twelfth. You will be performing in Montricher on the thirteenth and in Markneukirchen, East Saxony, on the twenty-eighth. These are only the only firm dates. Other appearances are bookable on an informal basis—for additional fees, of course. Otherwise, you may if you wish simply lecture, do research, or see the sights. You return to Geneva on the twenty-ninth and leave for New York that evening."

"Wait a minute, Mr. Mundel," I finally managed to break in. "This all sounds marvelous. But before we get into all of the details, I've got some questions. I mean, for instance, who is the Philomel Foundation?"

Mundel smiled thinly. "I'm not surprised that you have not heard of us, Mr. French. Ours is not a large organization, or one that is, how do you say, publicity-minded. But we do exist, Mr. French, I assure you. And in good time, you will learn all you need to know about us." He pressed the ivory button on his telephone. "Marianne," he said, "bring in the contracts for Mr. French. And the check." He turned to me with another smile. "The best argument for our existence, my dear Mr. French, is our readiness to proceed."

The contracts were typed up on creamy paper. While Mundel waited smiling, I thumbed through the pages. In legalese, they confirmed the arrangements already spelled out in the letter. Pinned to the top copy was a check for four thousand and no one-hundredths dollars U. S. drawn on the Credit Suisse of Zurich, Special Account, payable to Alan French. "This, of course, is only an advance. Nonreturnable, I might add. It will cover your initial expenses of preparing a program and rehearsal. The balance is payable on arrival in Geneva." Mundel produced a silver-barreled pen from his inside breast pocket. "If this is satisfactory, Mr. French, simply place your signature here, here, and here." He handed me the pen. I hate signing things. But I signed.

"This is excellent, Mr. French," Mundel said, retrieving his pen and carefully screwing the top back on. Again he pressed his ivory button. "Marianne. Mr. French has completed the contracts." A moment later, the receptionist came in, went over to the table, picked up the sheaf of papers and, neatly detaching one copy and the check, which she handed to me, took the rest outside. "Thank you, Mr. French," she said. "Thank you," I said inanely.

"Now, Mr. French, if you will from time to time notify this office in writing of your preliminary expenses, these will be reimbursed according to agreement. We're very prompt about such things. But we do hope your accounts will be reasonable. And perhaps you and your associates will give me the pleasure of dining with me the evening of your departure. Nothing elaborate, you understand. Just a little preliminary celebration. Now I must excuse myself. But do not doubt us, Mr. French, we are real." He wagged his forefinger at me, then used it to press his button. I stood up. By the time Marianne appeared, I was halfway through the door. We nearly collided, and for a moment her elegant face wore a confused look. Then she gave me a ravishing smile. "*Pardonnez-moi, M'sieu,*" she said. "*Je t'en prie,*" I said back. The French, I've found, loathe being addressed in French by non-Frenchmen, and Marianne would naturally detest being *tutoyer'd* by any stranger. But I couldn't resist trying to dent her aplomb.

It was a relief to board the elevator, travel lurchingly to the lobby, and escape into the shabby street. After Mundel and Marianne, it was a positive pleasure to locate a coffee shop, settle down at the steamy counter, and negotiate with a Clairol blonde waitress for a cup of inky coffee. It was a contrary pleasure to sip the coffee, refusing virtuously to order a Danish, with four thousand dollars tucked away in my wallet. Besides, I needed to think.

Musicians, even more than actors, learn to live with fear. Fear of hitting a wrong note, fear of forgetting the part, fear of the audience. You kid yourself about your fear. You call yourself neurotic or label your fear simply stagefright. You do things to overcome it. But no matter what, if you're a musician you become a connoisseur of fear, in yourself and in others. That's why I needed the coffee, and the time to get my thoughts together. Marianne had smiled the right smiles, murmured the right phrases, and walked the right walk. But when I nearly bumped into her, she shrank back as though a cat were stalking over her grave. Mundel himself, behind his Swiss correctness, had been as nervous as the same cat. My signing the contract had nothing to do with it. If anything, he'd become more tense afterward.

"Want more coffee?" If the homely waitress in her blue smock hadn't leaned over the counter at just that moment, I might have gone back across the street and called the whole deal off. But there she was, as unwholesome and as reassuring as New York itself. If she could survive, I could. I sighed and asked for more. They were all out of cinnamon Danish, so I had cheese Danish instead.

There are many who play stickily, as if they
had glue between their fingers.

K.P.E. BACH, p. 149.

CHAPTER FOUR

THE DAY AFTER MY INTERVIEW, David Brodkey visited the foul-smelling shop of Jake the *luthier* (who insists on using hide glue, which is
what makes his shop so foul-smelling), and redeemed his lute. The day
after that, Ralph Mitchell bade the ballet school farewell for the nonce.
Four of Ralph's slender young friends moved his harpsichord across
town and into my studio, and Ralph moved in, too. In two more days,
Ralph had cleaned up the whole apartment. I talked him out of new
slipcovers for the chairs, but he did rent a forty-eight-cup coffee urn to
save trips to the kitchen. Terry Monza got his brother to fill in for him at
Emilio's in Queens, and Jackie took over as treasurer. And the Antiqua
Players were in rehearsal.

Other musicians, seasoned professionals, swear that our rehearsals
are insane. "Not even Toscanini makes people do the things you do,"
one oboist friend insisted. He's right, but we're not a 120-piece orchestra. What holds us together is the awareness that old music can't
possibly be faked. It's chamber music, subtle and nuanced. To sound
right, a chamber group has to do more than execute well. Its members,
whatever they're like as individuals, must be as close to each other as
the fingers of one hand. So our rehearsals are maddening. Sometimes
we're all high and the music has the special velvety sheen it should
have. Sometimes only one of us is off and we get away with it.
Sometimes the whole thing sounds like a bunch of silly people making
silly nursery noises. That's when I have to step in.

"O. K. everybody, take ten for chili." That was the night, three
years ago, when my oboist buddy decided we were all insane. But we

all put down our instruments, put on our coats, and fared forth for a thick china bowl of the hottest chile in North America. But don't look for the source, because two years ago Rafael Ortiz was bulldozed into a heap of smashed white tile and was urban renewed all the way back to Calexico.

Then there was the time we all did Yogic exercises for two hours. We were cutting rough tapes in a rented studio. But we were so nervous that I finally decided the hell with it. So while the minutes ticked away at two dollars each, we all got down on the floor, squeezed ourselves into the lotus position, and practiced various *asanas*. When the manager, peering through the glass of the control booth, saw what we were doing, he nearly called the cops. But the sound engineer came to our rescue.

This time, things didn't wait until our nerves were frayed. On the third day of rehearsal, Jackie stopped dead in the middle of a passage, stuck her bow under the strings of her gamba, and said, "I'm sorry. I'm just not *relating* to any of you people." Naturally, everything came to a stop. If David clowns around or Terry cracks up, it's one thing. But Jackie is the motor that keeps the rest of us moving. I decided to assert myself.

"What's bugging you?" someone asked.

"Christus, I don't know. Yes, I do. It's you." She looked at me.

"What's the problem?"

"Nothing, that's just it. You sound dead."

The trouble was, she was right. I'd told none of the others, not even Jackie, about Mundel and his strangeness. I'd given the check to Jackie and explained the arrangements to everybody, but I'd kept my worries to myself. Now music was letting out the secret. Not in ways that you could hear, but in tiny little flaws: an entry a split-second behind the beat, a vibrato a shade too impassioned for the music. A lot of the work in music is gaining control over your own ears, so that you can hear what you really sound like. If you're distracted, you stop listening to yourself and everybody else. Then the distraction shows. That's what Jackie had heard.

"Stick around for some head shrinking after the rehearsal," I told her. We went on working, but I dropped out and forced myself to listen. Without me, they sounded better.

About ten, Terry and Dave left and Ralph went off to one of his parties, leaving Jackie and me peacefully alone. I drew her a paper cup of coffee from the urn, shoved the cream container in her direction and sipped at my own cup. Before she sat down, Jackie finished rosining her bow and put it carefully away. Then she dropped into a chair. "What's wrong?" she asked. I didn't want to tell her. Instead, for about the ninety-fifth time I wanted to ask her how she managed to keep her long hair from getting tangled in the strings when she played. Or how she kept her eyes so bright and her complexion so girlish in an atmosphere consisting mostly of cigarette smoke. But I denied myself and told her about Mundel. To my surprise, she laughed. "I don't blame him for being nervous," she said. "Look who he's doing business with. I mean, he probably thought he'd get a call from some big agent representing you, and here you walk in yourself and just sign on the dotted line. That must have flipped him out."

"I had the feeling he expected me," I said.

"Even so, you do come as a bit of a shock."

"Listen, I'll have you know I shaved and put on a necktie."

"Well, never mind. The first check cleared and we'll have round-trip tickets."

"But Jackie, he was really scared. As if someone or something was really threatening him."

"If you ask me, you're the one who's scared."

"I am, in a way. I don't know this guy, and I'm supposed to take four other people with me on a tour out of the country."

"That's not what you were telling me two weeks ago. Two weeks ago, you were saying that this was your chance, mine I mean, to get back to Europe with money and really enjoy it. So I canceled everything for May and got out of lessons to rehearse and started to look forward to the trip. Now you're copping out." She looked at me as sternly as Jackie can ever look. "I even bought a new long dress," she added disconsolately.

What could I say? I said, "Look. I'm not saying we shouldn't go. I'm saying that there's something strange going on. We should keep our eyes open, that's all."

"With you, there's always something strange going on. You keep your eyes open when you're asleep. Well, don't be so damn suspicious. And you better start to practice, because we're *going*."

Oddly enough, after Jackie finished I felt better. Mundel was an oddball, but so is everyone in music. As for that dig about practicing, Jackie was right. Not that I have any daily dozen to do, but there was some passage-work in one of the suites that needed looking over. "Okay," I said. "I've done my duty. But do me a favor, will you? If we get a chance, I'd like you to meet Mundel. Tell me what you think of him." I picked up my flute and blew a little riff. For the first time that night, it sounded like music.

"Hey, pretty good," Jackie said. "You think you're out of your gloom?"

"Maybe," I said. So we tried the two outer parts of one of the weird little syncopated dances we usually play to open a program. And it sounded great. In this music, you have to throw away phrase after phrase the way an actor throws away his choicest lines. If you can't let things go, you sound earnest and dull. All of a sudden that night, Jackie and I were letting go. I don't think we've ever played better than we did then, all alone in the studio with no one but ourselves to hear.

This is the hidden heart of music that only musicians know, the beating heart that speaks quietly beneath the pleasing, exciting noises other people hear. With her music, Jackie was telling me things. About her childhood in the small Indiana town where her father ran the drugstore, and the wide streets with no curbs and the big trees, and playing the piccolo in the high school band. About the train trips up to Chicago and sitting at night in Ravinia Park to hear the Chicago Orchestra, and then back to saw away at the cello while other evenings descended on the lawn outside her window and the summer crickets began their song. About winning the scholarship to Oberlin and the strangeness of Ohio after Indiana and the sophistication of the kids from the East who had had private lessons ever since they could walk. The men she had met, nearly all of them musicians, and the two or three she had slept with, and that was strange, too. And it was strange to learn that she, not the others, had talent—"Maybe it's our milk in Indiana," her mother had said—and strangest of all to come to New York and play so well and be so young and live alone.

We're professionals, but it happens to us just as if we were kids learning our first little songs. What my playing had told Jackie, I had no idea. But we both knew, after we quit playing, that things were rearranging themselves between us. It suddenly didn't seem like such a bad idea to go trouping off to Switzerland with this girl and our little platoon of minstrels. And Mundel could be dealt with in the cool light of day.

Jackie finished tucking away her gamba, closed up the case, and put on her coat. She did this all quite gracefully, I noticed. On her way to the door, she stopped in front of me and looked at me gravely. I noticed that one of her eyebrows had a tiny tuft of hair sticking up like a miniature cowlick. Then Jackie kissed me on the mouth, picked up her paraphernalia, and slipped out the door. It didn't even squeak when it closed behind her. After she left, I practiced for two hours and went to bed.

Never undertake more than can be kept under
control in a public performance.

K.P.E. BACH, p. 151.

CHAPTER FIVE

THE COUCH IN WALTER MUNDEL'S living room was a small marvel of
space-age craftsmanship in chrome steel and soft black hippopotamus
hide. It was two horizontal couples long. Occupying it at the moment I
arrived were Ralph Mitchell, a friend of Ralph's named Paul (I thought
I recognized him as one of Ralph's harpsichord movers), Terry Monza,
and David Brodkey's girlfriend, Rhoda from Woodmere with the
boutique and the big plans. Even with the four of them as tenants, the
couch looked almost deserted. Instead of taking out a lease of my own,
I made for the little rosewood bar. Mundel greeted me and gave me a
sherry. Of all of us, Mundel alone wore a dinner jacket and black tie.
"Mr. French. You and your charming group are all ready?" We
were. Rehearsals were over, the round-trip tickets were nestling snugly
in Jackie's folder, and Ralph's connection in Antwerp had sworn to
have the best harpsichord in Europe at the hotel when we arrived. We'd
all been injected. All of us, under Jackie's supervision, had trooped
down to Rockefeller Plaza to have our pictures taken and our passport
applications processed. Brodkey muttered something about free fron-
tiers and slaves of a fascist state, but the passport lady was too wrapped
up in her rubber stamping to hear him. When they told Jackie at the
airlines that she'd have to rent an extra seat—and pay a full fare—for
her gamba, we had made one of our few appeals to Mundel's office.
"Just send us the bill," Marianne said, and that had been that. All of
our other expenses had been smoothly accepted and processed. New
music covers? Floor racks to hold the instruments we weren't using at
the moment? Publicity shots? A young man with a camera, another

23

friend of Ralph's, had showed up at rehearsals. Squeaking with delight, he had covered us, as he said, from every angle. Mundel had paid. Surprisingly, the pictures were excellent. One of Jackie looking dreamy-eyed while in the background I glared at a score, we'd had blown up for the living-room wall. Because of the particular part of Ralph that appeared in one corner, we all called the shot "Ars Longa."

As I turned from the bar, I felt a touch on my arm. Marianne. After office hours, she marched to quite a different drum. Her sequined jeans had been applied with an airbrush, and a ribbed undershirt lovingly delineated every contour of her spectacular Swiss landscape. Her feet were bare. I found myself wondering where she'd acquired her creamy suntan. On some rich old sultan's yacht, no doubt. Or some rich young sultan's.

"Alan—I may call you Alan?" It wasn't really a question. "Everything is all right? You are content with us?" Marianne looked hopeful and eager to please. But ear training does strange things. Even when you want to be convinced that what you're hearing is right—and I wanted, I wanted—your ear still insists on picking apart the music. Marianne's music was well rehearsed, but not in my key.

"What could be wrong? You've done a great job. You'd make somebody a wonderful secretary."

"Now you're teasing me," she said. "But I'm serious."

"I'm serious, too," I lied. "You've set things up perfectly. It can't be fun, playing angel to a herd of neurotics like us."

"Oh, no," Marianne said seriously. "I enjoy my work. And you are not neurotic. You should know how demanding are some of the artists. This one has to have fresh roses in his hotel suite. In January, fresh roses! This one will not play in a hall with blue curtains. So tiresome, they are. But for you the work is a pleasure. And some of the things we arrange for you in Geneva will be special. You will see."

"See what, my dear?" Mundel materialized at just the wrong moment. Absently, he placed a hand, thin and freckled, on Marianne's bare shoulder, stroking the brown skin with his fingertips. Marianne shivered very slightly but made no effort to move away. "What were you telling our Mr. French?"

"Only that there would be parties in Geneva as well as work," she said.

Mundel let his hand fall to his side. "This is true, Mr. French. My colleagues and I have taken the liberty of arranging a few receptions for you and your associates. But you will be told more about these when you reach Geneva. Believe me, there is nothing that will interfere with your schedule."

Marianne and Mundel drifted away, to be replaced by a pale thin girl in a pale thin dress who said she did publicity for the Foundation. She looked at me as if I wasn't particularly good publicity. But I got her a drink, and in gratitude she embarked on a long story about how difficult it was to arrange publicity for one of her Texas clients who had built, stocked, and endowed a museum in Houston.

"The poor girl spent ten million dollars," she said. "Don't you think she ought to get at least a column in the *Times?*" I said I thought she should, but things were tough in the art world. "Oh, they are," she said, "they definitely are."

I was glad to see Jackie emerge from the small crowd near the door and make her way toward me. By Marianne's standards, she was underdressed, in a long black jersey affair cut puritanically high. But jersey clings, and Jackie has more than enough for it to cling to. She tells me she's used to hearing people say, "But she doesn't *dress* like a musician."

We greeted each other, acquired drinks, and walked into what must have been Mundel's study. The drapes were drawn and the view of New York from the floor-to-ceiling windows made the city look like a huge, twinkling pinball machine. I never know what to think about New York's great top-of-the-heap views. They're beautiful. But if you know what's going on down in the glittery streets, they're embarrassing.

Jackie was excited about jetting to Geneva. When I muttered something dampening, she looked hurt. "That's just cultural shock," she said, "plus that old Alan French never-let-anything-show syndrome."

"Maybe I'm just scared of heights," I said placatingly.

"That reminds me," Jackie said. "I took your advice and went over to listen to some Caruso." I've been bugging the whole group to pay attention to the sustained phrasing of the great opera singers. "He's not hammy at all. Anyway, this type was waiting for my earphones—"

She never did get to finish the story. A servitor in a white linen jacket and a narrow black tie inserted himself between us. "Excuse me, sir and lady," he said. "It is Signor Mundel's wish that everybody be seated for dinner." His message delivered, he padded away with a dancer's exaggerated grace. Jackie's eyebrows and mine went up at exactly the same instant. We both burst into laughter. Other men's rituals are so strange, I thought, and we made our way into the dining room.

If Mundel's apartment was an event, his dinner was a whole happening. You expected the heavy white napery, the tall elegant candesticks, the Baccarat crystal, the fresh flowers. But as soon as we'd sipped our way through the soup course, the unexpected began. A door opened—to the kitchen? the pantry?—and in darted a crew of four Chinese chefs. Two of them carried a gigantic platter on which reposed, steaming, a huge whole roast pig. The chefs hustled their burden over to a side table, and as soon as the platter was in place the head chef, a squat, burly Cantonese, attacked the pig with an enormous cleaver. As fast as a percussionist executing a tarradiddle, the carver whipped into his victim. Slice after slice fell away from the carcass as the chef, sweating, worked away with his weapon. The candlelight cast weird shadows on his face. You could see from the twitchings of the jaw muscles and the tenseness of the lips that the man was in a trance of total concentration. He had to be; his free hand was constantly reaching into the platter. The cleaver, flashing up and down as it slammed into the meat, must have been as sharp as a guillotine blade.

Finally, after a last savage staccato of blows, there was silence. When the chef straightened up, smiling and out of breath, the whole table broke into applause. The moment was over; the bright lights went on; and instead of a demon with an assassin's blade, we were watching three Orientals expertly filling plates and serving dinner.

"God," my dinner partner breathed. She was the pale girl who did publicity. "Wasn't that marvelous?" At the head of the table, Mundel was smiling. We could hear him say, "Oh, yes, this is their specialty. It seemed to me very appropriate, at a party of artists, to invite another artist to perform. And of course, the symbolism, the violence, is so curious. We need to be reminded, do we not, that there is more to the act of eating than mere ingestion. If we are to live and thrive, something else, alas, must die and be chopped into pieces."

"I don't know about the symbolism," the pale girl said. "But I have to get that man for my next party. I mean, he's incredible." Her smooth hair fell lankly forward across her cheeks as she bent over her plate. "M-m-m," she said with her mouth half full. "It's delicious."

The food *was* good. But as I munched away, finishing what the chef had begun, I was thinking more about Mundel's motivation for providing such a strange, almost sinister, bit of dramatics. Granted, he liked his touch of primitivism. It went well with the slick apartment, the fashionable extra guests, the power of the patron. But why bother to impress us? I had the feeling that, before the evening was over, I'd find out why. Dinner wore on and on. The pork, it seemed, was only an appetizer. Plates were whisked away and freshly laden plates substituted. Bottles of wine were presented, uncorked, sampled by Mundel, and poured. A salad was served. Cheese and the thinnest of black breads. Platters of fresh fruit. A tiny concoction of chocolate, cream, and orange. Coffee. Then, dazed, we made our way back into the living room to slump into Mundel's yielding leather and steel and, aided by cognac, to digest our way back to reality. Terry, I could see, was making mental notes of things that would forever change the style of the restaurant business in Queens. Ralph and my pallid dinner partner—she had eaten her way through the feast as efficiently as a power saw—were deep in discourse about Chinese music. Marianne was being charming to Jackie, David, and Rhoda. The chatter of other assorted guests was background. When Mundel, drifting from group to group, finally wandered over to me, it seemed casual enough.

"Mr. French," he said, "I wonder if you could spare me a moment or two for a little private chat. Let us step into my study. It won't be long before I release you to your charming associates." The study was empty and quiet. Mundel closed the door behind us, and I thought I heard a lock click shut. Once we were alone, Mundel dropped into still another luxurious armchair and gestured for me to make myself comfortable. On a table between us was a tray laden with brandy, ice, a soda dispenser, and other man-of-distinction amenities. Mundel busied himself preparing fresh drinks, then leaned back and eyed me. "Mr. French, I must say that you and your group have cooperated admirably in all our arrangements. The Foundation is most pleased. We anticipate a splendid response to your tour. It may be that you can expect substantial Foundation support for future projects of this nature.

"But now I must ask you a question. Suppose that, in addition to your . . . musical responsibilities, there were certain other ways in which you could be helpful to the Foundation. Certain contacts you could make?

"Please, Mr. French. I beg you not to misunderstand." Hastily, Mundel held up a hand to keep me from interrupting. "We are not international criminals I assure you," his chuckle was almost a giggle. "I assure you we would ask you to do nothing that was . . . wrong. Nothing that your conscience would frown upon. Quite the contrary, in fact."

I had to say something. So I fell back upon cliché. "Mr. Mundel, I haven't the faintest idea what you're talking about."

"Of course not, Mr. French. How could you? Nothing has been said. There is no reason to say anything at this time. I have simply asked you a question. If the opportunity arises when you are abroad, and if the conditions are satisfactory, would you be willing to undertake a modest extra assignment on behalf of the Foundation?"

"Well, obviously the whole thing depends on what the assignment is. I can't imagine—"

"Mr. French, believe me, we would not ask you to undertake *anything* for which your qualifications—and they are excellent ones, excellent—were not appropriate."

"Well, in that case, if it's legitimate, I suppose I would. And if whatever it is doesn't interfere with the tour. Sure. Why not?"

"Ah. Excellent," Mundel purred again. "I am delighted, Mr. French. On behalf of the Foundation, I accept your offer."

"Wait a minute. I didn't offer—"

"No, no, of course not. That's just a manner of speaking. You didn't offer. *We* asked *you*. That is understood. Of course."

"What's the next step, then?"

"Next step? Why, nothing, Mr. French. At this point, there is nothing to concern you. Your plans are made, you are ready to leave, you leave. That is all. If something should come up, my colleagues will contact you in Geneva or elsewhere. There is nothing to worry about, nothing to distract you from the duties of the music." Mundel swallowed the rest of his cognac. "Now, we should rejoin the party."

As we padded back into the living room, the party seemed to be breaking up. A skinny brunette I hadn't met was being helped into a floor-length mink by her equally unrobust escort. "He is a heart surgeon," Mundel told me, "mad about the Renaissance; art, music, life. You will assuredly meet him again."

"Oh, Mr. French," the skinny lady said when Mundel introduced us. "I'm so disappointed that you and your friends didn't play for us this evening. The Doctor hoped so much to hear a little preview." My smile must have seemed sincere enough, because she squeezed my hand delicately and swore she'd bring the Doctor to every performance. I wondered if she meant that they'd actually fly to Geneva to do it.

Jackie decided that we all needed our sleep. With her usual minimum of fuss, she got us disentangled from the other guests, into our coats, and down in the elevator. We arranged to meet at the Swissair ticket counter the next morning and scattered to our various cars, buses, and subways. I volunteered to take Jackie home, but she turned me down. "I really am tired, Alan, and so are you," she said. But I did persuade her into a cab.

By the time I got back to my place, it was nearly one o'clock and I was yawning and ready for bed. But as I was fumbling with the key to the lobby door, someone came running softly across the pavement. It was Marianne, muffled up to the ears in one of those enormous sporty furs. "Quick," she said, "Mr. French, let me in with you. I am cold. And we must talk." When I glanced at her, I could see why her lips were trembling. Even the Swiss get cold walking barefoot in New York at one on an early spring morning.

The minute we got inside my apartment she made a beeline for the bathroom. I could hear the hot water running while I made coffee. By the time I carried the pot and cups into the living room, she had reappeared. She seemed warmer, but she still stayed huddled in her fur coat. I poured coffee, added a dollop of rum, and handed her the cup. She took a sip. "Marvelous," she sighed and leaned back in her chair.

"Now, what is all this?"

Marianne managed a weak smile and took another sip of her coffee. "Please don't misunderstand, Mr. French. I have to tell you something very important."

"It's Alan, and why do people keep telling me not to misunderstand? That's what your boss was saying a half hour ago."

"Alan, then. That's what I want to talk about. He asked you to do something, didn't he?"

"Who did?"

"Mr. Mundel. He did ask you. That was the whole purpose of the party."

"Wait a minute. Why should Mundel throw a party just to ask me if I'd do something for the Foundation? You're not making any sense."

"Then I was right. Alan . . . did you accept?" Marianne wasn't cold any more. She shrugged off her coat impatiently and dropped it on the floor by her chair.

"How could I accept or not accept? All he said was there might be something to do, something extra and not in any way dishonest or illegal. He didn't say what."

"Then listen to me. Whatever it is, whatever they want, don't do it."

"Marianne, this conversation is surreal by any standards, and I'm used to surreal conversations. You come in the middle of the night, you're freezing and scared, you waltz into my apartment, and you tell me not to do something the Philomel Foundation wants me to do. Now, there's obviously something strange about the Philomel Foundation. I've known that all along; you'd have to be an idiot not to know it. But as far as we're concerned, they've offered us a tour, paid our expenses, and even sent us you to keep us happy. So let me repeat my first question. What's this all about? Drugs, diamond smuggling, white slavery, or what?"

Marianne threw me a wan smile. "No, Alan, it's nothing like those things. It's—it's political in a way and yet not." She sounded genuinely troubled. Her enameled good looks had given way under fatigue and nervousness, and yet I found her much easier to be with. Her incredibly long eyelashes, I noticed with pleasure, were real. "Alan, can't you see? I can't tell you any more about this, this *thing* the people from Philomel will want you to do. But one thing I can tell you is, it's dangerous. It is even dangerous for me to be here. Please, when they ask you, it will sound innocent. But please, just refuse. Just go on the tour and play the music and—" she laughed shakily "—enjoy your journey. That's all."

"But, Marianne—"

"And please ask no more questions." She reached for her coffee cup, swallowed, made a face. "*Ouf*, cold. Now I must go." She reached for her coat.

"Smoke a cigarette first and have some hot coffee. Your feet must be freezing."

She giggled. "They are. All right, I will stay for a few minutes. But promise not to ask me any more questions. I know what," she said brightly. "Alan, please play for me one of your records, the dances of the court of Burgundy. I've never heard that one. Play it and we will just sit and listen. Then I'll go."

I had to shuffle through three-quarters of a big pile before I found the record she wanted. But I did find it, put it on the turntable, blew the dust off the pickup needle, and started the music. Then I brought my coffee cup over to the sofa and sat down. The sound was soft but it filled the room with the tap of the small drum and the plaintive response of the pipe. Marianne's face relaxed and she smiled. When I made an inviting gesture, she nodded and came over to seat herself beside me. My arm went around her, and for a while we did just sit and listen. But long before the first side was over, we were kissing deeply. By the second cut of side two, Marianne had wriggled free of her silver top and her jeans. She wore nothing underneath. There was passion as well as practice in her lovemaking, but also relief. While we were doing what we were doing, I could ask her no questions. The old magic of Burgundy, sensuous, lyrical, and impersonal, drove us beyond interrogations. After a while, Marianne slept lightly, wrapped in my jacket. I must have dozed off, because the next thing I remember was her tired, smiling face shadowed by the dim light. She was getting back into her clothes, getting ready to go. I made her slip her feet into a pair of old rubber-soled sandals and wear one of my aged sweaters. She refused more coffee, just washed her face at the kitchen sink and ran a comb through her hair. We said almost nothing, but everything was immensely friendly.

"*Bon voyage*, Alan," she said at the door. Then the elevator clanked open for her and she was gone.

Of course, it is only rarely possible
to reveal the true content and affect of
a piece on its first reading.

K.P.E. BACH, p. 147.

CHAPTER SIX

AT GENEVA INTERNATIONAL AIRPORT, the nice Swiss have installed a
people-mover to move people from landing gate to lobby. It's a brisk,
smooth trip to prepare your reflexes for brisk, smooth Switzerland.
Once you're spilled off the treadmill at Passport Control, the lobby
widens into the usual airport chaos. A huge bulletin board, surrounded
by anxious tourists and studded with messages in various tongues,
clogs the main concourse. "MR FRENCH AND PARTY," our message read, "PLEASE GO AT ONCE TO THE SIDE ENTRANCE ON
THE RIGHT. TRANSPORT IS LAID ON. A. DE SOTO."

At the glass entrance doors, an angular Englishwoman saluted us
with a wave of her umbrella. "Come along, Mr. French," she chir-
ruped, sorting us out of the crowd and herding us out into the bright
spring sunshine. Two huge gray Mercedes limousines swallowed our
luggage, our instruments, and us and still looked hungry. "We've
booked you into the International Plaza," said A. De Soto as I sank
back into the rearmost seat of the second limousine. Before we turned
out at the main airport gate, she had picked up the telephone mounted
on an armrest and notified somebody that we were on our way. Then
she turned to me and said, "Geneva can be absolute hell for visitors,
you know. It's awfully helpful to have someone about who can fix up
accommodations, answer questions, that sort of thing. So Philomel
keeps me on staff to greet visitors, do a bit of orienting: you know.
Naturally, you'll all be terribly busy. But if you do need a bit of help, I
am available." She handed me a card. It read, "Anne De Soto,

Communications, The Philomel Foundation,'' with a couple of telephone numbers. "This one's office, the other's home.'' She smiled encouragingly at me. As unobtrusively as possible, I edged away. For an official greeter, A. De Soto had shockingly bad breath.

The International Plaza was a block of expensive marble, glass, and concrete right on the lakefront. Almost before our cars had eased to a stop, blond Swiss boys were swarming out to whip open the doors and trunks and take possession of the luggage. We ourselves were ushered into the lobby by an assistant manager in a canary yellow tie. He registered us in a twinkling, collected our passports (I had to tell Tony and David to relax, they'd get their passports back in an hour), and even accompanied us up to our accommodations. On its own home ground, the Philomel Foundation obviously delighted in being hospitable. As chief guest, I'd been assigned a suite at least as big as my New York studio and decidedly more opulent. The *hotelier* fussed away, opening windows, showing me the view, closing drapes, switching on air-conditioning, and flicking open closets, cabinets, and a well-stocked bar. But when I offered him a five-franc piece, he recoiled in horror. "Oh, no, Mr. French,'' he said, "Philomel, you understand, has taken care of *everything*."

After he withdrew, with a final flicker of canary yellow, I was seized by the depression I always feel when I'm plunked down abruptly and temporarily in a strange place. The idea of unpacking, of surrendering my skimpy possessions to the cavernous closets and gaping bureau drawers of the International Plaza, was dispiriting. The thought that within forty-eight hours I'd be conducting a concert before an audience of courteous but uncomprehending Swiss was simply absurd. For this kind of mood, there's only one antidote. I mixed myself a stiff Scotch, ran a steaming tub, peeled off my clothes, and sipped and soaked myself into lassitude.

After about half an hour, a buzzer aroused me. I was just about to heave my dripping self out of the tub when I noticed the neat white extension phone on a ledge within arm's reach. Subsiding happily, I picked up the receiver. It was Jackie. "Hi,'' she said cheerfully. "We're all unpacked and thinking about lunch. And what about a rehearsal?''

"I'm in the bathtub,'' I said, just to let her know that rank hath its privileges.

"Well, hurry up.'' So much for rank, so much for privileges. I splashed out of the tub, shaved in front of a mirror lighted a flattering pink, and threw on a blue turtleneck pullover, slacks, and my new-for-the-trip crush-proof linen blazer—slightly crushed, of course, from the suitcase.

We met for lunch in the lemon yellow hotel dining room. Apparently A. De Soto had left her orders, because we were seated without delay and fed with dispatch. Following Jackie's example, we ate lightly, not an easy thing to do in a Swiss restaurant. Terry, thinking about his uncle's place in Woodside, explained to us why the International Plaza was a class establishment and folded up a menu for later study.

Somewhere between the strawberry tart and the iced coffee, the sense of strangeness wore off and I was left with a much more familiar feeling: panic. "Let's get out of here," I said. "We're supposed to be performing in this town and we've got less than a day to work. Does anybody know where we're going for rehearsal?"

"While you were wallowing in the bathtub, Miss De Soto gave me the directions," Jackie said smugly. "Furthermore, Ralph is in from Amsterdam, *with* his friend Kurt, and he *did* buy the Ruckers spinet, and he's meeting us at the Kursaal—that's the rehearsal place—in half an hour. And furthermore, there's a publicity party at five-thirty. So get ready, maestro, we're all waiting for you."

"A what at five-thirty?"

"That's what Miss De Soto told me, a publicity party. The press will be there, Miss De Soto will be there, Dr. Somebody-or-other Flachsmann will be there, and we'd better be there."

"Hugo," I said.

"Who?"

"Hugo. Flachsmann. *Doktor* Hugo. The Philomel Foundation guy. I want to meet him."

"So let's get going."

The Kursaal was a concert hall about five minutes from the International by Mercedes limousine. The management had allotted us a rehearsal studio on the third floor, a big room with a high, carved ceiling and a line of mirrors running along one wall. For some reason, the atmosphere made us all feel good. Ralph was there, and so was the harpsichord the Foundation had arranged for him. When Ralph pronounced the instrument excellent, we felt even better. Ralph has been known to bite people in rage over a bad or ugly harpsichord, but for once he was satisfied and we could all breathe easier.

Some rehearsals are businesslike. You set up the stands, pull up the chairs, open the music, play it through, and leave. Other rehearsals are dramatic. One of the performers is resisting the will of the group or is simply baffled by an interpretation. Then you repeat and repeat, knowing that even if everybody's exhausted and the mood is ugly, there's no choice, the problem must be solved. Once in a while, a rehearsal is something different. The players break new ground. Uncoerced, they begin to carve out some new way of making the music say whatever it has to say. If you're an outsider, what's going on will baffle you. The music, far from sounding elegant, will seem ragged or incoherent, or perhaps tentative. But if you're playing or conducting, this is what you pray for in rehearsal.

I remember, as we rehearsed that afternoon, catching a glimpse of the whole group in the mirror lining the one wall. The mirror, obviously, was meant for dancers, who must be able to see themselves in the act of performance. Musicians never need to know what they look like. There we always are, clutching and mouthing odd-looking tubes of wood and metal, hunched over boxes strung with bits of animal gut and wire. In the Kursaal mirror, our poses, movements, and gestures looked as bizarre as the antics of monkeys in a zoo. Yet our faces, grave with concentration, were like those of statesmen presiding over an international crisis or of lovers making love. The contrast fascinated and moved me. There's more than money in this business, after all.

We were playing one of the rarities on our program, an early Italian suite for consorted instruments, a kind of nonvocal set of madrigals, when we felt we'd reached a magical balance. So we stopped rehearsing, sensing that what we had begun to tap should be kept in the bottle for the concert itself. Ralph, sitting at the keyboard with his fingers poised over the final arpeggiando, said, "Well, my dears."

My palms were sticky. I felt wonderful, frightened as always before an approaching performance, but reassured. I was ready for a party.

Actually, we were whisked into a kaleidoscopic jumble of encounters. At five-thirty, we were back at the International, meeting the press. The press turned out to be a thin, graying gentleman who covered cultural events for the *Journal de Genève* and a plump, rosy miss who was the music critic for a glossy weekly. As Jackie had promised, or warned, A. De Soto was there, too, chattering away with ghastly cordiality. So were a number of other people; Swiss musicians, their wives, and a generous sampling of the strange types who pursue the arts in any city. Still a bit lightheaded from the rehearsal, I found my way first to the bar and then into conversation with the music critic. According to Jackie, the critic was under the impression that we were members of a string quartet. I seem to remember a long lecture on the technical aspects of yodeling. But I also remember Dave's interrupting to say, very excitedly, that music theory was at a critical state of ripeness.

"There's this theory in physics, you know, the one-electron theory—"

"Ze sound, wiessen sie, shtarts from ze diagram—"

"—one electron in the whole universe—"

"—ja, ja, dia*phragm*—"

"—moving so fast it creates all matter—"

"—open op ze lonks—"

"—like there's one note in music—"

"—ja, *longs*—"

"—linear like the electron—"

I clutched at Jackie as she was passing by. "Help," I said.

"What's that all about?"

"I think, voice training in the Alps with total temporal simultaneity in music."

"Oh. Well," Jackie was carrying a very large glass of sherry in each hand. "That man in the corner over there, that's Heinrich Wunschler, *the* Heinrich Wunschler. We're going to have a nice long talk." Wunschler, I knew, was the Pablo Casals of the viola da gamba. I would have liked to talk with him myself. Not only was he a superb musician, but he also ran a good-sized music school at a good-sized profit. I wanted to ask him how he did it. But he was Jackie's legitimate prey, so I left her to it and, making my escape, bumped into the grayhaired cultural reporter for the Geneva paper.

"Mr. French, if you can spare me a moment, there are some questions I'd like to ask you for my story."

"Of course," I said. "What kind of a story?" He led me over to a comfortable sofa.

"You see, I am also cultural affairs correspondent for a number of papers in France and also in West Germany," he began, "and I think in your visit here there is perhaps material for an article they would buy." I nodded, and he settled himself more comfortably. "So could I ask you, Mr. French? Your ensemble specializes in preclassical music.

This is very remote in time and mood, shall we say, from the unsettled world of the present. Would you say that your kind of art offers your listeners escape? That and nothing more?''

The man and his question reminded me oddly of my conversation with Mundel in New York, and of Marianne's vague warning, but I could see nothing wrong with trying to answer. "All art is escapist in a sense," I said. "Artists, composers, musicians aren't politicians or engineers. Our job, our role, is to play our music as well as we can and not to worry if people think of it as an escape."

"But Mr. French, this may not always be so easy. You cannot always be neutral, like a Swiss. You permit?" He reached into his breast pocket, brought out a slim cigar and lighted it with a gold lighter. "No, not so easy," he repeated. "You are like the manufacturer of a drug which is both useful and dangerous. You say, we produce the drug, it is not for us to judge what people do with it. But if too many people abuse the drug, you will be made to stop production. So you cannot say you have no reason to worry."

"Yes, but our music isn't some kind of opium, *Herr*—I'm afraid I don't know your name."

"Bauer, Mr. French, Ernst Bauer. No, your music is simply music, as the drug is simply a chemical substance. But what use you make of it, Mr. French, what *social* use—"

"*Herr* Bauer, please believe me. We've come over here to give a few concerts, that's all. We're instrumentalists interested in early music. Our first concert is tomorrow evening. If you come, I'm sure you'll understand why we play the kind of music we play."

"I shall attend, Mr. French. As it happens, I am very, very fond of the kind of music you play. But are you quite sure, Mr. French, that to play this music is the only reason you come to Geneva? The *only* reason?"

I tried not to let Bauer see my surprise. "What other reason could there possibly be?"

"Let me ask you something else, Mr. French. How much do you really know about the Philomel Foundation?"

"Well, they're our sponsors, of course." Bauer nodded his head. I read nothing in his expression. "They're a cultural group with headquarters here and an office in New York, they've arranged everything for us, and they're financially solvent. Obviously." Bauer nodded again. "Their director is somebody named Hugo Flachsmann. At least, he signs the mail."

"Have you ever met *Doktor* Flachsmann?"

"No. As a matter of fact, he's supposed to be here at this reception, but I haven't met him yet. Why? Do you know him?"

"I know *of* him, Mr. French. He is not here so far. But you will meet him, of that I am sure. He too is a great enthusiast of early music, and of other matters as well. He has tremendous wealth, so they say. When you meet him, Mr. French, I am sure you will be impressed."

"Fine. As long as he can pay our bills."

"He can do that, Mr. French. For your music and for other things as well."

"Like what, *Herr* Bauer? What other things?" But Bauer was levering himself out of his seat.

"I am sure you will find *Doktor* Flachsmann a most generous patron," he said. "That is all I meant. Now, you will excuse me. Our conversation has been very helpful. I hope I shall be able to incorporate some of these thoughts into a good article on you and your work, Mr. French. It has been a pleasure. *Auf wiedersehen!*" Bauer maneuvered his way through a knot of people at the door and disappeared.

Before I could even begin to sort out my reactions, I was shaking hands with a replacement.

"Mr. French? Bob Carroll, U. S. Embassy, cultural attaché." Carroll was a bulky man with a mop of brown hair. Some of the hair had migrated down to colonize a big handlebar moustache. He wore a checked shirt, a woolly woven tie, and a corduroy jacket. He could have been a Greenwich Village painter or a professor of English somewhere in the Midwest. "Just thought I'd drop by to see if there was anything Uncle could do, but it looks like you're meeting the right people. Yes, sir, this is a good crowd, very unusual for a musical organization. Now, when Norman Mailer came through, we had to alert the cops. But this is great, you're getting grade-A treatment. That guy Bauer, for instance, half the time if it's an American he doesn't even show up."

"Who is he?" Maybe Uncle could help me a little bit.

"Who, Bauer? He does a lot of writing on intellectual and cultural events. Mostly covers art, antiques, that sort of stuff. You know

Geneva's a headquarters for dealers. Very upper-upper guy, family owns a private bank, knows everybody. Why?''

"Well, he seemed to be convinced that we were here on some kind of political mission."

Carroll laughed. "Don't worry about it, he's just drumming up some excitement. When Mailer was here, we were getting calls from all over: did the State Department accept responsibility, did we endorse him? Hell, it was embarrassing. But you have to understand the European mentality. They just don't understand that our artists are on their own."

"Bauer asked me what I knew about the Philomel Foundation. Is there something I should know except that they're sponsoring us?"

"Well, you have to meet *Herr Doktor* Flachsmann. He *is* Philomel. Quite a boy. Made his money in industrial publishing: technical journals, catalogues, directories. Does a lot of business in Eastern Europe, but he's no Commie. Anything but." Carroll laughed. "Hal Fisher, he's our commercial attaché, could tell you about him. He knows Flachsmann. He's even been up to the castle. Flachsmann's got a huge chateau up in the mountains. Hal says the parties up there make Fellini look like Sunday afternoon in Sauk Center, but I wouldn't know, I've never been to one.

"Anyway, Flachsmann runs Philomel as a kind of hobby. You know, do something for the arts, get good publicity, meet the right people. But it's clean. I mean, as far as we're concerned, we've never heard a word against it."

I thanked Carroll for the rundown. "Oh, you bet," he said. Then I grabbed a Sion and seltzer from the bar and wandered out onto a terrace overlooking the lake. I watched the chilly Swiss spring evening start to throw shadows on the hills surrounding the city and tried to make some sense out of the situation. The thing is, I didn't really want to have to think. That morning, remember, we'd been in New York. Here we were, in the lap of luxury and in the middle of professional preparations. I *like* luxury, and the rehearsal had gone well, and I *like* rehearsing and getting ready for the stage. All right, Mundel had asked me to do him a favor and his secretary had warned me not to. Or rather, Mundel had said there might be some extra little thing and Marianne had said it might be a dangerous extra little thing. Then, some Swiss newspaperman had hinted mysteriously about the reason for our Geneva appearance. But the U. S. cultural attaché gave Philomel and clean sheet. What the hell, the important thing was not to let anything distract any of us while we were on tour. If Flachsmann or Mundel asked me to do something gross, I could simply say no. The worst they could do would be to cancel the tour. That would mean breaking the contract. Besides, we already had our return-trip tickets. So why worry?

Why, indeed? I felt uneasily cheerful, as if I'd given a bad performance and received a good review. But my party mood was over.

Play from the soul, not like a trained bird!

K.P.E. BACH, p. 150.

CHAPTER SEVEN

I ATE BREAKFAST in my room with the spring sunlight streaming in through the French windows and the advance copies of the concert program strewn across the bed. The orange juice was fresh, the omelette fluffy, the brioches yielding and buttery. The programs looked terrific. Mundel, or whoever was responsible, had used one of our rehearsal photographs on the cover, then vignetted the pictures of the individual performers for use with the blurbs identifying each one. It was cleverly done. And somebody had even prepared sensible program notes on the instruments and on the preclassical tradition. I was almost impressed enough to forget about *Herr* Bauer and his disquieting questions.

We all met downstairs in the lobby and spent the morning seeing the sights of Geneva, such as these are. By about twenty years, we seemed to be the youngest people on the streets. But the streets were very clean and the air as clear as a bell. The industry of Geneva is money, and making money leaves no smog to linger in the Swiss atmosphere.

When we found our way back to the hotel, there was a message awaiting us. The president of Krohl & Sohne, Zurich, would like us to be his luncheon guests. A. De Soto, materialized suddenly to explain that *Herr* Krohl was the head of the biggest, most important musical instrument firm in Switzerland. "Krohl recorders, I believe, are used in schools everywhere," she announced. "I think you might find it worth your while to accept the invitation."

So we all met at one of those Geneva restaurants where the only specialty is beefsteak, which you broil yourself in a pan over a burner at your table. The steak is eaten with a gigantic mound of sliver-thin french fries and washed down with beer. No conversation accompanies this ritual. Only later did *Herr* Krohl, a balding, anxious businessman, broach his idea, which was that during the concert we should all use the recorders produced by his firm. These, he assured us, were the world's finest. Indeed, we should visit the factory, where we could watch Swiss craftsmen, also the finest in the world, assemble these instruments. And of course, he himself would be delighted to present to us, as a gift, several sets of Krohl *Meisterstücke* recorders. These would be sent to the hotel or the Kursaal or wherever we wished that very afternoon.

Except for Ralph, who picked his way inconcernedly through his strudel, the whole Antiqua ensemble gazed expectantly at me.

It wasn't easy to keep a straight face, but I did it. "*Herr* Krohl," I said, "we are deeply grateful for your very generous offer. We are all keenly interested in the craft of musical instrument manufacture. But for us to switch from instruments we've used for years to unfamiliar instruments—"

"Bah," Krohl said. It was the first time in my life I'd ever actually heard anyone say "bah." "Recorders are all the same, sticks with holes in them. I should know. Play our recorders, Mr. French, play some other recorders, what's the difference? So play ours. We'll make it worth your while."

W.C. Fields, or perhaps Sidney Greenstreet, would have known what to say—something like, "Your arguments have proved absolutely convincing. How much?" Instead, I said, "I'm afraid not, Mr. Krohl. We're sorry, we just can't do it."

I must have pinked him in a tender part. "So now you are calling me Mister, eh, Mr. French? All right, the deal is off. You could have had an exclusive Krohl franchise. Our newest plastic models will sell in the millions. Not even the Japanese are cheaper. I thought I was dealing with a gentleman." On this note, *Herr* Krohl arose from the table and stalked indignantly out, conspicuously neglecting the check. We gazed after him in awed silence.

"Wow," said Jackie, "I thought musicians were the temperamental ones."

"Oh, dear," said A. De Soto. "I'm so terribly sorry. I had no idea. . . ."

"Please," I said magnanimously. "Don't give it another thought."
A. De Soto looked relieved. She'd probably had a vision of a whole

tableful of musicians, edgy with pre-performance anxiety, rising in angry pursuit of Krohl, following him out onto the street, perhaps pelting him with breadsticks and rolls, causing a shocking incident—then, in frustration, turning on her. What's the meaning of this? How dare you insult our artistic integrity? That's not at all what an official hostess wants to happen at a luncheon for special guests of her employer.

But even if we'd wanted to fling things at Krohl, it would have been impossible. Ralph, caught by surprise, was choking on his strudel and his laughter. David and Terry were collapsing in their seats. Jackie was digging into her bag for a Kleenex to wipe tears from her eyes. We really weren't much of a threat to anyone.

"What we should do," David said, "is run a credit line in the program. The instruments used in this performance supplied despite the courtesy of Krohl." By the time we'd exhausted the other, more venturesome possibilities, A. De Soto had appropriated the check. Since I suspected that the entire luncheon had been arranged between her and Krohl in return for some sort of commission, it seemed right to let her pick up the tab. When we finally did leave, still giggling, we were more relaxed than we would have been after two hours in the International's sauna.

By four o'clock, after a last session at the Kursaal, we could have used another dose of Krohl. As usual at a final rehearsal, nothing went right. David, tuning his lute, snapped a string. First, Jackie had to help him find his package of spares—in his jacket pocket—then we all had to wait while he wound a new string on his lute, stretched it, tuned it, and tested it. Then it was his turn to wait, while the rest of us ran through a Landini suite that called for the harpsichord, not the lute. He was furious. "Ragged, uneven, and off-key," he said smugly about our third try at a smooth start on the coranto.

"I am *never* off-key," Jackie said.

"Bullshit," David said. "You were off, Alan was off, Ralph was late, and Terry was late. You stank." Of such mature analyses are dress rehearsals made. "Try it again." We tried it again. "It's mostly Ralph."

"I *told* you," Jackie said.

Then Ralph joined the act. "You're accenting the entry too much. It's dee-dee-dee-DAH and two and three, not DAH-dee-dee-BLAM. Just walk into it."

Eighteen starts later, Jackie said, "Shit." She almost never said anything stronger than "damn." She put down her bow and turned to me. "How come you haven't told us what *you* think?"

"If I did, you'd just get mad," I said.

"No, go ahead and say it. I won't get mad."

"No, because you're already mad," I said.

"I am *not* mad."

"Well, then, I don't think there was anything wrong with it except that the coranto flows out of the alman without a break, just a little pause, and when we work on the coranto by itself you try to make it have a start it doesn't have. Let's start at bar 15 of the alman and play through and see." Jackie glowered at me, but everybody began at bar 15 and played through the end of the alman and the beginning of the coranto and it sounded fine.

"Now I suppose you're pleased because I was wrong," Jackie said.

"Can we do the lute trio?" David asked.

"I never said you were wrong or right or anything," I said to Jackie.

"Please?" David asked.

"Well, you should have said something instead of wasting all this time," Jackie said.

"Please can we rehearse the fucking lute trio now and get this fucking rehearsal over with?" David said. For a moment, I played with the idea of saying no, just to see what would happen. But I knew what would happen. I put down my treble viol and picked up my Baroque flute. We played through the trio.

"Yich," Terry said. "Awful."

"Now don't *you* start," Jackie said.

"It's after four," I said. "Rehearsal is over. We'll meet in the dressing room downstairs at seven-thirty. I'm going back to the hotel to take a nap."

"The one thing I hate about this group," Jackie said, "is that when we have problems nobody tries to straighten them out. Everybody goes back and takes a nap."

Ralph and I walked back to the hotel together. "What do you think?" I asked.

"Is there a shoeshine place at the hotel?" he asked me back. "I have to get my black shoes polished."

"Ralph," I said, "don't be maddening. What do you think?"

He smiled. "Things were just ratty enough so that it could be a great concert. Or it could all fall apart. But I don't think it will. Fall apart, I mean."

At the hotel, Ralph wandered off to get a shine. I caught up with Jackie at the elevators. "I'm sorry," she said, "I didn't mean to work everybody up. But Wunschler is going to be out there tonight and I'm *nervous*. Last night he told me he disapproved of American viol playing. Too broad, he said. Too free. Not enough discipline. Here, feel my hand." I did. It was icy cold.

"Listen," I said. "Forget about Wunschler. You have a worse critic to satisfy: me. If you start in with that wiry tone, no vibrato, dry scholarship chicken-picking garbage, I personally will climb over your music stand and wrap your bow around your sweet neck." Wunschler, I thought. Complacent Swiss bastard with a professorship. What does he know about Jackie Craine? "Wunschler's just jealous," I said, "or if he isn't, he ought to be." Jackie smiled.

"He's not, really," she said. "He's really very gentle and sweet. Only he makes me nervous, damn him. Oh, well. I better go up and press my dress. If anybody needs buttons sewn, I'll be in my room. See you later." She got out at her floor, the big instrument case clasped like a clumsy baby in her arms.

I guess every musician has his own private way of getting through the dead hours before a concert. My way is to do nothing physical. The fingers that anxiety makes into bunches of bananas are the same fingers that worked nimbly enough at rehearsals; they can be made nimble again on stage. So I avoid last-second practicing. It's the psyche that has the problems and needs the help. If I can, I lie down somewhere and let loose. Usually, my preconcert mental exercise takes the form of imagining that the concert itself is *over*. I seem to want to experience in advance the exhaustion, the sour sense that the minutes of performance have slipped by, the emotional letdown. I've gotten so used to this peculiar reaction that if I don't feel wrung out before a concert, I worry.

This time, I felt properly depressed. As always, I wondered what had prompted me to take up a form of music in which every technical slip, every error of interpretation, was instantly and humiliatingly apparent to the audience. Why couldn't I have settled for a safe career well back in the second fiddle section of the New York Philharmonic, where nobody hears the clinkers? Why couldn't I be back in my ugly, drafty apartment in New York, instead of pretending to be a chamber musician in Geneva?

Like a dental patient with a familiar toothache, I probed my angst with the tip of my metaphoric tongue and felt reassured. Before normal worry could give way to absolute panic, the psyche took the next step. I fell asleep.

The purring of the bedside telephone brought me back to life. Groggily, I reached for the receiver. "Mr. French? I am so sorry if I have disturbed you." The unfamiliar voice was soft and deferential. "*Doktor* Flachsmann has asked me to call. He sends his best wishes for your success this evening. *Doktor* Flachsmann will personally attend the concert. He also wishes to invite you and your colleagues to a little reception and dinner afterward. Nothing elaborate, you understand, only a small private gathering at the *schloss*. It will not be necessary to change. The cars will pick you up at the Kursaal direct. You will accept, I hope."

"Yes, we'll be happy to come."

"We shall expect you, then, soon after the concert. Thank you, Mr. French. Goodbye."

I glanced at my watch. Six o'clock. I felt rested and nervous, just the right combination. I used the telephone to let everyone else know about the post-concert party, then I showered, shaved, and started the ritual of dressing. Dress shirt, studs, cufflinks, black tie: all part of the act of turning myself into a performer. By the time I'd shrugged myself into my penguin suit, it was seven o'clock, time to get going.

When I got backstage at the Kursaal, Ralph was already on the empty stage in his shirtsleeves, fussing with the harpsichord. He held a tuning-wrench in one hand, an A-fork in the other, and a screwdriver clamped between his teeth, so he just waggled his eyebrows in greeting. I left him to his mechanics and went on with my own preparations. The black velvet cloth spread on the floor for the treble viol, the little rack for the flute and recorders and krummhorn, the rebec in its case. The music. Before I finished laying everything out, Terry and David came onstage with their gear. More recorders, handbells, percussion, viols, the lute. Mentally, I checked it all off; it's quite an array, a kind of musical hardware store.

Jackie arrived, a little out of breath from lugging her viol. She really had treated herself to something special for the tour. It was a long, fitted dress of yellow crushed velvet, tight at the waist, with a very deep, square-cut neckline, and Jackie looked gorgeous in it. "Wow," I said, and Terry and David said the same thing. Even Ralph, looking up from his labor, gave a whistle.

"Thank you, sirs," Jackie said prettily. "Alan, I've been talking to the ticket lady and guess what? They're sold out. Every seat in the house!"

"When they see you," I said, "they'll be swinging from the rafters. I want you to go on first tonight."

"All by myself?"

"That's what you get for looking so sexy, and don't hide behind your gamba. First you, then Ralph, then Terry, David, and me. Ralph, you get seated right away. We'll all stand for a second, then Jackie sits down and we follow. Come on, let's practice it." I made us all leave the stage and rehearse an entrance. Then we practiced an intermission exit: Terry, David, and I rising, waiting for Jackie to stand and sweep past us, then following her off with Ralph last. This may sound silly, but we're in show biz. With an attraction like Jackie to exploit, I didn't mind being exploitative. Anyway, nothing makes a worse impression than a group of musicians bumping around at random on stage.

At about five past eight, Ralph finished his tuning and we all went back to the dressing room for a final smoke. I sent Terry out on stage again a few minutes later, to make sure the lights on the music stands were switched on, and to keep him from driving Jackie crazy with his wisecracks about her dress. He came back with the report that the lights were turned on and that the audience was starting to fill up the house. "They're a lot of them wearing mink," he said. Suddenly, Ralph turned pale, gave a gulp, and disappeared into the bathroom. I gave him about three minutes and then followed him in, to find him in one of the cubicles, retching miserably. "Sorry," he croaked when he was finished, "just the usual thing." It was. Ralph plays in public ten or fifteen times a year. Before almost every performance, his system rebels this way. There's nothing much he or anyone else can do about it. I waited while he pulled himself together. "I'm cold," he said. "Could you get me my coat?" I went outside, grabbed it, and brought it to him. "Thanks, Alan. I'm okay. How much time?"

"We're on in ten."

"Okay." He huddled into his coat and put on his gloves. "I'll be out in a couple of minutes."

"He's all right, isn't he?" Jackie asked. "Christus, I'd hate to have to go through that every time. I don't know how he stands it." I didn't either.

A few minutes later, Ralph came out. He was still wearing his coat and gloves, but he'd stopped shivering and some color had come back into his face. To make us feel better, he said, "I know it takes guts to be a musician, but I wish it didn't take all of mine." To make him feel better, we laughed.

Then it was eight-thirty. We trooped out of the dressing-room and down the corridor, waiting in the wings to give the audience a chance to settle down. Ralph took off his gloves. "Here's the beat," I said. "One and two and one and *play*." And we went on.

We usually open a program with a medium-tempo dance-song, to give listeners a sense of our ensemble sound and to give us time to warm up. Our second number we make more exciting. That night, we'd picked a saltarello, a wild Italian dance in very fast triple time. We started it with two heavy drumbeats, raced through it once, then split up the repeats so that everyone had a solo with variations. It was driving, raucous, earthy music, anything but the polite scholarly tweeting audiences still seem to expect. And though I say it myself, it drove the Geneva audience absolutely wild. As soon as Ralph gave us the two drumbeats, I thought I could hear a little hiss of anticipation from the front rows. Three measures into the opening—we use a shawm, a krummhorn, and a rebec to generate plenty of bite and plenty of volume—the stolid Swiss were grabbing the arms of their seats. When I started my solo, I gave Ralph a quick wink. He eased his drumming just a hair, leaving me time to scribble some ornamentation with my tiny, raspy minstrel's fiddle. Terry followed me on the shawm, a primitive oboe that sounds primitive. The climax was Jackie's solo. She was a little excited herself, and she treated the big viol as if it were a violin. For about thirty seconds, her fingers were flying and her bow hand a blur. Long before she reached the end, she was pulling bursts of applause from the crowd. When we all came in together for the finale, the clapping and shouting nearly drowned us out.

After a show-stopper, you need something to get your adrenalin, and the audience's, under control. Deliberately, we had scheduled a group of quiet *chansons*. As usual, we did a lot of instrument-switching. For instance, *Plus ne regretz*, one of the great hit songs of the fifteenth century, we begin as a recorder quartet. David then plays one strain as a lute solo while the rest of us are dropping our recorders and snatching up our viols. To cover us in case somebody forgets, Ralph joins in, doubling the melody in octaves on the harpsichord. After four more bars, I fall out, grab back my alto recorder and rejoin on the top line. For the final repeat, we're a mixed consort: bass viol, bass recorder, tenor recorder, and wooden flute. Working out all this instrumentation so that it doesn't sound too choppy or too cute takes hours of rehearsal time. Sometimes we guess wrong, and instead of playing music we're playing musical chairs with the melody. This time, we had it right. Only after the final plaintive flute note died away did the applause begin. But it went on, steady and long, and we knew that for the rest of the evening, this audience would drink us in like wine.

The people quieted again for Ralph's first solo, a set of Sweelink variations on a beautiful hymn tune with an unpronounceable Flemish name, or maybe it was a Walloon name. Ralph belongs to the poker-face school of keyboard players. From his bland expression, you'd never have guessed that half an hour earlier he'd been ashen and quaking with stagefright, or that the music he was playing was hellishly difficult. I'm not saying that Ralph never camps in public. I've heard him play the delicate bonbons of the harpsichord repertoire with a shade too much delicacy, if you know what I mean. But Sweelink is harsh, rugged, and technically very demanding. That night, Ralph tackled Sweelink head-on and made him sing. He used none of the mechanical tricks of registration that harpsichordists can use to dress up their music. It was all in Ralph's fingers, and in the perfect phrasing you need to give shape to the endless strings of sixteenth-notes Sweelink sprays around like jets from a hose. After Ralph finished, there was a second of silence. Then came the ovation. They never give you that tiny pause unless they want you to play some more.

Under cover of the clapping and "bravos" we all exchanged glances. We had one more group of pieces to play before the intermission. If we kept on going at this pace, we might run out of energy ourselves and exhaust the audience with the whole second half of the program still to go. If we relaxed too much, we might cool off musically and lose audience rapport. Then, after the intermission, we'd have to start all over again. I'm making this sound like a reasoned analysis, which of course it never is. But I had to decide. Should I push us ahead or hold us back? What the hell, I thought, let's go for broke, nobody looks too tired. So I grinned and made a "right-on" gesture and picked up my next instrument, the flute.

The one-keyed wooden flute can sound so awful that, as soon as it was invented, flute-players began doing things to it. Because the fingerings were so tricky, they added more keys. Because the embouchure and tonguing were so difficult, they gave it a mouthpiece. To make it louder, they even changed the bore, from cylindrical to conical. Finally, when they'd loaded so much hardware onto it that its tone was dreadful, they gave up altogether and started making flutes out of metal. Today, no flautist in his right mind plays the old wooden flute. I struggle with the thing myself for only one reason: I love the original sound.

This explains why I chose the flute for my only long solo, on the last piece before the intermission. It doesn't explain what happened, or nearly happened. We'd taken the first two of the three dance-songs in the suite at fairly brisk tempi. The final one is more lyrical. When Jackie, Terry, and David started it, their start was slower, much slower, than we'd rehearsed it. As I brought the flute up to my lip, I knew what the slow start meant.

I was going to run out of breath. And except for one place about halfway through, there was nowhere in the solo where I could logically break the continuity of the music to gulp in a lungful of air.

There was no use in taking a huge breath at the very beginning. I'd still run out long before the end. Besides, it's just as hard to play with too much air in your lungs as it is with too little. If I did hyperventilate at the start, I'd probably lose all control over the tone of the flute. Or else blow too hard and sharpen every note.

Jesus. The only thing to do was to breathe normally. *Normally*. Keep going through the first long passage, take my breath halfway, and hope not to fade out before the end.

I wished I'd given up smoking.

I breathed, flexed my fingers, and came in on my cue. The tone was so good it surprised me. Lips and tongue were doing their job. I just tried to keep my fingers dancing evenly in their sequence, up, down, over the holes.

Think about the act of walking, you fall on your face. Think about breathing, you begin to pant for air. Moral: don't think about breathing. *Don't think about it*. Keep the fingers moving, watch the high passage-work coming up three bars ahead . . . two bars . . . one bar . . . now. Use up a little more air; you always need more on high notes. Forget that your diaphragm, taut with the effort to squeeze the breath evenly out of your lungs, is straining in tighter and tighter.

Halfway. Time to breathe. Wait for the breathmark. Breathe. Play.

Think about the audience. You could drop out and sit here gasping like a stranded porpoise and none of them would even notice. *They would notice.* Jackie would notice. Ralph would notice. They'd know; they've been through their ordeals and done bloody brilliantly, and I'm supposed to be the *leader* and they'd know.

The last twelve bars. The sound of the flute just right, floating out over the viol and the soft buzz of the krummhorn, captivating like the pied piper don't you wish you could breathe *now. Shut up, shut up,* keep the fingers moving deliberately, concentrate on tone, fingers, tone.

I ran out with four bars to go. Diaphragm pressed solidly back, no flow from the lungs, just what air was left in the bronchials and the little pocket at the back of the throat.

One bar. I was actually dizzy with anoxia, starting to feel faint as the body, its distress signals ignored, attempted to take over.

The low F finish. Hold for half a measure. It was *over* and the audience was applauding. I made myself wait one impossible instant longer and then I took the breath. The fainting symptoms still persisted until that first gulp of oxygen forced its way from the lungs into the bloodstream into the brain. Then I could really notice what was going on: the applause, the shouting, the little bustle on stage as we prepared to exit for intermission. When we stood up to follow Jackie offstage, my legs were rubbery, but the audience, God bless it, was cheering us.

Back in the dressing room, I lit a cigarette, took one drag, then put the thing out. "You guys nearly killed me," I said to Jackie.

"It was fantastic, wasn't it? We couldn't do anything wrong." Jackie was glowing. I eyed her sourly.

"Goddammit, you practically had lung tissue flowing," I said.

"What do you mean? What's wrong?"

"On the passamezzo. You were about half-speed."

"We were? Terry, were we slow on the passamezzo?" Terry looked bushed.

"Yeah, we were, a little. Alan, got a cigarette?"

"Here, take the pack. I'll never smoke again, I swear it. You were so slow I nearly died out there," I said.

"Why, what happened?" They both looked concerned.

"You know damn well there's no place to breathe except once in the whole piece." I took back the cigarettes from Terry's unresisting fingers.

"You mean, you played that whole fantastic solo on one breath?" Jackie said.

"It was easy," I said. "You guys sunk my boat." I lit another cigarette. The hell of it was, it tasted good.

"But that's fantastic," Jackie was saying. I interrupted her.

"Listen, everybody," I raised my voice. David put down his Coke and Ralph looked up from his music. "It went really well, but pay attention to tempo. You should all have your tempi marked on every piece, or make a little note to yourself. Terry and Jackie took the passamezzo too slow and nearly ruined me.

"Aside from that," I went on, sounding to myself embarrassingly like a coach between halves of a football game, "I thought you guys were great. Ralph, the Sweelink was beautiful. Jackie, don't be afraid to give them more fireworks. David"—his lute solo opened the second half of the program—"make them forget about Julian Bream. Terry, you're never going back to Queens.

"I love you all," I said. "I love what we've done out there and what we're going to do. And if any of you remind me at the next rehearsal of what I just said, I'll deny every word."

"Maestro, can I have your autograph on my program?" said David. They all laughed. But schmaltzy or not, my locker-rooming made a difference. Everybody likes praise, but artists hunger for it; don't think they don't. Praise is the great oleo of the performing arts, the only fuel that sparks singers and dancers and actors and musicians to do the impossible things they sometimes do. Like every other kind of fuel, praise is dangerous. Too much of it inflames the ego and kills the talent. Too little shrivels the ego and ditto the talent. So ration out your praise, use it only as directed, but if you're dealing with performers, don't ever forget to add it to their diet.

A musician cannot move others unless he too is moved.

K.P.E. BACH, p. 152.

CHAPTER EIGHT

THE BUZZER SOUNDED for the second half. "Let's not be too eager," I whispered as we lined up in the wings. As soon as Jackie paraded on, the clapping began. I even heard some whistling. With the house lights not yet dimmed, I could get a look at the audience. At home, our audiences are mostly the young, with a sprinkling of the scholarly or bearded older types who follow the arts. Here there were the usual clusters of students and beards, but whole rows were filled also with older, affluent-looking males—businessmen and civil servants, no doubt—and silvery-blonde women. We'd drawn the Geneva equivalent of the New York Philharmonic crowd.

The house darkened, and again we were isolated in the little pool of light onstage. Only now, instead of feeling strange, the playing area seemed familiar, even cozy. Terry came forward to place a small footstool in front of David's chair. To play the lute, you need a prop for your right foot. But this footstool, for some reason, was covered in needlepoint. "Did you swipe that from the hotel?" I muttered to Terry. He nodded. I thought it added still another domestic touch.

David must have thought so, too, because he sat down and played his lute as casually as if he were picking out music in his own living room. Occasionally he grinned to himself, and once or twice we could hear him humming along under his breath. He was perfect. He made the audience feel that it was overhearing a private performance, not sitting in a concert hall listening to a professional, and you could have heard the proverbial pin drop. At the end, when the applause began, David even had the chutzpah to look up from his fragile instrument with a startled expression, as if the noise had awakened him from deep communion with his personal muse. Then he stood up, gave the crowd his nicest boyish smile, and took his bow.

"Nice going, you ham," I said as he edged past me on his way to his regular seat.

"Screw you," he whispered back happily, "screw you." Thank God the mikes didn't pick it up.

The whole second half of the program went the same way. We were playing for fun and for each other and hardly even remembering that there was an audience, except at the end of each number when the applause broke through. Jackie sparkled her way through her Tobias Hume. Terry and David teamed up slap-happily on a group of Thomas Morley two-part canzonets. Their dialoguing was so witty that only a pro would have noticed the occasional dropped note. Ralph swept majestically through one of the great Byrd pavane-galliard sequences. Finally, we came to the set of instrumental madrigals we'd just begun to develop so intriguingly in rehearsal the day before. And, as I'd hoped, we broke through the outer shell of the music. If you're a musician, you'll understand. If you're not, I guess there's no use trying to explain. But we were *making* music together, not simply playing it well.

We had to play three encores.

Even after the house lights went on, half the crowd pushed forward toward the stage and stood clapping in rhythm while we paraded off and then, urged by a delighted young production assistant in a flowery bow tie, back on. Maybe it was Jackie's yellow dress and David's soulful smile, or maybe it was that we'd given the performance of our lives, you never know, but we'd certainly caught the fancy of the fans.

The dressing room was so mobbed that we hardly had room to put down our instruments. Jovial people kept coming up to me and saying, "You don't know me, but—" and trying to shake hands. A. De Soto was proclaiming that we were mahvlous, mahvlous. Wunschler the viol-player, his face wreathed in smiles like a Swiss Santa Claus's, rushed up to Jackie and embraced her. Carroll from the Embassy was there with a young lady who looked impressed when he introduced her. So were others I vaguely recognized, including, incredibly, the skinny heart surgeon and his wife who had been at Mundel's party in New York.

On the table, a huge silver bowl was stuffed with red roses. Tucked into the display was an engraved card. It read, "Congratulations on Your Outstanding Performance. The Philomel Foundation." For a second, I wondered what the message would have been if our performance had been other than Outstanding. But a touch on my arm interrupted the reverie. It was Bauer, the suspicious-minded cultural reporter. "Congratulations, Mr. French," he said. "You attracted a first-rate audience and I must say you dazzled it. A good performance, a very strong performance." After I thanked him, he went on, "I must say that I may have been mistaken."

"You mean about my having been a secret member of the CIA?"

"No, no, Mr. French," Bauer chuckled. "The CIA? God forbid. You are not, if I may say so, the CIA type. But about, let us say, ulterior reasons for making the trip. Motives—other than musical."

"*Herr* Bauer—"

"Mr. French, have I not just said my apologies? There is no need to berate me. You have convinced me, or rather, your playing has convinced me. You are a fine professional, Mr. French, I admit it, not an enthusiastic amateur whose main interest is," he hesitated for a second, "elsewhere."

"I've said all along that we came here to play music."

"Very true, Mr. French. If I am any judge of my countrymen," Bauer gestured at the crowd in the room, "you are about to become very busy with your success. So busy, I hope, that you will have no time left to do things that arouse the curiosity of an old bloodhound like me. Now I must go and write my review." He shook my hand and once again bade me *Auf wiedersehen*. I would have loved to pump him about the Philomel Foundation, but I wasn't too unhappy to see him leave.

"Ach, Mr. French! You were wonderful, marvelous!" Walter Mundel, soigné in a gray suit and a silver tie, slipped toward me through the crowd. "Permit me to congratulate you! We chose wisely when we selected you, of course, we knew of your accomplishments. But you are a hit! How fortunate that I had to be in Geneva for a meeting and so could steal the time to be here. Please congratulate the others, especially Miss Craine. She looked so charming and she played ravishly. I mean, of course, ravishingly." Ebullience was not Mundel's strong suit. "We expect to renew our acquaintance with you later at the *Schloss*. You will be there later, will you not? Of course. *Natürlich*, we will have a chance to talk. Now is not the time, eh? First, celebrate, then cerebrate. Good, then, until later." He nodded stiffly, smiled a stiff smile, and moved away. I noticed that, from across the room, Bauer followed Mundel with his eyes until Mundel pushed through the door and disappeared. Frankly, I felt relieved. Before too long, Mundel and Philomel were obviously planning to let Alan French know where he stood.

Several dozen congratulations later, the jammed room began to empty. The bespectacled young man lecturing Ralph on the niceties of the *pralltriller* finally gave up, clicked his heels politely, and excused himself for intruding upon the gracious *Herr*'s festive occasion. The clusters of enthusiasts surrounding Jackie and David began to thin out. The assistant in the bow tie, still looking delighted, was posted at the door, bowing the notables out, and denying entrance to latecomers still trying to get in. One of the latecomers, I noted with astonishment, was our friend Krohl, resplendent in a mouton-trimmed impresario's overcoat. He was insisting pompously that as a sponsor and patron he should naturally have access. . . . Bow tie raised his eyebrows inquiringly at me. I beckoned him over and said, "Tell him, don't call us, we'll call you."

"Pardon?" The eyebrows shot even higher. I should have known better.

"Say to Mr. Krohl that any proposition he wishes to make to us should be addressed to me in writing."

"Ah." I watched him relay the message to Krohl, who looked so disappointed that I almost felt sorry for him. Almost.

"Mr. French?" A. De Soto peered at me anxiously. "The car is ready."

"The car?"

"To leave for the Castle. The reception is scheduled to begin at midnight." Suddenly, I did feel sorry for A. De Soto, bad breath and all. She'd obviously been up and working since the crack of dawn, attending to details, writing up schedules, arranging the luncheon. Now it must be nearly eleven-thirty, and she was still on the job.

"We're not quite ready to leave," I said, "but we won't be long."

"Oh, do take your time," she said in the tone of voice that, coming from an Englishwoman, means, "Do for God's sake hurry up." So I cruised around and got the others to start packing instruments and putting on coats, and eventually we straggled out the stage entrance. Another one of those enormous Mercedes limousines stood waiting to receive us. A few minutes later, we were moving out of the heavy city traffic and climbing steadily on a road into the hills. Hills? To me, they looked more like Alps, although from the way the chauffeur whipped us around the switchbacks and hairpins turns, the Swiss obviously draw the line differently. The car was snug and warm. After a few minutes of excited chatter, we all quieted down. I must have dozed off, because the next thing I knew, we were rolling down the steep main street of a village—Montricher, I later learned—around a tight curve and then suddenly off the main road, through a set of massive gates and onto a narrow paved drive that seemed to lead straight up the side of a mountain. I sensed rather than saw the shadowy forms of big pines slipping by on either side. At one point, the Mercedes braked sharply. In the glare of the headlights, I caught a quick glimpse of a deer as it cut across the track to plunge fluidly into the woods. We picked up speed again, and a minute later we were driving through another set of gates into a courtyard and pulling up before a huge, looming pile of masonry.

"My God," Terry muttered. "This guy really does have his own castle."

"*Madame, messieurs*, please be careful crossing the bridge," the chauffeur warned as he opened our door. He wasn't joking. A lowered drawbridge presented itself, its chains gleaming in the light from a pair of torches bracketed onto the stonework. We clomped across hurriedly, passed through a kind of tunnel cut in the outer wall and found ourselves in a grassy interior courtyard. A flagged path led us to the main house, a slightly less medieval structure backed up against the rear wall of the castle itself. The house was brightly lighted, but although we'd seen a dozen or more cars parked in the outer courtyard, no sound was escaping those walls to let anyone know a party was going on.

The night air was more than cool, it was cold. We were glad to be inside, on the thick velvety carpet of the reception hall, with one servant pushing shut the heavy oak door and another relieving us of the raincoats we'd all thrown on over our fancy clothes after the performance. Jackie disappeared into the powder room. David, Terry, Ralph, and I waited patiently until she emerged. She made a face at us, murmured something about being a mess, and began to fuss with David's black tie. Just then, Mundel came padding out to greet us. "Mademoiselle Craine! Gentlemen! How good that you have arrived!" He led us down a richly paneled, heavily carpeted corridor into an enormous drawing-room. It too was carpeted, and over the neutral-colored carpeting were laid Persian and Turkish rugs that looked like collector's items. Unadorned, the stone floors of the castle would probably have been freezing cold, but this way the effect was something like walking on a trampoline.

A couple of dozen people were already in the room, some grouped at the carved table serving as a bar, others gathered at a buffet, still others in front of the immense sculptured marble fireplace. Most of the women and some of the men were in formal dress. It was an ad for gracious living on the grand scale.

"Please first stop for a drink," Mundel said, "and then come with me to meet the *Doktor*. *Doktor* Flachsmann is very anxious to meet you all." A barman juggled ice, glasses, and liquor for us, then Mundel escorted us over to the liveliest of the groups of guests. At its center, a drink in his hand, was our host.

From his name, his dealings with us, and what little I'd heard about his life style, I'd naturally assumed that Hugo Flachsmann was an elderly man, and the prototype of the rich, shrewd European. You know, either an elegant, ambassadorial aristocrat or else a gross, arrogant, but cunning self-made man. The only thing that had never occurred to me was that the fabulous *Doktor* Flachsmann might turn out to be a trim thirty-five-year-old American with blue eyes, an Ivy League side cut, and a let's-be-friends grin.

"Hi," he said, holding out a tanned, well-manicured hand to Jackie. "Welcome to San Simeon. Isn't this place the most ridiculous thing you've ever seen?" Before any of us could answer, he was introducing us around, saving the last introduction for a stunning-looking brunette. "This is Deborah," Flachsmann said. "She's the only thing in the whole castle that won't ever need restoring—except you, Jackie. Right, honey?"

"I guess so," said the girl, who was eyeing Jackie with something less than enthusiasm. Then she brightened. "You're the one who played the cello tonight, aren't you? I thought it sounded just beautiful." She very carefully did not say "bee-yoo-ti-ful."

"Thank you," said Jackie sweetly.

"I wish I could play something like that," Deborah said. "But it must take hours of practice. I'd never have the patience."

Flachsmann looked a little embarrassed. "It wasn't a cello, it was a viola da gamba," he said. I was surprised that he knew. "And it takes more than patience, Deb. It takes talent. Look at her hands," he ordered Deborah. "Have you ever seen such beautiful hands?"

"Beautiful," Deborah echoed. "My friend—I have a friend who's a specialist in hands—my friend says that hands with square fingertips mean a practical nature. Are you practical?"

"Very," said Jackie.

"There, you see, Hugo? I told you Larry could tell a lot about people from their hands. Hugo, Larry should be a consultant in Personnel."

"I don't know how we got off on this ridiculous subject," Flachsmann said. He spoke amiably, but Deborah immediately subsided. "What I want to talk about, Alan," he turned to me, "is the Antiqua Players. I listen to a lot of music and I thought you were simply outstanding tonight. Hey, everybody, didn't these people do an outstanding job?"

The four or five other people within earshot all answered yes, we'd been outstanding, terrific, they'd never been to a better concert. They were all Americans, and I couldn't help wondering if they'd ever been to another concert.

"I bet you get great reviews," Flachsmann said contentedly. "The Swiss really go for good music. I'd like to see what they say. Walter," he said to Mundel, "how about sending a car down to Geneva for the early papers? Let's have a look at the reviews. Alan and Jackie are probably anxious to know how they did." He laughed.

"We can send Hubener," Mundel said.

"No, don't send Hubener. He has to drive this gang back—hey, wait a minute!" Again he turned to me. "What are your plans for tomorrow?"

"I don't know," I said. "Sleep late, eat a big breakfast, read the reviews, maybe rehearse in the afternoon."

"Why don't you stay up here tonight? We've got plenty of room. Don't we, Debbie? Nobody else is staying over, are they?"

"Only Herb, and he doesn't know for sure, he's got a meeting in the morning."

"Oh, Herb. He can go in with Hubener," Flachsmann said a little impatiently. "Tell him he can see me late tomorrow."

"Okay," Deborah said. "He's such a problem," she sighed dramatically. "He brought Herb up here specially to brief him before the meeting."

"Look," I said, "if this is going to be too much trouble—"

"No, please stay. It will be fun. I never get a chance to be with artists. It's mostly businessmen. I love art, and artists are madly attractive."

Jackie was pulling at my sleeve. "Alan, will you *listen*? It's great to stay in a castle, but do you realize that we're all dressed to play and tomorrow we won't have a thing to wear?''

"Oh, don't worry about that," Deborah said. "Hugo's got lots of clothes. And I could lend you something." She seemed quite reconciled to having as houseguests five total strangers. "Come on upstairs," she said to Jackie, "I'll show you around and you can pick up some stuff to put on."

As the girls left to go exploring, Flachsmann said, "Hey, this is great. One of the chauffeurs is taking Herb into town, and he'll pick up the papers with the reviews. We're having him stop by your hotel in case there are any cables or messages for you, okay?''

"Sure," I said, "but isn't this a lot of trouble?''

"Hell, no, we do it all the time. People come up here on business, they fall in love with the place, and they just stay. Sometimes they stay a week. Besides," he added, "I really do want to talk to you."

This is it, I thought. "What about?''

"Oh, the Antiqua Players and the music business and whatever we decide to talk about. But let's do it tomorrow morning after breakfast. You don't want to talk business now and I don't want to bust up a celebration. Hey, where's Jackie?''

"She went upstairs with Deborah to look things over."

"Well, she ought to be here when we get the reviews." Multimillionaire or not, this clean-cut *wunderkind* certainly liked women. Watch out, Debbie, I thought, new girl in town. Furthermore, Flachsmann had what it took to make women like him. He was as fit as a ski instructor and almost as handsome, and he had the kind of self-deprecating charm I associated with certain very successful male actors, sports heroes, and now, business entrepreneurs. "She won't want to miss the reviews," Flachsmann repeated.

"She'll be down in a few minutes, I'm sure," I said.

"Well, I know it sounds ridiculous," he said, "but make yourselves at home." His gesture indicated the whole salon and the main body of the castle.

I laughed. "Tell me——"

"Listen, if we're going to talk, just call me Hugo." He extracted a Sobranie cigarette from a flat gold case and lit it with a solid gold Dunhill gas lighter. Then, remembering his manners, he held out the case to me, which is more than most of the rich people I've met would do.

"No, thanks," I said. "I nearly ran out of breath on one number tonight and it's making me nervous."

"Then I shouldn't tempt you," he said seriously and put away the case. "But that doesn't mean you can't have another drink. Phillipe!" he hailed the bartender. "Another Dewar's and soda for me. What are you drinking?" he asked me.

"A vermouth cassis." When the drinks came, he lifted his glass in salute. "Here's to Alan French and the Antiqua Players. May their tour be a brilliant success and their future brilliant, too."

"Thanks. Cheers," I said and everybody else said, "Hear, hear!" and we drank. Flachsmann put a brotherly hand on my shoulder.

"I like this guy," he said. "Alan, you don't come on like a musician. Now your good buddies over there—Dave and Terry, right?—well, Dave and Terry do. They act like real artists, with plenty of the old temperament. But I watched you up on that stage and you keep your cool."

"You don't come on like a big business executive," I said.

"I'm not one really. These other guys are the management experts. I'm just a kid who happened to be in the right place at the right time with the right idea." He caught me looking skeptically around the huge, improbable room and laughed.

"If you're thinking that this is a vulgar, ostentatious life style for someone who just got lucky, you're absolutely right." Since that was exactly what I had been thinking, I kept my mouth shut. "I have no right to live like this," Flachsmann went on. "Alan, I'll tell you a secret. My stockholders ought to throw me right out of the company on my ear for living here. But it's not my fault. It just happened, that's all. One day I saw the want ad in *The Zurich Express*. For sale, small castle, vicinity Montricher. I drove up to take a look. You'll see tomorrow, it's a hell of a piece of property. Great view, good water, right near town. I figured, let the company buy it and hold it, some day it'll be worth a fortune. So we bought it. I never thought I'd *live* here. We used to come up for weekends, camp out in sleeping bags, go hiking in the woods. Then I thought, why not remodel one of the old turrets, just as a getaway place? But some of these other bastards got jealous." He gestured around him in comic disgust. "They wanted getaway places, too. So we finally wound up spending a fortune, putting the main hall and one whole wing back in shape.

"So I moved in, and that's how come I live in a castle," he finished.

"The funny thing is, it's great public relations. I'm not sure the board would let me move even if I wanted to. If that sounds crazy, don't worry about it. It *is* crazy." He sounded so rueful that for a moment, I was tempted to believe him. But if you're a Hugo Flachsmann and you don't want to live in your castle, let's face it, you don't have to.

"Crazy or not, you love it," I told him.

"You're absolutely right," he said again. "I shouldn't, but I do. But let's not talk about that. I want to know about Alan French." For fifteen minutes, he quizzed me intently, about myself, about being a musician, about the business of making music. Other people were partying, some were listening, but Flachsmann had a way of making the person he was talking to feel as if he were the only person in the room. You and I are alone together, his manner hinted engagingly, those others are just part of our scenery. Because I'm young and rich and so dynamic, you too are someone very special . Otherwise, I wouldn't be dismissing everybody else to spend my time with you.

They teach this sort of technique at the Dale Carnegie School, I suppose. But when it's being practiced on you by fifty million dollars' worth of candid, likeable entrepreneur, you feel flattered. At least, I did. I was enjoying my *tête-à-tête* with Flachsmann, and when it was interrupted, I was sorry.

"Hubener is back, sir, with the newspapers." The barman had spotted the chauffeur as he came in. Mundel himself greeted the man and took from him the neatly folded journals. From across the salon, I saw Hubener nod in response to some request and salute respectfully as Mundel dismissed him.

"Walter, let's see them," Flachsmann said. "And somebody go find Debbie and Jackie." That must have been what Mundel had ordered Hubener to do, because a minute later the two girls appeared. Evidently, they'd made friends. At least, Jackie had changed out of her yellow dress into a black après-ski that could only have come from Debbie's closet. As she walked over, I could see Flachsmann's eyes brighten.

"Alan, this place is terrific," Jackie said. "Wait 'til you see what they've done upstairs. Mr. Flachsmann—"

"Alan calls me Hugo, sweetie. You should, too."

"Oh." Jackie suddenly woke up to Flachsmann's interest, his personal interest, in Jackie Craine. After about one second, she decided she liked it. "Well, Hugo, it's, it's—"

"Terrific," he finished for her gently. "If someone with your taste thinks so, then the stockholders' money has not been spent in vain." Jackie flushed prettily. "Alan, does he talk this way to all his musician friends?"

"Believe it or not, sweetie," said Flachsmann, "you and Alan are my only musician friends. I mean, I've met Horowitz and Isaac Stern and even Casals once in Prades, but that was just casual, for business. This is something different." He flashed her his ten-thousand-volt smile and then began riffling swiftly through the newspapers. "Ah, here we go." He raised his voice. "Ladies and gentlemen." People stopped their drinking and talking immediately. "Please listen. 'A new and vital musical organization tonight brought exciting life to old music.' That's the headline of the *Journal de Genève* review. Kass— he's the one who counts—Kass says: 'The sedate, scholarly perform- ance tradition that so weakens our appreciation of preclassical music was cast aside tonight by the Antiqua Players. The result was like that of peeling the layers of old varnish off Old Master paintings, a revela- tion of the color and power still possessed by great works even after centuries.' Then he goes on, 'The Antiqua Players, so subtly led that they seemed utterly spontaneous, played with complete technical sec- urity and, more important, *con brio* and *con amore*.'

"Alan," he laughed, "did you write this thing yourself?" I grinned, and he read us a few more phrases. " 'Jacqueline Craine, a virtuoso with much to teach our gamba specialists . . . David Brodkey, intense and sparkling . . . Ralph Mitchell, a harpsichordist of the first rank.'

"Ladies and gentlemen," Flachsmann said above the buzz of talk. "It's obvious that our guests of tonight, Alan French and his Antiqua Players, are the musical toasts of Geneva. Most of us heard them play earlier, so we're in a position to judge that the reviewers are absolutely right. I personally am very proud that our Philomel Foundation was instrumental in sponsoring this group and in allowing its well-deserved triumph." There was a spattering of applause.

"And now, at the risk of seeming rude," Flachsmann went on, "I would remind you that it's very late, nearly two o'clock, and that most of us have to be at our desks in the morning. So I suggest that we all now finish our nightcaps and head for home. Thank you so much for being here."

It sounded polite, it was polite, but it was an order. Within ten minutes, the room had emptied of everybody except Debbie,

Flachsmann, Mundel, and the five of us. Mundel lingered only long enough to congratulate us and to set up a meeting "with our publicity people" as soon as possible. Then he left, too. Flachsmann, glass in hand, prowled around the salon snapping off light switches like a suburban host. Debbie, curled up on a couch by the fireplace, yawned delicately, covering her open mouth with a ladylike hand. For a few minutes, we all sat cozily around the fire, passing the reviews back and forth and enjoying every word of them. Then the yawning became an epidemic. Flachsmann pressed a buzzer. He spoke in rapid German to the white-aproned housekeeper who apeared in answer. "Ursula says your rooms are ready," he announced.

"Aren't you coming up, honey?" Debbie asked as the rest of us said our good nights and, like tired children behind their nursemaid, got ready to follow Ursula upstairs.

"In a minute," Flachsmann said, and Debbie sighed. At the door, I glanced back. Flachsmann had settled in an easy chair, a briefcase open beside him. From behind some panel, he'd rolled out a large TV set. He was fiddling with the dials and the screen was flickering on. Debbie sighed again but kept on walking with the rest of us.

I vaguely remember climbing a wide stone staircase and being conducted along a passageway. Shiny suits of armor stood along one wall. I had to go through a Gothic arched doorway to get into my room. And I recall the musty smell of old woodwork and old stone, mingled with the limy scent of new plasterwork. But I was dead tired. I barely looked around before stripping off my tuxedo and boiled shirt and falling into bed.

Good performance can, in fact, improve and gain praise
for even an average composition.

K.P.E. BACH, p. 153.

CHAPTER NINE

FLACHSMANN EXPLODED HIS BOMBSHELL after breakfast.

I'd slept deeply and I woke up slowly, lying on my back and enjoying
in a mild way my disorientation. Only after I'd drifted halfway back to
sleep did a light tapping on the door bring me wide awake. A housemaid bearing a tray greeted me softly. The steaming pot of tea she left
me tempted me out of bed, and then I began reacting to the other
reminders that I'd spent the night in a millionaire's private castle. There
was the room itself, its narrow shuttered window opening on a vista of
green mountain meadow and tan plowland. There was the adjoining
bath, with thick towels and choice toiletries laid out neatly for the
guest. Back in the bedroom, I found that some silent servitor had
pressed my tuxedo and laundered my linens during the night. And the
clothes Flachsmann—Debbie, really—had promised to supply were
lying folded on a dresser: soft leather shoes that fit, a pair of jeans, and a
russet-colored cashmere pullover: exactly my idea of what to wear
when you wander around a castle in search of breakfast.

As I made my way down the stone stairs, the whole vast place was
silent. But at the main landing, the same housemaid who'd brought me
the tea accosted me. "The *Herr Doktor* is taking his breakfast on the
terrace. Will it please the gracious *Herr* to join him?" She led me
through a formal dining room large enough to hold a troop of dragoons.
I stepped through the tall French doors at the far end and out into a crisp
Swiss spring morning. The terrace had been built right into the ancient
fortifications. Tucked into an angle of one huge buttress, shielded from
the wind, was a small, sunny area set up outdoor-cafe style. Seated at

one of the tables was Flachsmann, looking relaxed in slacks, loafers, and sport jacket. He was drinking coffee and reading a business journal. "Hey, good morning!" He tilted his sunglasses up on his forehead and squinted cheerfully at me. "Have some breakfast? We'll get you some super ham and eggs." He rang a small silver bell and told the maid who appeared, "Margit, bring Alan the works." She bobbed and smiled and disappeared. Within three minutes, the food was on the table. While Flachsmann read and sipped from his cup, I waded through my ham and eggs. I was just washing down a fresh croissant with my first cupful of coffee when he threw down his magazine and said, "Alan, this is a great place for us to have a talk."

It was. From where we sat, we could gaze out over a sweep of landscape, across a valley and toward the mountain ridge beyond. The sun was warm; the sky was bright, bright blue; and the coffee at my elbow was delicious. I waited for Flachsmann to go on. Solicitously, he asked me how I'd slept, how I felt, and how it feels to wake up after a successful concert. Then he said quietly, "Back in New York, Walter mentioned to you, didn't he, that there might be some way you could help us out? I mean, apart from being a wonderful musician and a very, very nice guy."

I nodded. If I'd been one of the birds chirping at the far end of the terrace, he'd have had me feeding out of his hand.

"There is a way." He paused to reach for a cigarette, this time offering me the case before he extracted a smoke of his own. "There is a way," he repeated. "If you'd been a different kind of a guy, I might just make you the proposition. But I can't."

"Why not?"

"You have to let me explain, you have to let me give you the background." He inhaled and blew out a cloud of tobacco smoke, staring thoughtfully past me at the mountain scenery. "You see," he said, "I believe in art. If I didn't, you wouldn't be here, naturally. Naturally, I believe in business, too, in the almighty dollar or franc or dinar. Otherwise—otherwise neither of us would be here. All right. But business and art go together. Down through history, they've gone hand in hand. You understand?" He clasped his two hands together, then rapped one hand on the table to make sure I understood. "Okay. Well, as it happens, I do a lot of business with our friends behind the so-called Iron Curtain.

"Don't worry, Alan, that's got nothing to do with you," he said hastily, before I could even register surprise. "Nothing at all. And every subscription we sell, every catalogue we mail to Poland or East Germany or the Soviet Union, is sold openly and with the approval of the government." Did he mean the Swiss government, the U.S. government, or the Soviet government? I wondered, but I didn't interrupt him.

"Certainly, I do it to make money," Flachsmann said, "and you'd be surprised. Every one of those Communist purchasing agents and technicians pays in cash and on time. There's never a renewal problem, never even a second statement. I wish I could say as much for our cousins in Freedomland.

"But," he added fervently, "I also sell to those people because we're in the information business. And I believe that the free exchange of information is a great catalyst that will some day make all people free."

My God, I thought, he sounds like a Voice of America brochure. Flachsmann grinned embarrassedly. "I'm sorry," he said. "I must sound like a Voice of America brochure. I don't mean to, but this is so important." He hunched forward in his chair. "What I'm saying is, business information is already free. Even in Red China, in the trade bureaus of Peking, we have subscribers.

"But art, the other great inspirer of human freedom," he punctuated his words with little jabbings of his right forefinger, "art isn't free. Okay?

"Why, did you know that in the Soviet Union alone, thousands upon thousands of your fellow artists—musicians, painters, writers, even dancers—are forbidden to practice their art? If they defy the ban, some of them are sentenced to work camps in Siberia, or worse. Or worse," he repeated grimly, stubbing out his Sobranie in a china ashtray that had MOET-CHANDON printed across the bottom.

For a few seconds, Flachsmann allowed me to contemplate the terrible plight of thousands upon thousands of my fellow artists. "We've got to get organized on this," he said fiercely. "We've got to do something to call the attention of the whole world to these artists in chains. That's the gut purpose of Philomel—" He cut himself off as if he felt he'd said too much. Then he asked abruptly, "Alan, do you know Kobrand, the cellist?"

The closest I'd ever come to knowing Itzaak Kobrand was during his last American tour. One night, he was playing the Dvorak cello concerto with an orchestra in New York. The same night, I was playing with the same orchestra. Kobrand was the soloist. I was in the second violin section, third chair from the end on the right. Before the performance, he asked me for some rosin. With my rosin and his talent, how could he miss? He was a big, burly peasant of a man, I remembered, with a cropped haircut and broad, muscular hands. And he was exactly what his publicity called him, the greatest cellist in the world.

"I did meet him once," I told Flachsmann. "Several years ago."

"Do you know what's happened to him since?"

"Well," I said, thinking back. 'He was one of the people who led the protest against the suppression of Ivry's opera about Stalin. Wasn't that it?"

"Right," said Flachsmann. "And do you know what they did to him afterward?"

"No."

"Well, I'll tell you. First they canceled his passport, naturally, so he could no longer leave the country. Then they removed him from his faculty post at the Leningrad Conservatory because his teaching had 'cosmopolitan' tendencies. You know what that means?" I nodded.

"Correct. In his final class, he told his students, 'If belief in the universality of music is cosmopolitan, then I am proud to be a cosmopolite.' The authorities didn't like that. So the Soviet Musicians' Guild issued an official reprimand and started a boycott. Kobrand couldn't play with any orchestra. He couldn't even find an accompanist. So he announced that he would devote himself exclusively to the solo music of Bach.

"Six months ago, the Ministry of Culture decided enough was enough. They had Kobrand detained and they sent him to a mental institution for 'rehabilitation.'

"We're getting Kobrand out of Russia. And we want you to help get him the rest of the way out."

Jesus. So that was it. Inside Flachsmann's expensive cashmere, I quietly began to sweat. "But why me?" I asked, already half-knowing the answer.

"Because you're a musician and musicians can go anywhere." Flachsmann lit another Sobranie. "Because you're not in any way associated with Kobrand or his supporters. He doesn't even play your kind of music. You're not Jewish." He looked at me. "You're not, are you?'' I shook my head. ''Well, no one will suspect, when you go into East Germany, that it's anything but part of your tour.''

''You are really and truly crazy,'' I said. Flachsmann ignored me.

''We've arranged for Kobrand to be transferred from the mental hospital in Leningrad to a facility in East Germany that deals in the 'treatment' of dissident intellectuals. The specialists there processed most of the leaders of the Hungarian revolt and then later some of the key Polish labor officials.

''It's a quiet place, very discreet. Guess where it's located?''

''I give up,'' I said.

''Markneukirchen.'' The quaint village where the locals make replicas of old musical instruments. The quaint village where we were scheduled to perform in some sort of *festspiel*. I felt sick at the thought.

''You say *you* arranged Kobrand's transfer? How?''

''That's not your problem,'' Flachsmann said. ''Your problem is simply contacting Kobrand, arranging a time and place, and driving him out. It's easy, really. And we'll be helping every step of the way.''

''Ah,'' I said. ''You mean, all we have to do is get to Markneukirchen, wherever *that* is, probably ten miles up a dirt goat-track, pick up the phone and call Kobrand at the local madhouse, and tell him, 'Pack up, we'll be by for you in half an hour.' Sure. Easy. The cops won't even notice, let alone interfere. In fact, they'll check our oil and wipe the windshield.

''Hugo, old boy, you've been great and we're all grateful. But, no.''

''Alan, I was hoping you'd say that.'' Flachsmann assured me sincerely. ''If some crazy guy hit me over the head with this scheme, I'd feel exactly the same way. That's why you have to let me explain.''

''No.''

''Number One,'' Flachsmann went right on, ''you're already booked right into the middle of things. Number Two, there's a local festival in session, with people coming and going all day long. We simply have to work out the mechanics of separating Kobrand from his guards, getting him into a car, and driving him away.''

''No.''

''It's going to be like sneaking a note past your fourth-grade teacher,'' Flachsmann protested. ''How can you just keep on saying no?''

''If that was all there was to it,'' I said, ''you'd have done it yourself a long time ago. So there's something you're not telling me. Probably a lot of things. Besides, I'm a coward.''

"Well,'' Flachsmann said, "getting Kobrand *into* Markneukirchen isn't something you do whenever you want. *Ergo*, getting Kobrand *out* of Markneukirchen isn't a job you save up to pull off any rainy Saturday afternoon when you can't go skiing. Otherwise—you're right—otherwise, I would have done it long ago.'' Suddenly, he began to laugh. "Sorry, Alan,'' he said. "I'm certainly not making fun of you. But it *is* funny. I said to Walter Mundel last night, I told him you might be difficult. He said, 'Nonsense. French will want to help a great and suffering artist. Besides, he's naive. All musicians are naive.' Obviously, you're not that. And don't give me that stuff about being a coward.'' Deftly, Flachsmann poured us both coffee. "No. If you were a different type of person, I could make the proposition, sweeten it if need be, then sit back and watch you accept.''

I couldn't resist. "Sweeten it how?''

Flachsmann eyed me appraisingly. "Oh, there are ways,'' he said. "Some people, you'd just put some cash in a Swiss bank. Alan, you can't *believe* what risks people will take for plain old money. Not too much money, either. Hell, for ten thousand bucks, I could get a professional to go in, get a message to Kobrand, maybe even wait around to bring him out.''

"Why not do it that way?''

"Alan, let me tell you why not.'' As he looked guilelessly into my eyes, I knew with a sinking sensation in my ham and eggs that he was preparing a sleek, fat lie. "With a professional, you can't buy loyalty. Or enthusiasm. On this project, you need both. Plus, of course, the freedom to move around. Most of the professionals are known, and they'd be watched. They might not get caught, but there would be risks, and we want no risks. For once, and for this one time, an amateur would be safer.

"But forget all that. I wouldn't offer you that kind of deal; I'm not that stupid. Forget it. You'd have to want to do this job in the first place, and not only for money.''

"Don't flatter me,'' I said.

"I'm not flattering you. All I'm saying is, you haven't really considered the issues. If you'd said yes right off the bat, I'd have been worried. But you're saying no too damn fast, too. So cool down.

"My problem is, you're simply not greedy.'' In mock frustration, he shook his head. "I'm a salesman, and I have no way to sell you.''

I had no response. The whole conversation was casting a dirty gray shadow over the sunny Alpine morning. The last cup of coffee sat in my stomach like a memory of guilt. In fact, I was feeling some guilt. I felt guilty for refusing Flachsmann's offer: I had nothing against Kobrand, I would have wanted to help him if I could. Guiltier still for having put myself—and all of us—in a position where I had to listen in the first place. The Philomel Foundation. I'd been right about it from the start. They'd offered us too much, so that when their turn came they could get it all back. With interest. There had to be more to this than Flachsmann was telling me. It was time to find out how much more.

"Let me make sure I've got it straight," I said. "You believe in freedom of the arts. A noble spirit, that's you. So you activate God knows what kind of machinery inside Soviet Russia on behalf of Itzaak Kobrand. If you can get him all the way from Leningrad to Markneukirchen, you're right, it must be some operation. Christ, if you can do that, you ought to be able to charter Brezhnev's personal plane to *fly* him the rest of the way.

"But no, that would be too easy. No, oh Jesus no, no professionals; they'd be watched; amateurs are better. So you push another button, activate Mundel; he activates us. No trouble, no trouble at all. Get us from New York, set us up over here. To do what?" I was beginning to scare myself silly. "To drive Kobrand a few hundred miles through tank-traps? Come on, Hugo. Let's not hear any more about how easy it is. Or about the freedom of the arts."

One thing a musician does understand is the use of silence. Flachsmann sat impassively in the sunshine while the smoke from his Sobranie curled emptily into the air and the coffee in his cup went from hot to tepid. But I'd made up my mind to outwait him, and I won.

"All right, Alan," Flachsmann said. "I should have known better. If you must know, I'll tell you the whole story. But are you sure you really want to know?"

"No," I said, "I'm not sure at all. But tell me anyway."

There was another long silence. Then Flachsmann, for the first time looking nervous, moistened his lips with his tongue. "Do you—have you any knowledge of the KGB?"

Holy Christ, I thought. Siberia. The knout. The midnight knock on the door. "The Russian Gestapo," I said aloud.

Flachsmann laughed. 'Not really, not since Stalin's death," he said, "but in a way, of course, you're absolutely right. It's the Politburo's internal security organ, and it's got its nose into everything. Even culture. Or perhaps I should say, especially culture. Well, then, this Kobrand affair—"

"It's a KGB operation."

"Exactly," Flachsmann said. "But believe me, Alan, you're jumping to the wrong conclusion."

"No doubt," I said. "You want me to go in and snatch Kobrand out of East Germany. It's easy. And the fact that the KGB is probably guarding him with a regiment of undercover goons, not to mention squads of 200-pound police dogs who are fed, once a month or so, on human flesh—well, what the hell, I'm James Bond; no problem."

"Alan, goddamn it, will you *listen*," Flachsmann almost shouted. "The KGB is going to *help* you."

"Come again," I said.

With exaggerated slowness and patience, Flachsmann repeated himself. "The KGB, the Committee for State Security, will be assisting you in the removal of Itzaak Kobrand from Markneukirchen and in the trip from Markneukirchen to the Swiss border."

"Yes, of course they will," I said. "I'm sure the KGB would be delighted to ship the cremains to any point in the world."

"Alan," Flachsmann sighed, "please listen." Maybe I was wearing him down. I hoped so. He said, "The KGB isn't just a bunch of goons, any more than the FBI or the CIA is just a bunch of goons."

"You could have fooled me," I said, thinking about the FBI and the CIA.

"Let's not argue the point," Flachsmann said. "Take my word or read your history books. In Russia, the secret police has always been sociopolitically oriented in a way that no Westerner understands. It goes back beyond Stalin, beyond Lenin even, all the way back to the old Czarist Okhrana."

"Okay," I said, "In Russia, the KGB is a state within a state. So what?"

"So this. Itzaak Kobrand is an international celebrity. He is also a troublemaker. So much so that the Supreme Soviet would love to be rid of him. In the old days, they would have long since shipped him east or had him suffer a fatal accident. And frankly, there are still elements in the Politburo who would just as soon see him liquidated.

"But not the KGB. First of all, it looks terrible even in Russia to liquidate a great artist. It's *akulturny*, barbaric. The Russians are sensitive about that. But second of all, there's a better way to deal with embarrassing dissidents, a proven way. Instead of shipping them east, ship them west."

"You're thinking of Solzhenitsyn," I said.

"Exactly. Pack the guy up, escort him to the border, march him across, and warn him never to come back. Then say to the people, 'My country, love it or leave it; he left it, so draw your own conclusions. We're not inhuman, we let him go, and so on.' There's no mess, no blood on the state's hands; if the imperialists want him they can have him. That's the KGB approach these days."

"So you're telling me—"

"For Kobrand, the KGB couldn't get official approval of a Solzhenitsyn-type deal. There's a rumor that Milovich himself said the formal *nyet.*"

"Who the hell is Milovich?"

"Demechev Milovich, the Minister of Culture, the guy who came in after Furtseva died."

"Oh," I said. I wasn't much enlightened.

"Yekaterina Furtseva was the only woman in the Praesidium of the Party. A tough cookie. But she got into deep trouble over graft. They caught her building a quarter-of-a-million ruble dacha for her daughter with State supplies. Brezhnev let her keep her job, but she had to pay back the money. She was in even worse trouble because of her 'softness' on dissidents. They would have canned her for it, only she died. And the new boy, Milovich, wasn't about to let Kobrand become a Solzhenitsyn.

"But privately, very privately, he's told the State Security people, the KGB, 'Get this guy over the border, but make it look like a defection. That way, we're rid of him, he's discredited at home, *et cetera*. It saves trouble—and it saves Kobrand.' Comrade Milovich, it so happens, plays the cello."

In a Byzantine way, it did make sense. But enough loose ends were still dangling to stuff a mattress. "Fine," I said. "And when the KGB was looking around for a convenient pawnbroker to take Kobrand off their hands, who popped into their heads but Hugo Flachsmann, what a coincidence, ho, ho, ho. Hugo Flachsmann, dear friend and patron of the arts. And KGB operator."

Flachsmann flinched, but he fought back valiantly. "Alan, if I were a KGB operator, as you so quaintly put it, would I be telling you this scandal about a Politburo member? Be a little realistic. This Kobrand arrangement isn't a piece of espionage. Or counterespionage. To kick a bad boy over the border, the Russians don't need a *spy*."

"All right," I said, "you're no vulgar agent, you're a gentleman and a capitalist. I still want to know—"

"You want to know how and why the KGB people contact me. The 'how' is easy. They called me from Dzerzhinsky Square and set up a luncheon meeting to discuss it. Incidentally, they bought me a very good lunch.

"As for 'why,' I do a lot of business with the Russians. Profitable business. So . . . why not? We make a little money on the deal, which is nice. Nice for you, too, as you'll find out. But also—"

"Aha!" I said.

"Sure. The Ministry of the Interior runs the KGB. And the Ministry of the Interior also handles permits for imported publications."

"I get it," I said. "I absolutely get it. Business is business, so why not? If you play along, you make money, plus they leave you alone. If you don't, they yank your permits and you lose money. Very cozy. It's not quite capitalism, though, is it? Granted, it's not quite blackmail, either."

"Well," Flachsmann shrugged, "it's also less simple than you think, but what the hell? Say you're right, Alan. That still doesn't make me a KGB spy."

"Maybe not," I said, "but there's still the sixty-four-thousand-dollar question. Assuming everything you've said is true, why me?"

"I thought I'd already explained that to you. Because you're a musician and we can get you and your people into and out of the German Democratic Rupublic. Because you're not a professional who would be watched. The East German *Stadtpolizei* is not the KGB, you understand, and neither are the *Grupos* who guard the borders. They would know nothing in advance about any, uh, KGB arrangements. Of course," he added quickly, "you'd have documentation to get you through."

"Come on, Hugo. Why me in particular? Or did you just pick my name out of the Yellow Pages?"

"No, no. No, we didn't do that. I must admit that we did learn certain things about you."

"From whom?"

"From . . . various sources." Including Marianne, no doubt. "First of all, you're what I'd call a solitary, a loner. You live by yourself—

most of the time—you have few close personal contacts. At the same time, you're ambitious and, forgive the personal note, maybe a little frustrated that your talent hasn't won you wider recognition. Also, you're a leader. You can convince people to do things they might not otherwise do: this European tour is an example.

"Last of all, you are a performing musician. Musicians have in common some interesting traits. Like superior eye-hand coordination. Dexterity. Quick-wittedness and fast reflexes. Above all, good memory, an excellent sense of timing, and the ability to improvise. My executives are always talking about 'playing it by ear.' Musicians have to *do* it. Do you want me to go on?''

"Okay." I did and I didn't.

"Well, I could talk about self-assurance or platform presence or whatever you want to call it. Some musicians lack it. Others pretend they have it when they don't. You do have it. We've checked very carefully on that score, by the way.

"But for our purposes," he continued, "your most interesting trait is one that has nothing to do with music. Indeed, it seems rather rare among musicians, perhaps because they have to concentrate so hard on immediate tasks. But Alan, you yourself are insatiably curious. About odd things. About almost everything."

"The Elephant's Child, that's me," I said.

"Yes. Our evaluators think it must have something to do with your relationship with your mother."

"My mother?" I stopped trying to be dispassionate. "You people dug into my family background?"

"Family, friends, teachers, professional acquaintances, credit, everything. Oh, yes. We were thorough." Flachsmann's offhandedness was infuriating. "But rest assured. We found very little to worry about. Naturally, there's no written file."

"Christ Almighty," I said. "What right had you—"

"Oh, come now, Alan." His voice was patronizingly gentle. "A minute ago, you were pouting that we'd picked your name out of a phone book. Now you're complaining because we didn't. This is a major project. Wouldn't you expect us to do some research on our choice of the principal? That's what personnel departments are for."

It took me a couple of minutes to simmer down. Then I said slowly, "You've just told me two things. The first one is that you're very sure of me."

"Sure of you? Not at all."

"You mean I can refuse?"

Flachsmann looked shocked, or pretended to. "Of *course* you can refuse. What do you think—oh, I see, you still do think. That we're some kind of saboteurs or guerrilla warriors or something. That's right. Well, of course you can refuse. We'd be disappointed, frankly, because we think your qualifications are excellent. But," he continued smoothly, "this is a business proposition. We want somebody who *wants* the assignment, not somebody we have to, uh, *coerce* into it."

"What happens if I definitely don't want it?"

"We think you definitely will," Flachsmann said a little smugly. "Oh, not so much for the money," he added hastily, "although the money speaks for itself, and very nicely, too. But the publicity will be fantastic. The prestige will be enormous. And let's face it, the ego gratification is, too.

"But, if you turn us down, I guess you finish your little tour, go home, do what you want. We'll get somebody else."

"Suppose I go tell someone about this crazy project?"

"Alan, hey! I wouldn't do that if I were you. I definitely would *not*. Hey! That would, that will take it right out of the realm of business. I really don't know what might happen then. To you, I mean." Flachsmann was being anything but menacing. If anything, he sounded apologetic. But the hint of a threat was there. "Besides," he said, looking more cheerful, "who would you tell?"

"I don't know," I said. "The CIA, the embassy, someone."

"Oh, well," Flachsmann said. "If you did that, we'd have to go down and express our surprise and concern about this fantasy of yours. To the appropriate authorities. And if we did, I'm afraid you'd have far more, uh, difficulty then we would."

I had an uneasy suspicion that Flachsmann was right. In a contest, he'd be more credible by about a hundred fifty million dollars than I was. "Never mind," I said. "But the other thing you've told me is that what you want to do is a lot more complicated than just telling Kobrand, 'Maestro, your car for Switzerland leaves in five minutes.' A lot more dangerous, too."

Again, Flachsmann fidgeted with his Dunhill and his Black-and-Golds. "Yes," he said finally. "There is the possibility that making contact with Kobrand could get—complicated, I think you said. That's true. Some of the people around Kobrand aren't going to want us to get hold of him. That part, you're right, it could be tricky. It's going to take a lot of planning and a lot of work to get those people out of the way.

"But danger? No, not really. I mean, there could be a *delicate* moment or two, right at the start. But after that, I can't see that there'd be any danger at all. Who's going to put up a fight for Kobrand? Us? The KGB? The East Germans? Never. A nice piece of escape theater, that's what we're staging. Sure, the stage directions might get tangled up. But violence is the one thing *nobody* wants."

I was about to point out that there were lots of nonviolent ways to end up in an East German prison cell, but before I could open my mouth Flachsmann shifted his gears. "Alan, I don't expect your answer right now," he said crisply, very much the executive. "But we don't have a *lot* of time, either. Before you start to think this project over, why don't you let me tell you what it would be worth to us?"

"I suppose you may as well," I said.

"Okay. If the operations come off as planned and Kobrand gets away, we will deposit in a bank of your choice the sum of one hundred thousand American dollars. We'll even put this money in escrow before you leave, so you'll know we're not playing games.

"We pay all the taxes.

"We underwrite all the expenses.

"Within reason, we help you in your dealings with the authorities.

"We arrange for the Antiqua Players to get the maximum possible publicity out of being Kobrand's rescuers.

"Now, even if you, um, encounter difficulties and the operation is not a success, we would still pay you a portion of the total fee. Say, fifteen thousand dollars net after taxes."

All along, I'd expected Flachsmann to be generous. But a hundred thousand! Twenty thousand apiece if we all did the job and split the loot evenly. Tax free. Plus expenses.

"Well," I conceded, "that does make it harder to say no."

"Then you'll say yes?" Flachsmann's half question held a hint of self-satisfaction, as if he'd once again confirmed his judgment about every man's having a price.

'I doubt it," I said.

"What—"

"I mean, first of all, that I want to think about it myself. Then, no matter what I think, I have to tell the others."

"My God, Alan, you can't do that." At least Flachsmann no longer looked complacent. "This thing has got to be kept confidential."

"Listen," I said, "whatever your spies tell you about me, I'm not about to lead four other people blindly into your Kobrand Liberation Movement. I *like* these people, strange as that may seem. In the second place, I couldn't do it. Not with musicians. With musicians, it's a debate whether you walk across town or take a bus."

"Yes," Flachsmann said unhappily, "I know that."

"Good, I'm glad you understand. After we've talked it over, I'll be able to let you know."

"All right," Flachsmann said, "I suppose it makes sense. But try to do it today, will you?"

"Definitely," I said. "But if even one of us says no, it's no."

"All right," he said again, "do whatever you have to do. But let me know by the end of the day." I wondered why he made no further objections. When I got up to leave, he even gave me a half-hearted grin and said, "I knew I should have picked a pianist for this."

"You're right." I said, "you should have. You definitely should."

"Next time, I'll know better," Flachsmann said seriously. He rang for more coffee, or maybe an *aperitif*. Of hemlock.

We shall see presently that many passages
allow for more than one kind of embellishment.

K.P.E. Bach, p. 82.

CHAPTER TEN

On the hillside below the castle wall, Flachsmann's architects had
perched a swimming pool. I located a slightly rusty folding chair, set it
up on the grass by the empty concrete shell, and stretched out to curse
my fate in comfort. Flachsmann's scheme horrified me so much that,
even in the shade, I was still sweating. But at least I knew now what
Philomel and Flachsmann really wanted, and in a way I was less
horrified. The idea of our being able to liberate Kobrand seemed crazily
unreal. Yet, from what little I'd read about Communist internal politics, the plot itself might well not be crazy. It might even cover us all
with glory, courtesy of the KGB.

One thought that made me sweat was that Flachsmann had gone to a
lot of trouble to get us involved. Well, why not? We were legitimate,
we were cheap, and, let's face it, we were expendable.

But the most chilling thought of all was that Flachsmann, damn him,
knew I'd find the thing tempting. And I did.

It wasn't only the money. Somehow, in the course of their "research," Flachsmann and his minions had made a guess about Alan
French. They'd guessed that inside Alan French the musician there was
a clandestine operator who liked the idea of maneuvering in the dark for
big stakes. And they'd guessed right. It was degrading. But it was also
flattering. They knew me better than I knew myself, and that scared
me.

Forget about all that, I told myself. What about the others? How
would you explain to Rhoda from Woodmere that, for the sake of the

international freedom of the arts, David Brodkey had blithely undergone martyrdom somewhere in the People's Democratic Republic of Germany?

With this fancy flickering through my brain, I was far from happy to catch sight of Jackie as she started down the steps from the terrace to the pool. Oh, Christ. Never mind Rhoda, how was I ever going to explain to Jackie that the whole tour was ruined unless we all took part in a little plot? Nothing serious, just a political rescue operation behind the Iron Curtain.

I never even had to try.

Jackie, in a highly distracting blouse and the shortest shorts in Switzerland, came down those steep steps like the goddess Diana after some nice fresh breakfast venison. She marched over to where I was sprawling and stood in front of me, her arms folded. "Alan French," she said, her lips trembling, "if you don't help get Kobrand out, I'll never forgive you. Never."

I was too dumbfounded to answer.

"I've just been talking to Hugo about it. We've got to help. We've *got* to. Kobrand's a genius, Alan. And he's a saint. We've got to get him out. If you won't go, I'll go by myself."

"Jackie, listen—"

"No, *you* listen. How could you look yourself in the face, how could anybody, if you had a chance to get Kobrand out and you didn't take it? What kind of person are you? Don't you *care*?"

Of all the possibilities, I'd never considered this one. Flachsmann, you cunning so-and-so. Jackie was still raging:

"Take you away from your lessons and pupils and tiny little concerts and you're not even human." She was almost in tears. "You'd let somebody die."

"Jackie," I tried again.

"Don't 'Jackie' me, you—you iceberg," she stuttered.

"Now, look," I said. "Stop it. Shut up for a minute." My astonishment was giving way to delectable, heart-warming righteous indignation. "So far, you've been doing all the yelling and screaming. Now it's my turn. Grab yourself a chair, sit down, and listen. Then, if you still want to yell and scream, go right ahead." Jackie, startled in her turn, did as I asked. "Okay," I said when she'd curled her long legs under her in a canvas chair. "What exactly did sweet Hugo tell you?"

"That Izaak Kobrand was a prisoner in East Germany, that we had a chance to help him get out, and that you didn't want to help."

"Fine," I said. "Did he also tell you that the Russian secret police were involved? By the way, he seems to be one of their leading representatives in sunny Switzerland."

Jackie looked startled. "No," she said. "Alan, are you sure? I mean, he's so rich."

"Jackie, be your age. What better cover could a Communist agent have?" As coolly as I could, I went over with Jackie the Möbius-strip politics and sketchy logistics of Flachsmann's plan. She listened intently, not interrupting, the way I'd so often seen her concentrate on a new musical score. When I finished, she nodded. "Alan, I'm sorry," she said.

"Don't apologize, but don't get carried away, either. If this thing backfired, we wouldn't lose out on Merit Badges. We'd be in jail. Or maybe even dead."

"I'm sorry I yelled at you," Jackie said. "I can see why you don't trust Hugo, though I just can't believe he's a secret agent. I can see why you're afraid. But I still think it's right for us to do something, and I think we should do it."

I started through all the arguments again, but Jackie wouldn't let me go on. She'd made up her mind. Kobrand was a great artist unjustly deprived of his freedom. We had a way to help him be free. The politics made no difference. As for the risk, even if there were risks, we should do it. And that was that.

"Jesus," I muttered. "You're dangerous. You and your ideals ought to stay out of the hot sun."

Jackie laughed. But then she said, "Alan, stop being so cynical. You know you're dying to try. You'd say it's for the money, or just for the thrill. But you'd be doing it for Kobrand, too. Well, give the rest of us a chance. We're all consenting adults. I bet we make a terrific rescue team."

"I bet we do no such thing." It was no use, but I decided to make one more appeal. "Look, Jackie. You're the den mother around here. Do you honestly think Ralph and David and Terry are going to want to risk their necks in a bloody silly caper like this one?"

"If you really want to know," said Jackie sweetly, "why don't you ask them?"

The idea of confronting three half-awake instrumentalists with the Kobrand crisis was as appealing as a visit to the dentist. But fifteen minutes later, I was opening wide. We found the others at breakfast, and Jackie interrupted the spooning out of the scrambled eggs. "Listen, everybody," she said briskly, "Alan has something important to say."

"We're in big trouble," I mumbled.

"Well, it's about time." Ralph, as dapper as a cat in white pajamas and a foulard dressing-gown, heaved a theatrical sigh of relief. "Ever since we arrived, you've been absolutely impossible. Slinking around with the most awful sorrowful countenance. I can't say I'm on tip-pytoes to find out why, my dear, but I really do wish you'd unbosom. You'll feel *so* much better, I swear it."

"Okay, here goes." I took a deep breath. "Itzaak Kobrand the cellist is being held in East Germany, and our host and need-I-remind-you angel wants us to help him get out."

"You mean Flachsmann?" Terry was so surprised he almost dropped his buttered roll.

"Right." Once again, I ran through the story from the beginning. Never in my life have I had a more attentive audience.

"But what's the payoff?" asked David. I told him. "Wow," he said.

"You mean, if we go in and pull Kobrand loose, it's a hundred big ones?" Not since his first tour as altar boy at St. Rose of Lima had Terry whispered so reverently.

"That's what Flachsmann says," I said.

"Well, Jesus Christ," Terry said. "What are we waiting for?"

"We could all get killed," David said.

"Yeah, I know," Terry said, "but we could all get rich."

"It's up to you," I said. "I told Flachsmann, if anybody said no, the whole deal's off."

"I don't especially want to die," David said thoughtfully. "We'd split the loot evenly?"

"Naturally," I said.

Oddly enough, it was Ralph who cast the die. As always when things were serious, his swishing and camping fell away and he talked calmly and with authority. "I think we should do it," he said. "Number One, there's the money. That's lovely. Number Two, if we pull this off, we'll be absolutely made publicity-wise, and that could be a lot more important than even the twenty thousand dollars apiece. Number Three, there is a moral issue at stake here. I mean, not to sound pious and all that, we mustn't ignore right and wrong. Not to do what we could for poor old Kobrand would be, well, wicked.''

I just stood there. What else could I do? But Jackie went over to Ralph, put her arms around him, and kissed his cheek. "Thank you," she said.

"I think you're all a bunch of innocents," I began, but Ralph cut me off.

"That may be, dear Alan. But truth to tell, it's your fault or responsibility or something that we're involved. Now, isn't it? Well, then. Don't let's have a round of recriminations; they're so banal. We're in this with you, to coin a phrase, and *we're* not complaining. Instead of scolding us, you should go straight to Flachsmann and tell him that we're at his service and all ready to conspire.''

Feeling half-relieved, half-sheepish, and about as effectual as an old sock, I left them chattering away about Kobrand and went back out to the terrace. Flachsmann was still there, but his henchmen had set up a bright beach umbrella for shade and plugged in a telephone for commerce. He was on the phone when I caught his eye, and he pointed me to a chair. "Okay," he said into the receiver. "*D'accord. Oui, c'est ça. Une milliard. Bien.* Okay, bye bye.'' He hung up. "Foreign exchange problems," he said to me, "they're a pain in the ass.''

"I know," I said. He looked at me blankly for a second, then he laughed.

"That's right, you do. What's the story?''

"I've talked to my fellow artists," I said. "They agree. For the sake of freedom, adventure, and, just incidentally, a hundred thousand dollars plus, the Antiqua Players will strike this heroic blow.''

"Great," Flachsmann said sincerely. "That's great. Now listen, here's what we're going to do. You just go ahead with your schedule. When's your next concert?''

"Tomorrow night.''

"Fine. You just rehearse, get ready for it, do whatever is normal. Today is what, Tuesday?'' I nodded. "Okay. By Friday, Friday at the latest, we'll have done some things. Then, you guys all come up here for the weekend and we'll start the briefings. What I'd like to have you do is give a small private concert here Saturday night. That'll be good cover.''

"When do we leave?''

"Well, that depends on what I find out between now and Friday. But I'd guess you'd go over the border some day early next week.''

"All right,'' I said. "There's just one more thing.''

"What's that?''

"The money,'' I said.

"What about it?''

"We don't think the escrow arrangement is too great. We'd like to see that hundred thousand in a bank account. *Our* bank account. We won't touch it until everything is over. But we'd like to know it's there.''

Flachsmann sighed. "I think you're being just the least bit dumb,'' he said. "But if that's the way you want it—''

"I'm afraid it is,'' I said.

Flachsmann pressed a button on his telephone. "Ask Linzer to come out,'' he said into the mouthpiece. A minute later, a gray-suited retainer appeared. "Franz, this is Alan French.'' The retainer bowed slightly. "Prepare a draft in his name—one 'l,' right Alan?—for one hundred thousand American dollars. Use the Zurich number three account. Then bring it out here.'' Without a word, Linzer bowed again and disappeared inside. "Okay. Now, you take this draft to—'' he gave me the name and address of a bank "—they'll fix you up. Tell you what. We'll even let you draw against the first fifteen thousand right away.''

"That's not necessary,'' I began, but Flachsmann waved away my objections.

"No problem,'' he said. "We want you to be happy.''

Linzer reappeared. Expressionlessly, he handed Flachsmann a yellow form and, along with it, a black Pelikan fountain pen. Flachsmann glanced at the draft, signed it, and waved it in the air to dry the ink. "Here you go,'' he said. On the draft, in addition to all the right names and numbers, some secretary had typed neatly: "Expenses in connection with concert tour.'' The draft itself was drawn on the Number Three Personal Account of Hugo Flachsmann.

I folded it and stuck it in the pocket of my jeans—or rather, Flachsmann's jeans. Nothing like having a patron from the skin out, I thought.

"All set, Alan?" I nodded. "Fine. Now, get lost, do whatever you have to do until Friday. You'll hear from us. When you're ready to go back to town, just give Anne De Soto a buzz. She'll have a car for you." Flachsmann grinned at me and waved me away. The Antiqua Players were formally filed away in his mind. Under C for conspiracy.

When only little time is available for the display
of craftsmanship, the performer should not wander into
too remote keys.

K.P.E. BACH, p. 431.

CHAPTER ELEVEN

BY THE TIME Flachsmann's limousine spun us back down the mountain
roads and into Geneva, it was midafternoon. Nobody felt like working,
so I called a rehearsal for seven-thirty that evening, just a run-through
of the program for Wednesday night. Would the Kursaal be open for
us? Indeed it would: in a minor-league way, we were celebrities. At the
hotel, we found a stack of messages and mail, including one cabled
invitation to appear at something called the Shropshire Festival of the
Arts and a letter asking us if we would so kindly perform for the
crippled children at a hospice near Sion. We turned the Shropshire offer
over to Anne De Soto for further inquiry and fee haggling. We couldn't
decide about the hospice. Jackie, naturally, wanted to go. Ralph had no
opinion except that he couldn't see how we were going to haul his
harpsichord up what he was sure was a mule-track. So we compro-
mised. Jackie, Terry, and David would go on Thursday afternoon,
David doing continuo on the lute.

Meanwhile, Flachsmann's money was burning a hole in my pocket.
How would you feel with a hundred thousand conspiratorial dollars
nestling next to your International Auto License and vaccination certificate? Taking Jackie with me as bodyguard, I left the others on the hotel
terrace and fared forth in search of the bank Flachsmann had recom-
mended. Its brass plate gleamed discreetly beside the door of a tall,
narrow private house on a street of tall, narrow houses. As we went
inside, I wondered if all of them were banks. We introduced ourselves
to a tall narrow gentleman in a gray cutaway coat and striped trousers.
He listened attentively to our request, displaying about as much emo-

tion over our hundred thousand dollars as a subway clerk in New York displays over a crumpled single. Our draft in hand, he disappeared into the inner recesses of the bank, returning a few moments later with a sheaf of forms for us to complete. Yes, a numbered account would be in order, as long as we were prepared to prove that these dollars had not actually been transferred from the United States without notice to the federal government. *Herr* Flachsmann? Yes, of course. Then in that case could he suggest. . . . It went on and on, but in the end we had agreed on some strange type of interest-bearing account on which we could also draw checks up to fifteen thousand dollars before Friday, checks on the balance subject to countersignature by an official of Flachsmann's own bank. Sign here, Sir, and here and here, and if the lady would sign here and *here*. . . .

Finally, exhausted by the effort it took to become a capitalist—"a capitalist *lackey*, you mean," Jackie quipped—we escaped into the bright sunlight. We were about to stroll back to the hotel when Jackie grabbed my arm. "Look." We were a short block away from the lakefront park, and she'd spotted, at the entrance to a little wooden dock, a sign advertising sailboats for rent. We had an hour or so to kill, and the sunshine was dancing on the water as innocently as childhood. It took us only a moment to strike our bargain with the brown-faced, smiling proprietor; then we were clambering down into one of his brightly painted wooden dinghies, casting off, and hoisting the little sail. The breeze was offshore, and while Jackie trimmed the sail I let us run well out. Then, we simply tacked back and forth along the Geneva shoreline.

For a few idyllic moments, the tiny problems of navigation were our only problems. The creak of the rigging and the delectable *slap-slap* of the waves on the hull were great tranquilizers. Flachsmann and his plans, politics, the preposterous venture we'd agreed to undertake, even the money—all were diminishing into insignificance. I knew I had to start thinking about these things. But for now, I could be a kid again, afloat on a pond in the Adirondacks, my sole worry whether or not the breeze would freshen enough to blow me home in time for dinner. Well, not quite my sole worry. There was Jackie, now in blue jeans and white tee shirt, sitting easily on a thwart, ready to take in or let out sail, as expert at this as she was at music. The wind ruffled her hair. The sun made her squint as she grinned happily at me. She worried me, too.

"Listen, Jackie." I had to raise my voice against the wind. "I love you," I said, ducking as a generous splash of Lake Geneva found its way inboard.

"That's wonderful, Alan," she called back. "I love you, too. But I'm still not going to sleep with you."

"You don't understand," I found myself saying. It was funny, I thought, how the little interlude with Marianne, the friendliest and most casual of one-night encounters, had sharpened rather than blunted my feelings for Jackie. Maybe that casualness had simply made me aware of what I really wanted, something that would last and last. "You don't understand." Another faceful of spray inhibited conversation. "I think we should get married."

"What? You *what*?" This was getting bloody ridiculous, I thought. Here I was, proposing marriage at the top of my lungs, and the object of my devotion couldn't even hear me. "Watch out," Jackie yelled suddenly, "we're going to jibe!"

Just in time, I pushed the tiller away from me and brought the dinghy back into the wind.

"I said I think we ought to get married, Jackie," I repeated. "Soon," I added, looking at her and feeling love—ordinary, healthy, spring-afternoon love—thicken in my throat.

"Darling Alan, do you know what you're saying?" She was still laughing, but her eyes were soft and serious and she looked very young.

"Yes," I yelled back. "I am in full possession of my faculties and I know that what I say may be taken down and used in evidence against me. But I don't care. I love you." Yet another wave slopped damply over the gunwale. "Jackie, please let's get married."

"If you're not more careful, skipper, we'll both be lost at sea before the honeymoon," Jackie said, and my heart began dancing a little gavotte.

"All my proposals involve a certain amount of risk," I said with dignity.

"True. Well, then, do you suppose the captain of this vessel would marry us before we hit an iceberg?"

Neither of us said another word until we'd sailed the little boat back to the dock and paid and extravagantly tipped the startled boatmaster. Then, walking hand in hand along the waterfront, we both started talking at once.

"After this is over—"

"And we can support each other in the style we're accustomed—"

"I'll sell my fiddle and buy a ring!" We laughed together, and, for the first time since we'd met so many years ago, we kissed. Fortunately, no passersby came near enough to notice. God knows what the Swiss would have done.

"Alan, you do mean it, really and truly?"

"I really and truly do," I said.

"Then, you'll give me some time." There was pride as well as appeal in her voice. As urgently as Jackie might want me to sweep her off her feet, Jackie was still Jackie. I was asking her to decide something momentous, and for her this meant breathing space long enough to let her cool off and think. This was how she managed her music, and, as I well knew, this was how she managed her life.

"Okay," I said, "but don't make me wait too long." She squeezed my hand.

"I don't think it will take too long," she said.

"Good. Let's go back to the hotel."

"Oh, no, darling," she said hastily. "We're going to the Kursaal. We've got a rehearsal."

"You make it sound like an Auden libretto," I said.

"Idiot!" My God, I thought bemusedly. Why didn't I propose the moment I saw her?

"Seriously, Alan," she said. "Let's not *do* anything until later."

"Why the hell not?" But I knew what she was thinking. The others would be pleased enough about us. But musicians are unpredictable. The balance of emotional relationships among all of us would be bound to change, and so would our playing—perhaps for the better, but who could be sure? And as for the Flachsmann plot, I didn't even want to stir up any ideas. I hated the thought of Jackie's involvement. But I knew what would happen if I tried to talk her out of it. Besides, protectiveness be damned, I wanted her around. I *needed* her.

Just how much, I found out five minutes later. We arrived at the Kursaal and climbed the broad staircase that led past portraits of Swiss worthies to the rehearsal floor. As we entered our room, we saw that Ralph was there. He was sitting slackly at the harpsichord, dapper in a blue blazer, check knit trousers, and a yellow silk open-neck shirt. At least, he would have looked dapper if it weren't for the blood. It dripped languidly from his nose, just missed the tip of his chin and fell to soak his shirtfront. We stood in the doorway watching for what seemed like an hour. The late afternoon sun, gleaming through the tall windows, made the blood look redder than red.

Jackie's sandals clacked across the parquet. "Oh God," she whispered. "Ralphie. What happened?" He moved his head as if exhausted. I stared, fascinated, as the newest drop of blood was diverted to trickle along his upper lip and down his chin.

"I was practicing." He forced the words past swollen lips. "They threw open the door. Grabbed me. Two of them. I was surprised." He paused, wincing, for breath. "They grabbed me," he repeated, "and just began smacking away. My face. Whack, whack, whack. I started to bleed. I was bleeding." Tears formed in his eyes and ran down his bruised, puffy cheeks. "Then they stopped. They just—dropped me and left. One of them said, 'Next time, *junge*, we'll stomp your knuckles.' " Ralph quit talking. His eyelids flickered. I caught his shoulders as he fell forward. Otherwise, he would have smacked his forehead on the keyboard. The blood on his shirt smudged my—Flachsmann's—sweater as I eased him out of the chair and onto the floor. While I was doing my best to make him comfortable, Jackie was working the pay telephone on the landing. I hear her asking the hotel operator for Terry's room. In a minute, she was back.

"I told Terry that Ralph had had an accident," she said. "He and David are both coming. They're bringing towels and ice. Alan, should we call a doctor?"

I wasn't sure. Ralph's face, where the blood hadn't caked, looked pallid and sick. But he was breathing easily through his puffy nose and the rest of him seemed undamaged. I didn't think he was seriously hurt. But then, I hadn't been the one to go through the wringer.

"No doctor." Ralph mumbled the phrase without opening his eyes.

"What?" I wanted to be sure I'd heard him correctly.

"No doctor. Don't want the police." Of course, he was right. A doctor would have to call the police, and a police investigation might uncover anything. From our new point of view, cops were people to be avoided. By the time I'd reached this conclusion, Jackie was already back on the telephone.

"Flachsmann's out," she reported. "I left word for him to call us in person, here or at the hotel. I didn't tell anybody why."

"Good." None of us added anything else to the echoing silence in the room. Jackie sat down on the floor and gently eased Ralph's head onto her lap. Ralph heaved a sigh and attempted a grin of thanks. The bleeding from his nose seemed to have stopped, which I took to be a good sign. But there was really nothing at all we could do except sit there in the sunshine by the harpsichord and wait.

About five minutes later, the rescue mission arrived. Terry was carrying a whole pile of bath towels: he must have robbed the International's linen supply room. David clutched a bright yellow plastic bucket full of ice cubes.

"Wow, *baby*," Terry said. "Somebody must have really got next to you." Jackie folded one towel under Ralph's head, wet the corner of another towel, and went delicately to work mopping up the blood on his face. As calmly as if it were a familiar routine, David knotted ice into still another towel and passed it over. Jackie applied it to the patient's battered nose. Ralph groaned as the cold bit into the soreness.

"Does he know who did it?" Terry asked me.

"No."

"Must be the Kobrand caper. It has to be. But why?"

"That's it," I said. "Why?" My first thought, naturally, was the Russians. But which Russians? Unless Flachsmann was lying, the KGB *wanted* Kobrand liberated. Beating up an ally was a poor way to begin our bright new era in Soviet-American cultural endeavors. And maybe my childlike innocence was showing, but I didn't think Flachsmann was lying about the KGB. So it must have been some other Russians, or some other somebodys, who had a keen vested interest in terrorizing us. I tried, but I couldn't imagine who. For all I knew, it could have been an anti-Kobrand faction on the faculty of the Leningrad Conservatory.

Ralph was sitting up. He was bruised and bleary but surviving. "Ugh," he said with distaste, "somebody help me off with this shirt." David gave him a hand and he wriggled out of the blazer and the stained yellow silk. I couldn't help noticing that, for all his slightness, Ralph was surprisingly strongly built.

"Here, baby." Terry volunteered his sweater. Ralph must have caught my glance at his physique, because he grinned mockingly.

"Oh, yes, my dear, I go to a gym regularly. If those two brutes hadn't surprised me, I might have surprised *them*. I hope I catch up with them some day," he added venomously. "I'll know what to do." On his feet, he took a few painful steps and paused to pull the baggy sweater gingerly over his head. "Thanks, love," he said to Terry.

"Listen, Ralph, have you any idea who could have done it?"

"Well, they weren't wearing fur caps and speaking with Slavic accents, if that's what you mean. One of them had on a brown suit and a red tie. The other one was holding me from behind, and I didn't get more than a glimpse at him. But I think he had a beard. Oh, my God, I'm a *mess*." He'd caught sight of his face in the mirrors lining the wall. "Anyway, I can tell you this, they were experts. They knew how to hurt me without really hurting. I mean, even while it was going on, I knew they weren't going to kill me. They didn't want that. They were like cops."

"Like *cops*?" I thought I knew what he meant, though.

"That's right. You know, nothing personal, sweetheart, just a job, got a wife and kids, have to eat. Sorry. Next time, it's your hands." Ralph looked quickly at his hands, looked away, then let them seek refuge deep in his pockets. Smashed hands, the musician's nightmare. Empathy made me shiver.

Out in the hall, the telephone was ringing. Jackie ran out to answer it. Jackie! We hadn't had time to give each other a thought. Suppose she'd been the one to wander over early to warm up? The thought knotted my stomach.

Jackie came back. "It's Flachsmann."

"Good." I went to the telephone.

"Is anything wrong, Alan? Didn't the money go okay?"

"Fuck the money. Listen. . . ." I told him what had happened. He swore. Then he said, "Okay, just sit tight and stay where you are. In about ten minutes, a car will pull right up in front of the Kursaal. *Don't go downstairs*. One of the men in the car will come all the way up to get you. His name's Yuri. Go with him. They'll drive you back to the hotel and take you up through the garage. When you get set at the hotel, call me. I don't think anything more will happen, but let's not take any more dumb chances. Okay? Talk to you later." He hung up.

The routine unfolded exactly like a movie scene. From the window, we watched one of Flachsmann's limousines draw up to the door. The first man out of the car stationed himself out of our line of sight, but presumably in a position from which he could cover the entrance, the sidewalk, and the limousine. The second man out was Yuri. He was a short, thin, nervous-looking clerk of a man, not at all my idea of a bodyguard. But he came out of the limousine on the street side and walked around the back of the car before crossing the sidewalk and starting into the Kursaal lobby. Nearly five minutes went by before he appeared in the doorway of the rehearsal room. "Yuri," he introduced himself. "Who got hurt? You?" I shook my head. "Oh. Good," he said to Ralph, "you're up and around. Fine, let's go." We all went down the stairs together. One at a time, we slipped outside and scampered for the car. Ralph went next to last, with Yuri right behind him. Before Yuri had his door closed, the limousine was moving away from the curb. "Very good," Yuri said. As far as I could tell, our movements hadn't caused even a head to turn. Rush-hour Geneva was too busy thinking about dinner. But maybe Yuri knew better.

When I opened the door to the hotel suite, the telephone was tinkling. "You're all okay?" It was Flachsmann. "Look, Alan, you and what's-hisname, Ralph, be ready at eight o'clock. I'm sending the helicopter down. We have to get together tonight. Okay? Yuri will put you aboard." I started to say something about rehearsals, then gave up. A helicopter ride would do more for Ralph than rehearsing would.

Instead, I said, "Well, we've met the enemy and they are you."

"What exactly do you mean by that?"

"Nothing," I said. "But let's hope the leak in your security doesn't let all the gas out of the helicopter's tank tonight."

"Now, just stop worrying, everything's under control."

"Tell that to Ralph."

"I will. 'Bye, now."

I flicked the receiver toggle a couple of times, then dialed Ralph. "Oh, no," he groaned, "I was just going to order dinner in my room and go to bed. I'm in the tub now. Must we?" But when he learned about the helicopter ride, he cheered up. "If you don't think he'll mind my *face*. I'm all pink and blotchy and awful."

"Ralph," I said, "I don't think he'll mind. And if it were me, well, I think you're a hero to be able to joke about it."

"Oh, we get used to it," he said cryptically, but he was making pleased noises when I said goodbye.

Halfway down the hall, I could hear the sound from Jackie's room. How typical. Before lunchtime, we join a political conspiracy. By midafternoon, we're in charge of a hundred thousand dollars. While the tourists are sipping their aperitifs, one of us is being smacked around by

thugs of unknown origin. Two of us have decided that it's the right time
to fall in love. Now, the chief conspirator has ordered an airlift to his
mountain lair. But still, no day is really complete for this woman
without at least a couple of hours of practice.

"Who is it?" she asked when I pushed the buzzer.

"It's Franz Liszt, your demon lover."

"Just a sec, silly." She was propping the gamba carefully against
her chair, hanging the bow on the edge of the music stand, pushing a
strand of hair back from her face. I could almost count the beats before
she opened the door. Then she was in my arms. The whole sequence
was as strange and as familiar as a dream.

"You scare me," I said.

"I do?"

"What were you playing when the blade dropped on Marie Antoin-
ette?"

"Don't, Alan, it's not funny." Surrounded by music, she'd been far
away from a world in which men and women did grim things to each
other for money and power and glory. I'd broken the spell.

"Flachsmann did call," I said. "He wants to fly Ralph and me back
up to Montricher."

"Tonight?" Jackie was dismayed. "Is it safe?"

"I don't know," I said. "I think so. I think Flachsmann has found
out something. And we sure as hell have to rearrange things."

"Why?"

"Well, Jackie, it's obvious that somebody knows we're up to
something, and they probably know what. Somebody in Flachsmann's
own organization. Either he plugs the leak or as far as I'm concerned
the whole bloody thing is off."

"But what about the money?"

"We'll give him back the money. You can't spend what you don't
have. And if you're dead you can't spend anything."

"But what about Kobrand?"

"Look, love. It's not going to do Kobrand a bit of good if we get
chopped into pieces a week before we even make the first move. We're
blown, Jackie. Our cover story is worth zero. I'm frankly hoping
Flachsmann will call the whole thing off. It's his own bungling that's to
blame, after all." As I said it, I felt a lot better. But not Jackie.

"But maybe what happened to Ralph is just some weird thing that has nothing to do with Kobrand. Oh, Alan, I hope so. I mean, it's so easy to be cynical and frightened and just give up. I want to say, Look, let's get out of here and go back home and play music."

"And get married?" I asked her gently.

"Yes, damn it, and get married and be together. Now, you keep your distance," she added hurriedly as I reached for her. "We've got to straighten out this Kobrand thing first."

"Jackie, you've got Kobrand on the brain," I said meanly. I felt mean and anxious. "Is there any way at all I could convince you to get on the next plane and disappear until after this thing blows over?"

"Why, Alan French the great big hunter want to keep his, his *squaw* stuck away in a nice, safe cave while he goes on the prowl. You *chauvinist*."

"Okay, Jackie, you don't have to give me any lip; I knew there wasn't hope."

"Hey," she was grinning at me.

"What?"

"We're having our first lovers' quarrel." This time, when I grabbed for her, she didn't move away. On the contrary, she pressed quite a lot of herself against me and offered me a good chance to do some advanced nonverbal communication. She only stopped when she felt the edge of the bed against the backs of her knees and sensed the direction in which I'd been steering her. "No, darling, *please*," she said unconvincingly as we collapsed onto what the International's brochure styled our "luxury sleeping accommodations."

"All right," I muttered, making my hands cease their exploration. "You're courting rape, you know."

"Oh, I am, am I?" Settling herself next to me, Jackie held my face between her hands and began bestowing little soft kisses on it. "I am, am I?" she repeated softly. "Good. Do I make you want to get me naked and beat me to make me behave?"

I thought about it. "Why, yes," I said with great conviction. "Now that you mention it, that's exactly what I'd like to do."

"Well, do you realize that you have to go on an airplane?"

"Helicopter."

"Helicopter, then. And work out a way to get Kobrand out of East Germany? And also get ready for a concert tomorrow night that we haven't even begun rehearsing?" She stopped kissing me, sat up straight, adjusted her clothing, and regarded me primly.

"For a shy classical musician, you have a remarkably sensual nature," I said. "Plus a horribly overdeveloped sense of responsibility. Couldn't I tie you up naked first?" We laughed. I was beginning to realize that if we ever did get through the Kobrand mess, living with this woman would be the beginning of a new Alan French.

I made Jackie promise to eat dinner with David and Terry in her room. She could fill them in on what was happening. "If you can stand it, you might even do some rehearsing." Jackie made me promise that whenever we got back from the castle, we'd call her. We told each other that nothing alarming was going to happen. But neither of us wanted to say goodbye.

The accomplished musician must have special endow-
ments and be capable of employing them wisely.

K.P.E. BACH, p. 153.

CHAPTER TWELVE

AT EXACTLY FIVE MINUTES to eight, Yuri tapped on my door and
gestured me into the corridor. Ralph was already with him. Aside from
a strip of tape across one cheekbone, Ralph looked not too battered. But
I didn't like the expression in his eyes.

Yuri steered us silently down the hall, slowing us as we approached
the elevator alcove, then moving us quickly past it toward the un-
marked door at the end of the corridor. Our feet made no sound on the
International's thick carpeting. We slipped through the door. We were
on a landing of the fire stairs. In the glare of the fluorescents, the rough
distempered walls and the crude utility of the firehose fixtures made the
place look grim. Yuri peered over the edge of the steel handrailing to
glance at the flights of stairs below. Then he turned and led us upward.
There were only a couple of flights to climb. Another steel fire door
opened silently, and we felt the cold night air.

The helicopter's engine was already turning over, and almost before
Yuri had hustled us over the cement of the landing pad the pilot had
upped the RPMs. Over the chattering roar, Yuri was exchanging
shouted comments with the red-headed pilot as Ralph and I buckled
ourselves into our seats. The cabin door slammed shut and we were
swinging up in a crescendo of noise. As we lifted away from the roof, I
saw a gleam of light from the entryway. Yuri must have left as quickly
as he'd come.

With a grin and a downward jerk of his head, the pilot signaled me to
stare at the view below. I was sitting to the pilot's left, the instrument
panel and controls in front of me duplicates of his own. We were

encased in a Plexiglas bubble, and the lights of Geneva and the glitter of the moon on the lake moved weirdly between my feet. Behind us, in one of the two other seats, Ralph was gazing from his own window. But within a couple of minutes, the lights had disappeared behind us and there was nothing to see except the dark wooded landscape and, ahead of us, the looming shapes of the Swiss alps. After one look at them, I glanced hastily away. They made me cold.

Somehow, I'd expected that the flight would annihilate time and distance entirely. But helicopters don't travel that fast. We were in the air a full fifteen minutes, time enough to get through an entire third of a concert program. I thought about Jackie back in the hotel with those two characters, eating her room-service dinner, clearing away the table and dishes, taking out her gamba, tuning it, starting to rehearse. You can have the glamour of flight. More than anything, I wanted to be back in that room.

Then, like a giant yo-yo at the end of its string, the helicopter was swinging downward in the darkness. I peered at the instrument panel to try to read our altitude. But all the gauges and dials looked alike, and anyway, by the time I'd remembered they would all be calibrated in meters, the helicopter was hovering in midair above a clearing in the forest near a bulk of architecture I knew must be the castle. As I watched, lights came on below us, defining the oval of the landing pad, and the machine descended gingerly. We were there. Before we'd stopped rocking on our skids, the door had opened and Hugo himself appeared. "How'd you like the flight? Fantastic, huh? Hurry up, there's someone I want you to meet."

A nod of thanks to the pilot, a quick walk over graveled paths, and there we were again, at the same brightly lighted entrance we'd swept up to the night before. Good God, I thought, did this whole thing really only start one night ago?

Incredibly, there seemed to be another party going on. But Hugo walked us past the great parlor—I caught a glimpse of a girl in a white dress dancing raptly to a snatch of disco music—and down some stone steps into a corner of the building I'd never visited before. Suddenly, we were in a suite of offices. The floors were carpeted, doors with nameplates on them were discreetly closed, and I could hear the tapping of a typewriter.

Hugo motioned us past him through a door. It closed silently behind us. We were deep in executive country. A huge desk squatted at the far end of the room. Behind the desk, tall French doors gave blankly onto the darkness of the terrace where we'd breakfasted that morning. Directly ahead of us, a fire crackled merrily in a massive stone fireplace. Landscapes and hunting prints adorned the walls. Everything smelled leathery and rich.

Seated on one of the two sofas near the fireplace, his feet cocked up on a low cocktail table, a glass in his hand, was a man wearing a greenish tweed jacket over a striped shirt and a striped tie. As we entered, his big head turned inquiringly toward us. Ralph gave a start.

"That's one of them!" Inadvertently, Ralph's hand came up to cover his mouth.

"You're quite correct, of course," Flachsmann said. "Allow me to introduce formally *Herr* Karl-Heinz Schnittemann, known to his friends as Heinzl and until recently a sergeant in the Bavarian Civil Police. Lately, Karl-Heinz has become a freelance specialist in physical violence."

"We've already met," Ralph said steadily. But his hands were shaking.

"No hard feelings, *junge*," said the man in the jacket. His tone was embarrassed. He pulled at his drink and dipped a beefy hand into the bowl of salted almonds on the cocktail table. "All in a day's work, eh?"

"You bastard," said Ralph with hatred in his voice. The man looked puzzled. He was upset the way a craftsman would be upset if a customer, instead of being grateful, chewed him out for sloppiness.

"Unfortunately, Karl-Heinz's business associate cannot be with us," Flachsmann said smoothly. "But Karl-Heinz is perfectly willing to explain to us how he happened to pay his attentions to you this afternoon. Go on, Karl-Heinz."

"*Ja*, sure, no problem." Amiably, Karl-Heinz turned to face us. "This morning, we get a call from Colonel Jerzy. He's, well, he's *active* in Geneva. And the Colonel tells us, 'Look, there's this *Ami* musician, and he's paying too much attention to one of the violinists in the Swiss Radio Orchestra, and one of the trustees doesn't like it, it's his boyfriend, see? You'll find the *Ami* in the Kursaal about fifteen-thirty. Go persuade him to lay off." With one gulp, Karl-Heinz disposed of the rest of his drink. "So that's what we did. We found you and we persuaded you."

So that's what we did, and that's what we are. Former cops, I thought to myself, with nothing but their police skills to sell. Ex-soldiers with no other trade except soldiering. Men-at-arms. The original hardhats. Stolid men making a living the only way they knew how, with their hands. Hired like tradesmen by well-dressed people in offices and once in a while interrogated politely by other well-dressed people in other offices. That last job, it just wasn't satisfactory; you were on the wrong side; what went wrong?

"Thank you, Karl-Heinz," Flachsmann said politely. "If you'll just wait here for a few minutes more, we'll have somebody drive you back to town. You've been very helpful. Maybe you better go away for the next few days."

Karl-Heinz, too, remembered his manners. His betters were about to leave the room. Putting down his empty glass, he stood up politely. He started to say something to Ralph. He held out his hand. I remember being surprised to see Ralph reach out as if he were going to shake the hand of a man who'd helped beat him bloody. But I don't remember exactly what Ralph did do. Only, Ralph was suddenly dropping to one knee. And instead of lumbering toward him, Karl-Heinz was first staggering and then sailing past Ralph to smash face-first on the carpet.

"Oh, my Christ!" Flachsmann hurried over to Karl-Heinz and bent beside him. Ralph, a tight smile on his face, stood up and flexed his fingers. After a second, Flachsmann went over to his desk and spoke into the intercom. "Have Carla come up to take a look at Herr Schnittemann. He's had a little industrial accident."

When we left, Karl-Heinz was sitting up groggily, supported on the arm of a tough-looking Swiss woman in a white uniform, and the odor of smelling salts was strong in the room.

Flachsmann led us into the next office, fitted up with maps as a conference room. "Now, that's what you don't understand," he said with exasperation. "It was just an accident. Karl-Heinz picked the wrong American." He did indeed, I thought, watching Ralph. He picked one who went to a gym.

"What are you?" I asked Ralph. "Some sort of black-belt champion?"

"Oh, no," he scoffed, "nothing like that. Only, you know what New York is like. I mean, you have to be able to protect yourself."

Slowly, my mind began to function again. "An accident?" I said to Flachsmann. "You think what happened to Ralph was pure coincidence?"

"It looks that way," Flachsmann said, but he didn't believe it.

"Who's this Colonel Jerzy who goes around arranging these accidents for visiting American musicians at fifteen-thirty in the Kursaal?"

To do Flachsmann justice, he looked miserably embarrassed. He began to fumble with his expensive smoking equipment. "Well, he's a Pole, Colonel Jerzy, naturally. Sort of a private investigator in Geneva. In fact, he's done a couple of jobs for our organization. I've put in a call for him but he's not at home and he's not at his office."

"When he's not working for you, what does he do, collect old Palestinian silver?"

Flachsmann's mood changed to one of defiance. "All right, Alan. I admit it. Jerzy may have found a leak somewhere. Not here, not in Geneva. Possibly in New York. We're checking, believe me. But he can't know much. All he knows is that some American musicians are mixed up with me. So he figures he'll send in a couple of goons to stir up trouble; maybe he'll find out more. I know the guy; that's how he works."

"He's going to find out something just as soon as Karl-Heinz gets over his headache," I said.

"Sure he is," Flachsmann said, "but what? That you and Ralph know me and that Ralph knew a judo throw."

"That may be," I said. "But I'd feel a lot happier if I knew who this Colonel Jerzy was and what he wants."

"I know what he wants," Flachsmann said impatiently. "He wants what they all want, to get something on me, then to come to me and get paid off for keeping it quiet. I know the guy," he repeated. "That's all there is to it."

"And if you don't pay off?"

"Then he goes and sells the information. To the papers, to the Swiss government, to the CIA—"

"Who?"

Flachsmann looked amused. "Alan, you've got to get things in perspective. In the States, the CIA is a super-bureaucracy. It starts wars, it taps phones, it runs the government; anything you want, okay, the CIA does it. But out here, it's just another seeker after information. A guy like Jerzy, he calls up Bob Carroll at the Embassy—"

"Carroll?" The name registered. "I thought he was the cultural attaché."

"He is, he is, but he's also the resident U.S. spook." That nice, artsy-looking man with the big moustache. I was disappointed. "Anyway, he's the one Colonel Jerzy calls to say, 'Hey, you know Flachsmann's Philomel Foundation? Let's have lunch about the Philomel Foundation.' So they have lunch, who cares?"

"I care," I said. "The day we make an arrangement together, Ralph is beaten up. He's gone nowhere, said nothing, done nothing since this morning. Right?" I glanced at Ralph, who nodded. "All he's done is play a harpsichord. And yet, some thugs go to work on him. And *you* say don't worry, it's just some petty operator in Geneva. No dice, Hugo. I'm not that simple."

"Alan, I swear to you—"

I started to answer but Ralph broke in. "The question is, what are you going to do about it? It's too late to worry about who know what, Alan; that's obvious. But I don't mind telling you that no matter who knows what, I'm not going to have my hands stamped on by any hoodlum. As far as I'm concerned, rescuing Kobrand is perfectly ducky still. But I want some protection and that's *it*. I mean, don't *you* have some goons you could send around to guard the bod, that sort of thing?"

"Cor*rect*," Flachsmann said triumphantly, as if he'd just won a major point. "All we need to do is to tighten up on security, and that solves the problem. That's why I sent the helicopter for you tonight, and why from now on Yuri and his people are going to be around, and I mean all the time. You may not know it, Alan, but Yuri's at the International right now, keeping an eye on things. Meanwhile, we're checking all down the line."

"You ought to do one other thing," I said.

"What's that?"

"Follow Karl-Heinz and see what he does." Flachsmann grinned.

"We're doing a lot better than that," he said. "Karl-Heinz's girlfriend works for one of our divisions. Oh, we've known about it for several years," he added when I raised my eyebrows. "In fact, we've used both Gerda and Karl-Heinz before. Otherwise, Karl-Heinz wouldn't have called us."

I had been wondering about that. I nodded, and Flachsmann went on.

"After he, uh, visited Ralph, he was at Gerda's and she was telling him about the concert last night. Right away, Karl-Heinz put two and two together."

"Yes," I said, "and came in fast to make his peace with you."

"That's right," said Flachsmann. "Anyway, we've programmed Karl-Heinz. He's to lie low for a day, then call Jerzy and report. He's to tell Jerzy the absolute truth, that we found him, you identified him, and we let him go. That should take care of the problem. That, plus tighter security."

"You think Jerzy will believe him?"

"Oh, yes. Why not? Karl-Heinz is a freelance. His reputation depends on his reliability. Jerzy will believe him, all right."

In my mind's eye, I could see the scene. Karl-Heinz, after the Kursaal episode, splitting from his pal to wander over to his girl's flat, probably wanting a Pilsen and a session in bed. Then learning the identity of the "Ami" and hurrying to the telephone to cover himself and to avoid a tongue-lashing from his girl. Delightful Gerda, charming Karl-Heinz.

Flachsmann went to the door and peered out. "Karl-Heinz has gone," he reported. "Let's move back into my office." A businessman shifting a meeting, he fussed over drinks for us, then used the intercom to alert the helipad that we'd be coming shortly. "Unless there's something else?" he asked politely. Ralph shrugged and I couldn't think of any way to say, "Look, the fun is over, let's call it off." So Flachsmann walked us through the French doors, down the terrace steps, and back through the grounds to where the aircraft was waiting. "Friday, don't forget," he yelled as the rotors began to flail in the air. I waved an acknowledgement and we were airborne, and Flachsmann was a tiny figure casting an odd long shadow on the floodlit grass. I wondered if he'd be going back to his party.

Crossing and turning . . . must be applied
in such a manner that the tones involved . . .
flow smoothly.

K.P.E. BACH, p. 58.

CHAPTER THIRTEEN

THE TRIP BACK from the castle was uneventful. If you call a helicopter descent to your hotel roof and an armed escort to your bedroom uneventful. We held a brief midnight conference with Terry, David, and Jackie, of which I remember only the random detail of the lamplight on Jackie's anxious face. Then we dragged ourselves off to bed.

All the next morning, we spent in rehearsal. Ralph and I were dead tired, and the others were far from being bright-eyed, but we had no choice.

The rehearsal work did us good. Musically, as you might expect, it was a fiasco. Ralph especially had trouble with the notes and everybody's timing was off. We were *anticipating* too much, David said. It was hard not to be nervous when you knew that outside the closed door a professional gunman was keeping watch. At least, I knew for sure about the gunman part. When we were coming into the Kursaal, Yuri's coat blew back in the breeze and gave me a glimpse of the ugly, stubby-looking revolver he wore slung butt downward in a shoulder holster.

Two things brightened the day. One was a message from an excited A. De Soto, delivered to us by Yuri. Would we care to tape a short concert for the Swiss radio network? The fee was straight scale but the publicity value was excellent. Yuri advised against it. "It's too hard to cover you in the street," he complained. "If anything happens, I get in trouble." We reminded him that if anything did happen, *he* might be in trouble but some of *us* might be applying for admission to the busy harpists' local in the sky. Eventually, Yuri conceded defeat. We broke off, packed up, and drove off without incident in the big limousine. Ralph said that the studio harpsichord made him feel as if he were banging the plumbing for more heat. But to my surprise, we played well. The very first take was good enough both for us and for the placid, gum-chewing sound engineer.

Then we discovered the sauna at the hotel.

If the ancient attendant was startled when five tired-looking guests, one of them a girl, lined up at the admissions counter, she concealed it expertly. She simply gestured us inside, and in a few minutes we assembled in the International's elegant teakwood version of the Finnish hot cabin. The electric elements were already glowing redly. The crone said something unintelligible and shut the door. A moment later Terry said, "The hell with it," stood up, and stripped off his towel.

"Hey!" Jackie protested. Grinning, Terry sat down again on the scorching slats of a bench, his back partly toward her.

"Christus," Jackie muttered. Her hair hung limply about her face. Beads of perspiration popped out on her forehead, hung there for a second, then evaporated. She looked very uncomfortable. I never thought she'd surrender her own towel. But she did. She unwound it gracefully and folded it neatly to use as a seat-pad. That's how I first surveyed the unclothed form of the girl I was hoping to marry, through slowly frying eyeballs in a room where the thermometer on the wall read 57° Celsius.

"Very sexy," I said as the wax in my ears began to melt.

"Oh, shut up," Jackie said, and we all laughed.

Our reason for going to the sauna was that Ralph's tender face and aching muscles needed therapy. But sitting around naked, baking and laughing, turned out to be good therapy for the rest of us, too. Someone said, "This is absurd," which it was. But the heat felt wonderful, and the tribal atmosphere was soothing and protective. From chili parlors and Yoga to a sauna in Switzerland: What next for the Antiqua Players? Group salt harvesting in Siberia? I said it out loud, and our mood was such that everybody laughed harder.

We were still laughing when the crone heaved open the door, flicked off the heaters, and opened up on us with a needle-spray hose of icy water. Then we were dancing around furiously, yelling for her to stop. Through the billows of steam leaking from the cabin, I caught sight of Yuri, resignedly professional, keeping careful watch over the wicker furniture in the dressing-room. What would it take, I wondered, to get him out of his clothes and shoulder holster and, giggling and screaming, into a sauna hut? I decided not to ask him.

Finally, the Wicked Witch of the West gave up and shut off the cold spray. She passed out sisal-fiber mittens and instructed us to massage one another until the circulation got going again. "You must be all over *redt!*" she commanded in her cracked voice. I was ready to give Jackie a few experimental rubs, but Jackie shrewdly handed back her mitten to the witch, who did the job instead. That left me to contend with Terry's remarkably hairy dorsal surfaces.

Half an hour later, respectably dressed but still tingling, I said to Jackie, "I love you for doing that number in the sauna."

All she said was, "It seemed like the right thing to do at the time." But she blushed right down to her neckline, and presumably beyond.

"It's curious," I said. "Naked in a sauna, you were aesthetically interesting but nothing more. Yet here, in the tea shop of this proper establishment, fully clothed and ready to face the threatening male world, you're driving me absolutely crazy. How do you account for that?"

"You're thirsty, that's all. Order us some tea."

"That's *not* all," I said. But I ordered the tea. "Is our life together going to be full of my questions and your irrelevant answers? One lump or two?"

"One, thanks. Yes, probably. Alan," she added, stirring the tea in her cup as neatly as she did everything else, "you still do mean it, don't you?"

"Mean what?" I tried unsuccessfully to keep my face expressionless.

"I hate you!" Looking around to be sure nobody was watching except the neutral Swiss, Jackie kissed me. "Now we drink our tea," she said.

So we drank our tea, ate our tiny sandwiches, repaired our metabolisms, and watched the office workers and schoolteachers. And we tried not to remember that a man with a gun was unobtrusively posted a few steps away, to protect us against other men, big men with heavy red faces and, I suspected, heavy red politics, too. "You know," I said, "I haven't even thought about the money."

"Neither have I; isn't it strange?"

"No, it is not strange at all that a beautiful, gifted young woman does not think of money! It is normal, thank God." With the ease of an aristocrat or a dance instructor, the man who had just interrupted us swept up a chair from the next table, planted it at our table, and sat down. His dark hair was sleeked back smoothly from a high, pale forehead. His small moustache sprang into stiff little points. "I will have English tea with you, my friends." A wave of his hand summoned the waitress. Opal links gleamed in his cuffs. He smelled of *eau de javel*. "Koblinski," he said, "an honor, a delight. Colonel Jerzy.

"You excuse?" he said. With a silver match, he lit a small tan cigar, replacing the match in the waistcoat pocket of his beautiful suit and inhaling carefully. "Ah-h! You are artists, you are cultivated people, you will understand." His tea arrived. Briskly, he poured from the pot and added sugar and the heavy Swiss cream. "*Thé à l'anglais*," he said. "I learned to love it in England during the last war, the Great Patriotic War. But I forget, you are children, you do not remember."

"Well enough," I said.

"No, excuse me, you cannot," said the Colonel. "And even if you do, this little one does not. It is not possible.

"But you do not wish to listen to the reveries of an ancient about his furloughs from a war that was over before you outgrew childhood. No, thank God, not. Instead, you ask yourselves, 'What does foolish old Colonel Jerzy want with us? How dares he to drew up a chair—?'"

"Draw up," Jackie said.

"Yes, draw up. To interrupt our *tête-à-tête*?' Well, I will tell you: to apologize. More hot tea!" he suddenly shouted to the waitress.

"Absolutely, I apologize. To the charming young man my associates so shamefully mistreated yesterday. To my dearest friend Hugo Flachsmann. To you. I, Colonel Jerzy, have made a mistook."

"Mistake," Jackie said.

"Mistake. All, all is wrong, is misunderstood on my part, not? You, sir, and you, *ma fille*, and your friends are artist, musician here to play concert."

"It's true," I said.

"Exactly true," exclaimed the Colonel. "All other things you do, whatsoever, they not mean anything. Pay visit to special private bank? Not. Is to deposit fees for your art. Go in limousine to castle? No other musicians visit my dear friend Flachsmann in limousine. Only you. But this means nothing. Colonel Jerzy is old senile suspicious fool to imagine different. Other fools with fists are worse fools." His moustache tips drooped remorsefully. He plunged into another cup of tea. "So," he said. "There was no reason to make little warning."

"What happened to Ralph was a warning?" I asked. But the Colonel ignored me.

"Your young friend I am sending a little present, a *bagatelle*. But—" a gold ring winked in the light as he wagged a finger "—you go here, you go there, you do nothing. But maybe sometime you go where you should not be, where there is difficulty, not? Then, is time to contact Colonel Jerzy." A small parchment card materialized in his hand. He passed it to me. Written on it was a multidigit number and a few words in what I took to be phoneticized Polish. "You call *this* and you say *this* and tell what is difficulty and maybe we arrange. Okay?"

"No," I said, "it's not okay."

"How not?"

"You're forgetting to tell us why."

The Colonel looked reproachful. "My dear boy! You have right! It is not allowed always to tell why. Only, I will tell you one thing." The Colonel's eyes, suddenly very cold, bored into mine. "This thing that you are *not* doing, thanks be to God. It is dangerous."

"Well," I said, "since we're not doing it—"

"Of course," said the Colonel. "Be careful." He drained his teacup, wiped his moustache delicately, plucked his cigar from the ashtray, flicked away the ash, and rose to his feet. "My dear, dear friends, I have much pleasure." He smiled his wolf's smile at Jackie. "*Ma jolie.*" He bowed to me. "Sir! Goodbye!" Sidestepping an overburdened waitress, he dodged his way to the street entrance, twinkled at us once, and disappeared.

"Good God," I said.

Jackie laughed. "I liked him. He's a spooky man but charming, charming! Are all spies like that?"

"Karl-Heinz isn't," I said. Here in the tearoom, amid the silver and the porcelain, the idea of violence seemed absurd. But it wasn't. "Karl- Heinz is a mercenary and a thug. Your charming Colonel, may I remind you, is Karl-Heinz's employer."

"I know." Jackie shivered. Probably, like me, she was thinking about Ralph. Reaching over the Colonel's cooling tea, I squeezed her hand. "Still," she went on slowly, "I think he means it."

"About being sorry?"

"Yes, in a way. And he's warned us. So now he can leave us alone."

"I hope you're right," I said. I didn't know why, but I thought she probably *was* right. The Colonel was disconcertingly well informed about our comings and goings. He almost certainly knew something about our extracurricular plans. His professional curiosity was sniffing and scratching at us. But—I told myself—he wasn't sure. The Antiqua Players were certainly the unlikeliest undercover team ever put together. And so, at least for now, the Colonel was calling off his German shepherds. After a warning.

"We better get back," Jackie said.

"Right." To myself, I shrugged. The only thing we could do was to keep going. We had to play the concert. Playing well was our best cover. The place to deal with Colonel Jerzy, I told myself, was in the Friday meeting at Flachsmann's.

I signed the check and we headed back through the hotel lobby to the elevators. Out of the corner of my eye, I saw Yuri move away from the pillar against which he'd been leaning and drift toward us. "You had company at your table," he said politely.

"Yes. We would have invited you to join us, but Colonel Jerzy was in a big hurry." The elevator doors slid open and the three of us stepped inside. Yuri pressed a button to make the doors close sooner.

"Ah, I see," he said.

"The Colonel says he regrets the trouble we had."

"Ah."

"He said we would not be troubled again."

"Ah."

"Is that all you can say? What good is this so-called security if Colonel Jerzy can walk right up to us any time he pleases?"

Yuri regarded us wearily. "Look, my friend, I know my job. Hugo says provide security cover until further notice. In the restaurant, I leave you alone. Why not? The Colonel is not violent in public places. But my personal opinion is that you are still spitting blood."

"Spitting blood?"

"On the spot, if you prefer. Hot. A potential target for physical coercion or violence." Yuri folded his arms and leaned against the metalwork of the elevator car. Poor guy, he must have spent most of his working lifetime leaning against things and waiting for physical coercion or violence to happen to somebody. The elevator slowed as it reached our floor. As the doors opened, Yuri pushed us gently to one side. For a second or so, long enough to screen us from any intrusive gunman, he stood in the entrance. Then he darted out into the elevator alcove to cover our exit. The alcove and the corridors leading off it were deserted. This should have made Yuri's lunging and peering look comical, but neither Jackie nor I felt like laughing.

"See you about seven."

"Bye, Alan." As Jackie was about to unlock her door, Yuri silently held out his hand for the key. She hesitated, looked over at me. I nodded. She gave it to him and he slid it into the lock, swinging the door open hard and momentarily disappearing inside. Then he reappeared, gave back the key, and stepped back in the corridor to let her enter. Watching him made me think disquieting thoughts. Yuri wasn't just doing bodyguard duty. He was our jailer as well.

A couple of hours later, fiddle in hand, black tie tickling my chin, I was inspecting the audience from the wings of the stage in the Kursaal. The house was full. It was also Old Home Night. Among the music lovers, I spotted Karl-Heinz in his green tweed jacket. He was sitting alone. From time to time, he wiped his tough cop's face with a white handkerchief. Further down toward the front, where the seats cost 28.50 Fr.Su. apiece, sat Colonel Jerzy, deep in enthusiastic conversation with a pretty girl. When she looked up laughing, I recognized Debbie. The seat on her left was vacant. Flachsmann, I assumed, would be joining her. But when I went backstage to be with the others, he still hadn't arrived.

Finally, the audience settled down and we played. "Now I know how the jazz piano-player felt when he saw Capone at a ringside table," Ralph whispered to me between pieces. He'd been inspecting the audience, too.

But nothing bad happened and nobody threw anything at us, unless you count the bunch of wild flowers, weighted with a block of wood, that thudded at Jackie's feet during the applause after her solo. She smiled at this homage from the students squeezed into the balcony. It did our popularity no harm when, after intermission, she came onstage wearing the same nosegay as a corsage.

At the end, there were more flowers.

We gave them our two encores, took our final bows, and trooped off for the last time. In the wings, Jackie paused and tucked into Yuri's buttonhole a rose from the enormous bouquet Hugo Flachsmann had just bestowed on her. "Remember, Yuri," she said happily, "make love, not war."

"Sure thing, Miss," he said, "that's right. Blessed are the peacemakers.'' All the same, he kept his eye on the people who were beginning to filter backstage. The dressing room crowd was smaller this time, but it was still enthusiastic. Total strangers kept patting my back. Once again, Jackie was surrounded by a gang of gamba players, Wunschler's students, and embraced by the beaming Wunschler himself. And then Colonel Jerzy made his entrance, arm-in-arm with Debbie and Flachsmann like a mini-*blutbruderschaft*, to proclaim as *he* embraced Jackie that beauty and talent were, thank God, still to be had in the world.

All of a sudden, I felt exhausted. Before everything began to blur, I grabbed Yuri's arm. "It's time we got out of here,'' I said. He nodded. Within a few minutes, he'd cleared the room, seen that the instruments were locked away, and found our coats. He almost chased us down to the car.

I don't know about the others, but the last thing I remembered before I dove into sleep was the faint smell of the rose in our jailer's lapel.

The keyboard is and must always remain
the guardian of the beat.

K.P.E. Bach, p. 33.

CHAPTER FOURTEEN

"Ladies and gentlemen, good morning! Welcome to Field Operations Briefing."

At nine o'clock precisely, the wakeup messages had made our telephones buzz. Any lingering drowsiness, the International Plaza's chicory-laced coffee had dispelled. By ten o'clock, Yuri was ushering us into our limousine. It was now ten forty-five and sixteen seconds. We were seated around the big slab of oiled teak that was the conference table in the room next door to Flachsmann's office, the same room in which Flachsmann, Ralph, and I had met after Ralph had shaken hands so satisfyingly with Karl-Heinz. At the head of the table, a pointer in her hand, stood A. De Soto. "The morning session," she intoned, "will be devoted to an overview of your assignment."

"What the fuck is Field Operations?" Terry mouthed at me.

"We are," I said.

"If unit members will hold their questions until the overview session is over," A. De Soto said without the trace of a smile, "we will proceed. First, will each of you take his or her briefing book from the pile on the table and position it for convenient subsequent reference."

The briefing books were pale blue vinyl three-ring notebooks stuffed with materials. I positioned mine carefully by dropping it on the table in front of me, and I sneaked a look inside. Maps, charts, graphs, and pages of typescript were all nicely subdivided by index-tabbed sheets like the ones you remember from the schoolroom.

"Please do not open your briefing books at this time," said A. De Soto. "Merely have them positioned for convenient future reference."

In the clipped singsong of the professional Englishwoman, she went on: "The field assignment, as you are aware, is the assisted withdrawal of Itzaak Kobrand, cellist, from the Chemnitz-Plauen-Erzgebirge Sector, German Democratic Republic. The withdrawal is scheduled for Wednesday, April 10." As she droned on, she pressed a button. The room lights went off. On a lighted screen, a slide appeared. It read "FIELD OPERATION 66," and in smaller letters, "Withdrawal of Itzaak Kobrand." The letters were white against a pale blue background.

For the next hour, we watched slides. We looked at maps of East Germany, at larger-scale maps of the southeastern region, and at charts of towns and cities. A. De Soto's pointer traced routes of entry, primary penetration routes, inner penetration zones, target points, secondary penetration routes, and emergence vectors. "Emergence vectors" I finally translated into "getaway routes." There didn't seem to be too many of these.

When she grew tired of slides, A. De Soto showed us films. We watched an Agfacolor propaganda history of the *Deutsches Demokratische Republik* from its birth in 1946 to the present day. We then switched to the other side; and learned about the dismantling of East Germany's industrial plant and the shipment of its productive facilities eastward to the U.S.S.R. We watched the Wall go up. We heard Kennedy tell the Berlin crowd, "*Ich bin ein Berliner!*" and it made me feel sad.

There was a sequence filmed in arty black and white, of Itzaak Kobrand playing the cello in a studio in Leningrad.

The direction was heavy on angle shots of the great man's hands and his bowing technique, and my visual memory is decidedly poor. But even so, after sitting through the whole film three times, I would have recognized Kobrand anywhere. He was a big man, barrel-chested and heavy-shouldered. In the film, he wore a white dress shirt with its sleeves rolled up and its collar open. His forearms were powerful, his wrists thick, and his hands stubby-fingered, square, and strong. His gray hair was cropped almost in a crewcut. His eyes were set deep in a lined, expressionless face. He looked exactly like what he was, a consummate professional, a master.

I could believe the story A. De Soto told us. During his imprisonment, the authorities allowed Kobrand to practice his music. Taking for granted that the microphones and cameras were monitoring even the innermost mutterings of his flesh, Kobrand had given in return something wonderful to watch and to hear. For four hours every day, he played only the low note D, filling the room with the sound, filling the microphones. The doctors and staff attendants assigned to him listened with puzzlement, annoyance, and finally alarm to these fruits of his reunion with his instrument. In answer to their frantic questions, he would explain blandly that for years he had been dissatisfied with his low D. Now, with no concerts, no rehearsals, no pupils to distract him, he had time enough to find out what was wrong.

A man capable of this much intensity—this was the moral of the story—would set a high price on his freedom. Kobrand would be ready.

Finally, the projector stopped whirring, the screen gleamed blankly white, and the house lights went back on. I rubbed my eyes and looked around at the other members of Field Operation 66. Terry was doodling. Ralph was playing with the solid gold felt-tip pen that was Colonel Jerzy's little gift. Jackie was staring abstractedly at the table. David had out a pad and pencil of his own. Even upside down, I could make out what he was doing. He was composing, a dangerous habit about which I'd warned him many times. David composes when he's bored, and the music *sounds* bored, which is what makes the habit dangerous.

"With respect to the material just presented, are there any questions?" At A. De Soto's question, Terry looked up from his doodle.

"Well, so far this is mostly bullshit," he said pleasantly. "How about we get down to the ballbreaking?" Poor A. De Soto.

"The details of the field operation will be discussed during the afternoon session," she said severely. "At this time we have shown you something of the sociopolitico-economic matrix in which the operation will be bedded. Have you any questions about *that*?" Clearly, there was no need to waste sympathy on A. De Soto.

"Christ, forget I asked," Terry said.

"Well," fluted A. De Soto, "if there are no questions, there will be a sixty-minute luncheon break. Please report back at one o'clock for the afternoon session. The cafeteria is the third door on the left. The loos for ladies and gentlemen are just beyond."

The cafeteria offered soup, plastic-wrapped sandwiches, candy, and tea or coffee from big shiny machines. You could munch and sip these delicacies at brightly colored Formica tables slightly too small for the numbers of chairs grouped around them. While the others were joking about our status as a "Field Operation" unit, I slurped the tea and dug into my briefing book. It certainly looked and felt important. See, its size and weight proclaimed, see how much time and money we've spent amassing information for you. On some subjects, like reindustrialization and local government, the amount of detail was remarkable. The biographical profiles of East Germany's political leaders were revealing and cleverly written. But on social and cultural life, the briefing book was skimpy. For example, the section on music mentioned only one or two orchestras. On organs and organ building, a specialty of the East Germans, there was a bare paragraph. On groups playing pre-classical music, nothing.

At least, the section tabbed "Chemnitz-Plauen Area, Geography" was helpful. It held a map, one so detailed it had to be folded out of the notebook to be read. In reassuring detail, it marked what seemed to be every hamlet and knoll in the area. And what pleased me most was the map's date, in tiny letters in the lower right-hand corner. It was less than six months old.

Still, I felt as if the briefing book had been put together for some other, different purpose and handed out to us solely to impress. I sipped more metallic cafeteria tea and hoped fervently that no East German would call on me to comment on the musical life of the nation.

The afternoon session was more useful, I must admit. For the first time, we learned the outline of the program we were to follow. On the next Tuesday, we were to fly to Frankfurt, picking up the E5 *Autobahn* just south of the city and be driven via Wurzburg and Bayreuth to the East German border. That evening, we would play a concert at a school in Plauen, a small city about 40 miles southwest of Karl-Marx-Stadt, the district capital.

The next day, we were to drive from Plauen through the Erzgebirge mountains to a village called Markneukirchen.

We had an unassailable excuse for going there. Markneukirchen is the center of East Germany's most specialized industry, the manufacture of string, woodwind, and other musical instruments, especially those of the preclassical era. If you want a grand piano, go to Erfurt. Better yet, go to Astoria, Queens, U. S. A. That's where they build Steinways. But if you want a shawm or a rauschpfeif, a krummhorn or a kortal, a crwth or a gamba, a lute or a cylindrical-bore medieval recorder, then Markneukirchen is the place to do your shopping.

Once a year, on a Wednesday in April, Markneukirchen displays to would-be buyers both itself and its wares. It celebrates a combination of *Festspiel* and miniature trade fair. Booths are set up in the village square, and the little place fills up with instrument makers and dealers, antiquarians, music historians, and even a few tourists. To entertain this year's visitors and to make a gesture to international amity, the sponsors of the fair had engaged the Antiqua Players from faraway New York.

As well as the fair, Markneukirchen boasts other amenities. For instance, an excellent *Ratskeller*. Superb views of the Schwarz and Elster valleys. A soothing bucolic atmosphere. Indeed, the peacefulness of the place explains why the government, years before, had taken over a resort hotel outside the village and turned it into a place of rest for those who were from-the-so-great-responsibilities-of-leadership-under-strain.

It would be only natural for a world-famous musician, a guest at this hospice, to want to pay a visit to the fair. Permission would be granted for the guest, suitably escorted, to take a glass of spring wine at the *Ratskeller*, to stroll among the booths, to listen to the quaint music, so different from his own repertoire, perhaps even to greet the performers.

That's how we were to make contact with Kobrand.

As far as I was concerned, the most beautiful feature of beautiful Markneukirchen was that it's just 10 miles from the West German border.

To "familiarize unit members with the terrain," A. De Soto showed us color slides of Markneukirchen and its surroundings. These were the usual banal postcard views that could have been made of any pretty town. But watching the *Hohestrasse*, the gabled roofs, the church, and the vistas from the neighboring hillsides appear and disappear, I began to sense what going there would be like.

Next, also in color, came detailed maps of the center of town, showing not only streets and lanes but byways and alleys.

Then, with a click, the last of the color slides blinked off. Replacing it on the screen was a black-and-white photo of a man wearing a laboratory coat. The picture was blurry, as if the photographer had had to shoot in haste, and the image was grainy from overenlargement. Nevertheless, the face on the screen was clear enough. It was not a nice face. Somebody, probably not God, had started with a half-peeled raw potato. Using a sharp knife, the Somebody had cut a slit in the lower end for a lipless, inexpressive mouth. Two gouges represented nostrils, two more a little higher were good enough for the eyes. There was little hair. Potato Man would be in his late forties or early fifties. "Kranz, Joachim," announced A. De Soto. "The Direktor of the Markneukirchen treatment facility. An authority on the rehabilitation of disordered emotional responses. The Herr Direktor will undoubtedly assign himself the task of accompanying Herr Kobrand on a tour of the fair."

Compared to Kranz, the party whose face next appeared was a raving beauty. Hair drawn back in a bun, a woman of about fifty gazed out at us full-face. Her face was rather like a cat's, shield-shaped, with a pointed chin. Behind thick, wire-rimmed eyeglasses, the eyes were severe. But at least the mouth looked as if it had not forgotten forever how to smile. A. De Soto introduced her: "Fornova, Valentina. She accompanied Herr Kobrand on his journey from Moscow and is directly responsible for his physical safety. A trained physiotherapist, Fornova is also a medalist in this year's All-Soviet Women's Arms Championship Competition. Her rank is equivalent to that of captain in the Red Army. She, too, will insist on going with Herr Kobrand."

At this point, Terry began to worry. "Hold it," he said. "Let me see if I've got it all together. We're supposed to go to this spot with the chimneys and do our number outdoors, right? Kobrand's going to be there with these two heavies, right? We're supposed to get him away from the heavies and then we all split—him too, right?"

"Absolutely accurate, Mr. Monza."

"How are we going to do all that?"

"I think it's time we began to fit the last few pieces into place." Flachsmann spoke in a mellow tone from the doorway. He must have been timing his entrance. Nodding to A. De Soto, he eased himself into the armchair at the head of the table. "Thank you, Anne. I'm sure everybody here will agree that you've given a very lucid presentation. There are just one or two points more." Flachsmann cleared his throat like an anxious tenor about to embark on a long journey through seas of upper-register sixteenth-notes.

"First, at twelve noon sharp on Wednesday next, a fast car, probably a German BMW, will be parked—Anne, excuse me, could you screen the town map again, not that one, *that* one, thank you—right here." With A. De Soto's pointer, Flachsmann indicated a spot on the north-south arterial road that runs one block over from the *Neukirchplatz*, the town square. "In that car, Alan French will drive Itzaak Kobrand from

Markneukirchen by a route we have worked out *very* carefully, to the West German border.''

"Hey," I protested, but Flachsmann forestalled me.

"*Please*, Alan. Please bear with me.'' Again Flachsmann waggled the pointer. He brought the tip down on a second location, one about half a block away from the first. "You'll all make the trip from Plauen to Markneukirchen in a red Mercedes van. The van will be parked right here. Between twelve-ten and twelve-thirty, all of you *except* Alan will rendezvous at the van.''

"And we'll be taking a different route to the border?'' Jackie asked expectantly. Flachsmann grinned broadly at her.

"Great thinking, Jackie, but wrong. Your driver has his instructions. They are, to drive you as fast as possible to District Police Head-quarters. It's only about a kilometer outside of town.'' There was a startled silence.

"You *are* joking, Hugo, aren't you? Well, *aren't* you?'' To judge from Ralph's acid tone, he found Flachsmann's joke no wittier than I did. Flachsmann flourished his white teeth at Ralph in an even wider grin.

"Of course I'm not joking," he said.

"But . . . why?'' I asked weakly.

"Okay. I'll explain. Reason One, once we separate Kobrand from his, uh, friends and send him on his way with Alan, you guys—'' he waved his hand at Jackie and the others "—are out of it. If you split up and run, it's a clear sign of guilt. You'll be hunted, and getting you out one at a time would just be impossible. So you stay together. If you jump in that van and go skating all over the scenery, you're going to make a lot of people nervous. Maybe you'll clobber a tree, maybe some border guard will turn trigger-happy, but probably somebody's going to get hurt. Whereas, if you go quietly and turn yourselves in, you'll be in the safest place in East Germany. And nobody will lay a glove on you.

"Reason Two, by late afternoon a colleague of mine will be in Markneukirchen. His job will be to sort things out with the locals and get you on your way. I want him to find you warm and cozy at police headquarters. It'll make his life a whole lot easier. You follow me?''

Again, Terry put things into perspective for all of us. He said: "You mean, first we pry loose Kobrand from the heavies and shoot him off with Alan. Then, we make tracks for Cop City and wait right there for the bail-out?''

"That's right."

"Hey,'' Terry said. "I like the part about going straight to the cops. Gives the whole operation a touch of class.''

"We think so, too,'' Flachsmann said, very pleased.

David looked up from his musical scribblings. "What story do we give the police?''

"First of all,'' Flachsmann said emphatically, "you speak no German.''

"Makes sense,'' said David.

"Then, you all tell the same tale. You're musicians, you were playing music, you know absolutely nothing about what happened. And your leader is missing. That's what you say. And you keep on saying it. The biggest thing in your favor is that you drove straight to the police station.''

Everybody nodded. It did make sense, in that any other alternative would have been suicidal.

"Any other questions?'' Flachsmann asked.

"Yes,'' I said.

"What's on your mind, Alan?''

"This. A minute ago, you were talking about getting Kobrand away from his guards.'' Flachsmann nodded. "What's the plan for doing that?''

"We thought we'd leave that up to you,'' Flachsmann said.

"Up to us,'' I echoed stupidly.

"Right.''

"We're supposed to figure out how to get rid of two highly trained professional-killer types—''

"Now, now,'' Flachsmann said, "Fornova's just a target-shooting expert. Probably she's never pointed a gun at a *person* in her whole life.''

"That makes me feel a lot better,'' I said. "Listen, Hugo, we're musicians, not hit men. You've got to give us some help. I know: Yuri comes with us. He's our chauffeur. When we're ready—''

"Uh-uh,'' said Flachsmann.

"What do you mean, 'uh-uh,' '' I said indignantly.

"I mean, nope. No violence. At least, nothing that makes a stink. The least fuss and you've blown this whole thing sky-high.'' We sat in silence. "Now, look,'' Flachsmann went on earnestly, "I can understand your being disturbed about this. But we just can't have, uh, a lot of commotion. Besides, how can we plan what we're going to be doing in the middle of a mob scene next Wednesday when we're sitting *here*? I mean, you have to leave some room for flexibility.''

In the race to see whose stack blew first, Ralph won by about half a heartbeat. ''That's nice, *sweetie*,'' he said to Hugo in his flattest drawl. ''But my wee life is on the line. As far as I'm concerned, *chiefie*, either we have a solid plan or it's no go. Mommy's little Ralph-child will be on the next plane to Paris.'' He sat up very straight and folded his arms to indicate finality.

For a moment, I thought Flachsmann was going to hit him.

Hugo, you silly bastard, I thought, why are you so upset? Hasn't anybody ever told you off before? Then, of course, I realized: nobody ever has. Nobody ever does tell off a rich business hotshot. In his whole lifetime, Hugo Flachsmann had probably heard fewer words of personal criticism than any one of us hears during an average two-hour rehearsal. Poor Hugo! I almost felt sorry for him.

Eventually, Flachsmann did calm himself down. He stopped trying to shoot Ralph with his super-executive death ray glower. ''Okay, Ralph, okay,'' he said. ''I accept what you're saying. Of course, we need a plan. I just thought that since you guys are going to be the ones on the scene, you should have first crack at coming up with one. If you need support, naturally we'll see that you have it. So why don't you brainstorm it for a while?

''Not now, though,'' he added hastily. ''It's been a long day and we're all tired. I think we should all break and have a drink and think about this some more.''

''What about weapons?'' Terry was mumbling.

''What about *what*?'' Flachsmann repeated.

''I said, what about guns? Are we going to be carrying any?''

''What for?'' Flachsmann asked.

''Shoot the heavies, take them out, *you* know.''

''Shoot the heavies,'' said Flachsmann. ''I see. Monza, you are *not* going to East Germany to start a gang war. You're going to East Germany to help a cello player who, if he even thought you had a gun, would refuse to go near you. If any situation arises in which a gun is needed, which God forbid, a professional will supply the need. So forget about guns. Also, knives, blackjacks, and hand grenades.''

''Okay, okay,'' Terry said.

"Okay!" Flachsmann echoed enthusiastically. He wiped his hand across his face as if he were trying to clean off all oily traces of conspiracy. Then he made us a present of his warmest, friendliest grin. "We make a great team," he said. "We're on our way to a great goal." As he intoned these profundities, his voice grew smooth and confident. "We mustn't allow petty differences to stand in the way of working together to achieve that goal." He paused to be sure we were all absorbing the thought. "Ralph," he said earnestly, "I'm afraid I allowed my temper to get the better of me back there. I apologize. I ask you to accept my apology and shake my hand." Manfully, he extended his right hand.

To my relief, Ralph kept a straight face. "Sure, sure," he murmured, and let Flachsmann shake his hand.

"Now, look, folks! It's Friday night." Flachsmann could have been reminding us that it was the eve of Judgment Day. "Let's all forget work and go have a drink."

In the uneasy peace that descended upon us like a shopworn Sabbath dove, we did have drinks, and after drinks a big meal in the baronial dining room. By turns, Flachsmann was charming to the gentlemen and gallant to the lady of Field Operation 66. He worked hard at it. By ten o'clock, when he said, "You folks, please stay, just ring Tonio for more coffee and brandy," and excused himself, the tension had eased somewhat.

"Welcome to Markneukirchen," Ralph said after Flachsmann had made his exit. "You may never leave this beautiful town."

"Don't *say* that," Jackie said.

"Nah, it's not gonna be like that," Terry said.

"What do you think?" David asked, and they all looked at me.

"I don't think it's going to be like that, either," I said. "*If* we can figure out a way to get rid of the goons, I think we can pull off this thing."

"Got any ideas?" asked Terry. Nobody answered.

"See what I mean?" Ralph said. "Welcome to Markneukirchen."

A fantasia is said to be free when it is un-
measured and moves through more keys than
is customary in other pieces.

K.P.E. BACH, p. 430.

CHAPTER FIFTEEN

"IT'S OUR FAREWELL, our swan song," Ralph said. That Saturday
night, we played as if it were true.

One of the things said about early music is that it's not dramatic, not
eventful like Beethoven or Brahms. Maybe not. But much early music
is the stuff out of which drama is fabricated. Think of the fanfares and
flourishes rulers demanded as decor on state occasions. Think of the
orchestral suites written especially to accompany the suppers of kings,
trumpets resounding as the food, forkful by delicate forkful, made its
way from gold dish to royal mouth. That's not Brahms, but it certainly
is drama.

For us, the Saturday night concert was a poignant prelude to our
adventure. It was part of the rightness of things that for Flachsmann's
uncaring friends, the same music was nothing more than high-class
Muzak, music for a social occasion. "Swan song, hell," I muttered to
Ralph between numbers. "It's music to pluck geese by." He almost
laughed out loud.

Before and after the concert, we did the very little there is to do in a
castle tricked out as a weekend place when the tennis courts have yet to
be installed and the swimming pool is empty. Jackie and I took walks
and contemplated cows. We all slept late and ate voluptuous meals.
Once a day, we rehearsed. But not until the very last rehearsal, on the
chilly Monday morning before we were to leave, did I figure out what
might be done about Kranz, Joachim and Fornova, Valentina.

"Lighter, two, three, four, *lighter*! Try it two in a bar." David

127

looked up from his lute at Jackie. "I'm sorry, David," she said, "but, Christus! It *is* a dance, after all." I was sitting there, nodding in absent-minded approval, when the bells began to ring and the whistles began to blow.

Dance.

People moving rythmically. In patterns. I could have danced danced danced all night.

"Dave! Jackie! Shut up! shut *up*, I tell you, I've got an idea." Like respectful children, everybody gathered around and I explained what had popped into my mind.

When I finished, Ralph said, "Huh." But it was a thoughtful grunt, not a hostile one.

"It might work," said Terry. "*Maybe.*"

"Let's try it on Flachsmann," I said. I thought Flachsmann would like my idea. It had a kind of inventiveness that would appeal to him. And it was the only scheme anybody, Flachsmann included, had actually brought forward.

"Can you really do it?" he asked.

"Consider the alternatives," I said. And so, after too many glasses of Bernkasteler Doktor 1967 and too many lightly grilled *bratwurst*, Field Operation 66 packed up its instruments and accessories and caught an afternoon Lufthansa flight for Frankfurt.

The Swiss morning chill turned into a German afternoon chill as our TriStar swept onto the runway at Frankfurt and taxied us up to immigration and customs. The cold accompanied us down the endless fluorescent-lighted corridors of the terminal and crept with us into our car, another one of those huge black limousines Flachsmann loved. Maybe it was just the air conditioning, I thought. But it wasn't. It was fright.

"Germany is an orderly country," we'd read in our briefing books. The trim farms, woodsy-looking woods, and gingerbread castles we glimpsed on the way to the border were set out as neatly as in an illustrated *Hans Und Gretl*. The crossing into East Germany, which I'd dreaded, came and went with all the drama of a tollbooth stop on the Pennsylvania Turnpike. A few minutes at the red-and-white-striped barrier on the *Autobahn* and we were finished. The pole swung up and our car sped on into country only a bit greener, hillier, and more *gemütlich* than the country we'd left behind.

Plauen, too, was a surprise. The Erzgebirge district, we'd been told, was the most heavily industrialized sector of East Germany. I could hear A. De Soto repeating in her fruitiest voice: "Ever since pitch-blende, the ore from which uranium is extracted, was discovered in the area, the entire Erzgebirge has been sealed off from Western eyes." We were expecting something like Tolkien's Land of Mordor, a grim, gloomy place studded with slag heaps and belching smokestacks. By the time we eased off the Autobahn at the Plauen-Öst exit, the day had turned gray and drizzly. But only as we actually entered Plauen did we see any smokestacks, and these looked no more bleak than the smoke-stacks of, say, Fall River, Massachusetts.

"It looks as if time had stopped," said Jackie, peering from a rain-blurred window at the street scenery. I could see what she meant. The brick houses and the gleaming streets, wide but almost empty of traffic, did resemble an American town in the days before the country had 100 million automobiles. A town or even the quieter reaches of a Midwestern city like Cleveland or Cincinnati.

The sense of familiarity lasted about sixty seconds. Then we were pulling up in front of the hotel, and the distance between Plauen, Germany, and the red-brick cities of the U.S. heartland went back to being five thousand miles. Architecturally, Plauen's Interhotel Engel-seitz was startling. "It's a gargoyle warehouse," Ralph said as we got out of the limousine and stretched our legs briefly in front of the entrance.

"Hell, no," David contradicted him. "It's the original of all of those chinaware castles you put in the bottoms of aquariums."

"You're being horrible," Jackie said. "I like it. It is a lot like a mastodon. It has charm."

Curiously, Jackie turned out to be right. Whatever you made of the exterior, the interior was warm and welcoming, full of heavy gilt, faded blue plush, and old polished paneling, and as unlike the image of a Communist hostel as it's possible to imagine. The manager, a very young man with straw-colored hair who was wearing snappy gray flannels and a blue blazer, announced in quite comprehensible English that the main salon had been set aside for us as a rehearsal room and that the chef, a music enthusiast—as who on the staff was not?—wished to prepare for us a special dinner. This would be served to us and our guests after the concerts entirely with the compliments of the En-gelseitz. In the meantime, if there were any small services he or the staff could perform. . . .

The floor of my bathroom was paved with marble tiles. The tub was an ancient monster that stood on lion feet in proud defiance of time and circumstance. In one or two places, the enamel was quite badly worn, and the piping gurgled asthmatically. But the water was steaming hot and the soap lathered as luxuriously as if it had been bought in Paris or Geneva.

On tour, we bathe, we eat, we rehearse, we perform. There's not very much else to do. Here, as in Geneva, the steaming tub, the cake of soap that persisted in sinking somewhere in the treacherous shoal-laden waters just off my right thigh, the scratchy hotel towel (it said KÖNIGSHAUS MUNICH on it, how naughty of the Engelseitz management), all diverted me. As I lay soaking, absently tracing the cracks in the ceiling paint to their common source in one big missing flake, I quit worrying about Kobrand. I did start to think about the concert. Unbidden, a new way to treat the theme in the third, allegro movement of the final piece began to insinuate itself into my innocent thoughts, like the snake in the Garden of Eden. Jackie would have to take the opening fraction of a second sooner. *Then* I would come in on the flute *and then* Ralph. . . .

I sat up splashily. A couple of days ago, Jackie and the rest of us were playing games in a sauna. Tomorrow we're going to be rescuing Kobrand from the Commies. Tomorrow we could all be dead. And Alan French, is he sleeping with his girl like Robert Jordan in *For Whom The Bell Tolls*? No: he's working out how to handle one four-measure theme in a sonata by J. J. Quantz, an eighteenth-century composer of remarkable obscurity.

When relaxed moods are shattered, we'll do the shattering. I wrapped myself in the scratchy towel, ran more hot water—this time in the basin—fished out my razor, and shaved. The individual regarding me glumly in the mirror was definitely not Robert Jordan. We made faces at each other. "The hell with you," we said.

As soon as I'd climbed into my clothes, I called around on the house telephone and announced a brief reheasal in ze salon, *ja*, in fifteen minutes, be so good. It was petty, but it made me feel better.

As a matter of fact, the theme did sound better the new way, which almost made up for the dirty look Jackie gave me when she showed up with soaking hair. She hadn't had time to dry it when I called. "Don't drip so loud, will you?" I said after a few bars. "It's very distracting."

There was no harpsichord in the salon, only an ancient and unplayable grand piano, which meant that Ralph could do nothing more than nod intelligently when I explained what I wanted.

"Man, for this you call a rehearsal?" David, perched on a frail rococo chaise, his lute belly-up beside him on the red plush upholstery, also had nothing to do.

"You're making me feel foolish," I said. "Class dismissed; we'll meet here at seven-thirty. That gives us an hour. Don't eat too much."

At the *Hochschule*, they'd done as well for us as they could. The auditorium, which obviously did double duty as a gymnasium for the youth of Plauen, was a dingy old place. The rows of old-fashioned wooden seats, attached to one another in groups of three, asserted the Puritan character of the East German educational establishment. I was happy not to have to wear out my *sitzfleisch* on one of those chairs.

On the low, narrow stage across an end of the room, they'd placed a set of chairs for us that looked and felt more comfortable. A big two-manual harpsichord had been shipped in—so the greeter at the door told us—from Dresden, where there was a factory. When Ralph saw it, he made a *moue* of distaste. "Ugh, how horrible," he said. "Impossible to regulate." He wandered over to it, sat down, and struck a few chords.

"Well?" I asked. He shrugged.

"It will do," he said. "Just." He began his usual tinkering with the machine's innards, leaving me to contemplate a decor that consisted, apart from the usual complement of music stands and lights, of two tall vases filled with fresh lilies, one placed at each side of the stage. Their odor mingled with the smell of the floor wax and the sweat of ten thousand gymnastics classes. Perhaps because the whole scene brought back the terrors of first school recitals, my normal preperformance nervousness suddenly gave way to a spasm of genuine panic. Everywhere else, if you give a bad performance you get bad reviews. Your competitors snicker at you, your friends avoid you, you miss out on good jobs, you lose money. Here, if you gave a bad performance they shot you. Or, no, they'd never do that; it would be inhumane; they'd make you give up music and turn you into a potato farmer—that would be it, potatoes. *Kartoffeln*. All you could dig, forever.

Surreptitiously, I wiped my hands on the black velvet I was spreading for the instruments.

While we were setting ourselves up, the audience must have been gathering outside in the rain. At exactly eight-twenty-five, the doors of the gymnasium were thrown creakily open and people began filing silently in. It was a mixed house: some young, some old, nobody looking too prosperous, nobody too eccentric. There were schoolchildren; there was one bent old man in a wheelchair. In about the fifth row center, a stocky man with a lined face, a short haircut, and powerful hands was seating himself. Kobrand. I knew him at once from Flachsmann's films and still photographs. On either side, also totally recognizable, sat his watchdogs. It was fascinating, it gave me a voyeuristic thrill, to be watching *them*.

Just then, the same elderly functionary in a brown cardigan who had let us into the building limped into the wings and began throwing the switches, so we had to start.

We were playing basically the same program we'd given in Geneva, and I don't remember one thing about the music. I suppose it went well enough. Applause followed every solo and every group of pieces, and at the intermission and the finale the clapping was heavy, solid, and lasting. We had to play our encores, and afterward we remained onstage while a heavyset individual in black alpaca lectured the audience on the wonders of musical artistry and of friendship between great peoples. My German soon buckled under the strain, and none of the rest of us onstage caught as much as I did. But we were lucky. The personage in black repeated his entire speech in careful English, just for us. All the while, Kobrand sat impassively on his wooden chair, his big hands folded in his lap, listening and watching but making no sign either of gratification or of displeasure. And all the while, I was eyeing Kranz and Fornova and wondering whether our plans for them were really going to work.

As the audience crowded toward the doors, I tried to keep my eye on them. No use: caught up in the swirl of departing music lovers, they vanished into the damp evening. If Kobrand had hoped to make contact with us, his hope had been vain.

But as we were gathering up our gear, one odd thing did occur. On my music stand, tucked in among the dog-eared scores and battered books of dances, I found a brightly printed brochure. It was the owner-driver manual, in German, French, and English, for that year's Bavarische Motor Werke BMW sedan, the 2002tii. For a second, I stared at the booklet in bewilderment. Then I crammed it into my briefcase and covered it with the *Glogauer Liederbuch*.

A stirring performance requires an alert
mind.

K.P.E. BACH, p. 148.

CHAPTER SIXTEEN

THE FLAT SUNLIGHT of early spring shone through the window,
neutralizing the fluorescents but casting deep shadows in the corners.
The motes of sawdust that danced in the air glittered where the light hit
them. Stacked in small piles on the plank floor, unfinished backs,
bellies, and frames gleamed skeletally. On the varnished instruments,
hung up by their scrolls to dry, the light was screamingly bright.
Everywhere, harsh as the sunshine itself, the smells of sawn pine and
maple, of glue and varnish and turpentine, filled our nostrils.

The hum of the machinery climbed the scale toward a snarl as the six
ganged bandsaws bit abruptly into their breakfast of wood. When I
flinched, the operator in charge grinned at me and nodded. I watched
the saw blades carve out a new batch of parts for violins. Over the
noise, the operator shouted something. I couldn't catch the words. But
the interpreter yelled in my ear: "He says production this year is 15
percent greater than last year." I took his word for it. I wondered
whether the sawyer's missing left thumb had fallen victim to the
stepped-up production rate.

In this part of the plant, nobody was worrying about "the traditions
of hand craftsmanship and dedicated devotion which for centuries have
distinguished the instrument-makers of Markneukirchen." That in-
flated language was for the salesman in the showroom at the front of the
shop. Here, the idea was to mass-produce the violins, violas, cellos,
and basses cheaply enough to meet the alarming competition of the
imperialist robber barons from Japan.

The first few times, it had been amusing to see the elaborate machinery set to work, not on prosaic furniture or kitchen cabinetry but on the

frivolous reverse curves of stringed instruments. In much the same way, it had been amusing to be awakened at seven-fifteen by a solicitous hotel manager and to have been given VIP treatment in a style no capitalist establishment could have bettered. But since our arrival in Markneukirchen at nine o'clock, we'd toured three instrument factories, and the novelty was fading fast.

Strangely, although we were all edgy, our mood was cheerful.

Our interpreter-guide, eager to please, must have noticed our slackening interest in production-line instruments. "This time, *Fräulein* and gentlemen, I take you to the shop of a real *meisterstreichermacher*. Old Hans still uses nothing but hand methods. Oh, yes, very good quality." Then, remembering his loyalty to large-scale enterprise: "But the bigger shops, very good also."

We were on our way out of the factory yard when the first event of that long, eventful day took place.

"Sir, sir, excuse me, sir." It was the saw operator whose left thumb had gone missing. He'd followed me out of the shed. When I stopped, he touched my sleeve with his maimed left hand. In his right hand, he held something that flashed silver in the sunlight. "Excuse me," he said again. "you have dropped this."

On the cheap tag bearing the BMW imprint were two shiny car keys.

As I accepted them, my pulse began to beat hard, the way it sometimes does when I walk onstage at the beginning of a concert.

The others, walking on ahead, had barely noticed the delay. I slipped the keys into my pocket. There was just time to nod thanks to the sawyer. In his stolid, sun-browned face, one blue eye winked. Then he turned away and I hurried on to catch up with the group, my hand still in my pocket.

"What has happened?" the guide wanted to know.

"It's nothing," I lied politely. "I dropped my lighter. The man in the shop returned it."

"*Ach, so.*" The guide gave a creaky smile. But he added sententiously, "Be very careful, please, with your lighter. It is strictly forbidden to smoke anywhere near the woodworking facilities."

"I'll try to remember," I promised.

Our guide led us down the *Hohestrasse*, the main street, past the old church, and into a district of small old frame-and-plaster houses. As we walked the few blocks, I noted that traffic was growing brisk. At the corner of a crooked side street, before we turned, I caught a glimpse of the market square with its fountain and the booths set up for the fair.

There was no sign on the door of Mlocek & Sohne. The shop needed none. The man at the table in the bowed front window was sign enough. In one big, knife-scarred hand, the man was cradling the neckpiece of a new violin. In his other hand was the gouge, its curved blade peeling a long, exquisite spiral of shaving from the scroll.

Inside, the shop was bigger than it looked from the street, stretching back dustily into the interior of the ancient house. Our nostrils filled again with the powerful smells of the solvents and varnishes used in the finishing process. Along one wall, in glass-enclosed racks padded with green velvet, was the stock of finished instruments. Some of them looked crude, with the uneven varnish and rough detailing that stigmatize all cheap fiddles. But others were not crude. David was already peering at the half-dozen lutes that rested, bellies down, on a table in a corner. Jackie, ooh-ing over a gamba, was looking around for a bow.

The man at the table worked on imperturbably, stopping only momentarily to answer the questions our guide was asking in very rapid German. The charm of the shop began to relax me and make me forget about unpleasant matters like political rescue missions.

That's when the next thing happened.

Through a door at the rear of the shop came a broad-shouldered man. He moved easily, not pausing as he threaded his way through the tangle of heavy furniture, carpenters' equipment, and partly finished instruments. It was Kobrand. With him was another, smaller man, a man with a face like a half-carved potato: Kranz.

I made myself stand absolutely still, my eyes focused on the rebec, the primitive violin I'd been inspecting. Without turning away from the display case and attracting attention, I couldn't see how the others were reacting. But the seconds passed and, to my relief, I heard no gasps, no dropped instruments, nothing. Either nobody had noticed or else we all were taking Kobrand in stride.

Suddenly, sharply, Kranz spoke in German to our guide. He must have been asking about us, because in the guide's reply I caught something that sounded like *Spielmenschen am Antikinstrumenten*. More deferentially, Kranz addressed Kobrand in Russian, presumably passing on the information. There was a pause, then Kobrand himself came up to me.

"Pardon," he said in quite passable English. "You are the American musician who will perform later at the fair?"

"One of them," I said. "These are the others."

"Ah. Very interesting, the old music," he said dismissively. "I will come to listen."

"You're very kind," I said. I added the only other thing I could think of to tell him. "Be sure you have a good place down in front for the dances."

"Very well," said Kobrand. He exchanged a sentence or two with his watchdog, nodded indifferently at me, and went through the entrance out into the street.

A few moments later, we, too, left the shop. Outside, blinking in the bright sunlight, I muttered to Jackie: "Did you hear what I told our friend?" She nodded. "Did everybody else?"

"I think so. *Christus!* My knees are shaky. Ask if there's somewhere we can sit down." The guide let loose a flood of apologies for fatiguing the *Herren und gnädiges Fräulein*. He led us immediately to a glassed-in cafe on the *Neukirchplatz*. The cafe was already crowded with locals and visitors to the fair, but our guide had a word with the dark, Alpine type in waiter's garb who was the proprietor, and a choice table was hurriedly vacated and set up for us. We ate small, sticky cakes and sipped weak coffee. I stood Norbert the guide a cherry brandy and we all looked through the windows at the action in the square.

From the Flachsmann briefing, I'd assumed that the Markneukirchen fair was held exclusively for the trade in musical instruments. I was wrong. From what was happening outside, I realized at once that the fair was much more, in fact a regional market for everything from livestock and agricultural implements to clothing, housewares, and even pets and caged songbirds. The booths of the instrument makers, although they were more elaborate than the others, took up only one corner of the square.

Great, I thought. For us, the more hustle and bustle the merrier.

Directly in front of the instrument makers' booths an area had been cleared of traffic. There, as we watched, we could see workmen knocking together a small platform, its planking raised perhaps a foot above the cobbled paving. Our bandstand. "When do they start putting up the guillotine?" Ralph said.

"Don't be a ghoul," Jackie said at once.

"That's right," said David, "shut up." Our guide was looking interested but confused.

"It's always this way," I said, "before we give a performance."

"Of course, of course," said the man soothingly. Yet actually, as in the shop, I was feeling only the merest prickle of t e tension that I thought—I feared—might wash over me. And froൢ their relaxed chatter, I was sure that the others were as unflustered as I was. The delectable sun warmed us through the cafe window; the cheerful crowds of fairgoers milled and flowed just yards from where we sat. In these surroundings, it was impossible to be tense. Reality was the friendly hubbub of the cafe and the apricot taste on my tongue, not the business that had brought us to this pleasant, alien place.

I smiled at Jackie. She smiled back, sighed, stretched herself like a cat in the sunshine. We might have been a couple of tourists. Before she opened her mouth, though, I knew what she was going to say. I glanced at my watch. "You're right," I said. "We'd better be getting along."

By the time we'd extricated ourselves from the packed cafe, the workmen had finished the platform. We strolled over to take a look. As I'd spelled out in my instructions to the guide, and he in his to the authorities, a space had been roped off in front of the platform. On the side of the platform nearest the booths, more ropes and stanchions defined a narrow lane we could use for entrances and exits. The lane ran for fifteen or so yards to the nearest of the booths. There, the guide would be stationed to look after whatever gear we weren't using onstage. And for certain essential changes in attire, we could use the tiny space inside the booth as a dressing-room.

"Good," I said to the guide. "Everything is right. You've done an excellent job."

Pleased and embarrassed, he said, "*Bitte sehr!*" several times.

A few steps from our improvised backstage, at the edge of the *Platz*, was the entrance of Mlocek & Sohne, the last of the instrument-making establishments we'd visited that morning. We continued our walk past the doorway, down the narrow street that led away from the *Platz* and along the wider street that intersected the first one. From the briefing and now from actual observation, I could see that the rear entrance of the Mlocek shop opened onto this second street.

Exactly where it was supposed to be, the red Mercedes van stood at the curb.

As soon as the driver saw us, he opened his door and jumped out. As if to show us how cooperative he could be, he unlocked the van's rear doors quickly and swung them wide. Then, with more German punctiliousness, he and the guide helped us unload our equipment trunks and instrument cases and hump them past the Mlocek rear entrance, down the narrow side street and into the square.

Up on the stage, a rangy, pimply youth was fooling with the cables and microphones of the public address system. We had to clamber around him to set up our stands and instruments. Why do all sound technicians suffer from acne and shuffle around like old drunks? "David," I said finally, "you're the big hi-fi expert. Get hold of Norbert the guide and the two of you tell Charlie-boy here that he's making me very nervous. All he's supposed to do, tell him, is make the music really loud and really clear. And tell him that if anybody trips over his goddam wires, he'll be stringing cable in *northern* Siberia." David laughed.

"Hey, if I didn't know you better," he said, "I'd think you were nervous."

"Just do it," I said. A minute later, I was comforted to hear Norbert being emphatic to the soundman.

Preparing for an outdoor concert is trickier than preparing for one indoors. There are the obvious anxieties, like making sure everybody's music stays put on the stands and doesn't blow all over the place—and for that matter seeing that the first breeze doesn't topple the stands themselves. There are problems of crowd control. Outdoor audiences are much less inhibited than audiences indoors about crowding up close, asking questions, and expressing enthusiasm—or the reverse.

Finally, there's the simple matter of being heard. A brass band, a string orchestra, even a solo piano, will be audible over quite a surprising din of shuffling in the audience, bird song, and traffic noise. But the merest whisper of wind sets up eddies around the vent of a recorder. Even with a special windscreen, you can barely play the thing at all, let alone play it loudly. Likewise, I knew we'd have volume problems with our viols and David's lute. We did have with us some louder instruments. The shawm, krummhorn, and cornet can be as raucous as the funkiest jazz saxophone. Terry would be sounding forth on our sackbut, the Renaissance version of the trombone. Wherever I could, I was substituting these noisier instruments for quieter ones. Still, I wanted to be very sure that once we began, our music making would be impossible to ignore.

So we put up with Charlie-boy, watching him climb around, cables trailing, screwdrivers and wire cutters stowed in the pockets of his soiled canvas work apron. The minutes ticked away. Lunch hour arrived, and Charlie-boy perched on the edge of the platform and washed down with a pilsener his huge sausage-and-onion sandwich. Lunch hour went, and Charlie heaved his ladder around and climbed awkwardly up the façades of nearby buildings to rig his loudspeakers. We regrouped our chairs to avoid being blinded by the afternoon sun. We fingered our instruments. We voice-tested the microphones. They seemed to work, although there was no way to know how well.

Finally, Charlie-boy stuffed away his pliers and nodded. Across the *Platz*, the ancient clock in the church tower wheezed through its routine and chimed two o'clock. We couldn't wait any longer. We took our places and I gave the upbeat for the first number.

The sound was fabulous.

Ralph was handling percussion. At the first snap of the stick on the big military drum, we heard an echo crack back from the stone buildings lining the square. The municipal jackdaws, which had just settled back in the tower of the church after the two o'clock bell, rose up again in an outraged cloud like a revolution of seminarians. There must have been a couple of thousand people at the fair, and every head swiveled in our direction. Before we were six bars into the piece, a march-tempo basse dance we'd scored for sackbut, krummhorns, rebec, and drums, people were flowing into our corner of the square. They came from all directions: only the rope barriers held them back from the platform and the small, cleared area in front of it. Six or seven deep, orderly as you'd expect a German crowd to be, and yet craving excitement, our audience assembled within a minute. No doubt about it, the music was doing what it was supposed to do. It resounded in that old town square as I've never heard music reverberate, before or since. I remember thinking with a kind of exultation: This is what we came for, this is what matters.

We repeated the last strain, very broad, Terry braying on sackbut, Ralph on drum, and the crowd ate it up. There were shrieks, whistles, yodels that sounded like rebel yells. I saw one round-faced *Frau* in dignified black actually skipping up and down in her excitement, while her small, round-faced daughter, prim in red jumper dress, tried to restrain her.

Right in front, where I'd hoped he'd have the sense to be, was Kobrand, impassive in the middle of the applause. On his right stood Kranz, watching incuriously the action of the crowd. The woman, Fornova, on Kobrand's left, was as unsmiling as the other two, but every so often I saw one of her feet tap to the music.

Terry sat down, Jackie and I stood, Ralph remained standing for the contrasting second number, a slower, more melodic *chanson*. Jackie played recorder to my flute. I thanked Orpheus for making the breeze die down. And I thanked Charlie-boy silently for the wonderful acoustics that gave such snap to Ralph's finger-cymbals. I felt marvelously light-hearted, ready to try anything.

When we ended, we drew another hand from the crowd. It was fascinating, the way a little music was making these sober-seeming East Germans let themselves go. Whatever the sociology behind it, the crowd's mood suited our purposes. I glanced at my watch. Two-oh-seven: as good a time as any. "Okay," I said to Jackie under the cover of the applause. "Duck out back and get yourself ready. Hey!" I had to call after her as she started to leave the platform. "Take your fiddle with you! Take me, too!" She smiled at me, grabbed the gamba, and went on her way, and Ralph, according to plan, went with her. For a moment, I fooled around with the reed of the shawm I was going to be playing next. Good: Jackie and Ralph were slipping into the empty booth that was our dressing area. I checked the crowd. Kobrand and his disciples were still standing quietly just behind the rope. "Norbert!" When the guide saw me beckon, he jumped onto the platform.

"Yes, Sir?"

"I want to say something to the audience about the next part of the program. Will you be able to translate?" Norbert looked indignant.

"Of course, Sir. I am graduate of Leipzig Interpreter's School with advance certificate."

"Fine, fine." I turned to the nearest microphone and plucked it off its stand. "Good afternoon, ladies and gentlemen," I intoned. "Welcome to this performance of the Antiqua Players. We are happy to be playing here today as a celebration of the friendship between our two great peoples." Flachsmann had insisted that I put it in, and it drew a spattering of applause. I handed the mike to Norbert. As he bellowed his translation, I glimpsed Jackie and Ralph on their way back to the platform. Suddenly, urgently, I didn't want this crazy business to go on. I wanted to hide, to run away. Rather badly, I wanted to use a bathroom. But Jackie and Ralph were here and Norbert was shoving the mike back at me and it was too late to tell Flachsmann, Keep your money, we're not prison breakers, we're artists, we're too pure.

Into the microphone, I said, "Ladies and gentlemen, the music we are performing for you today is music that is meant for dancing." The crowd got the point at once. "*Ja! Ja!*" I heard a couple of voices say. "*Für Tanz!*"

"So we thought you would like it if we showed you a little of how the old dances are done." Over to you, Norbert. The idea pleased the crowd. I saw nods and beaming faces. The *Amerikanishen Spielmenschen* were really putting on a show. What a thing to tell Gebhardt and Ilse; what a shame they didn't want to come today.

"Now," I said in my best impresario manner, "allow me to introduce my colleagues, *Fräulein* Craine and *Herr* Mitchell, who will begin the demonstration together." Side by side, the two of them stepped forward and executed a formal curtsy and bow. More applause. Ralph had gone to the trouble of slipping an embroidered silk shirt over his regular shirt. Its full sleeves and floppy collar gave it the look of a costume. Jackie had done rather less—or rather more. She had simply unbuttoned to her slim waist the front of her plain dark frock.

As I put back the mike and resumed my seat, I sneaked a glance at Kobrand and his friends. Kobrand's face was as unreadable as ever. I couldn't see Fornova. But Kranz I could see. He was staring at Jackie in a way I normally wouldn't have cared for at all, the slimy Red Peril. What we were going to do would jolly well serve him right.

I caught the eyes of Terry and David, gave a little upbeat, and we whipped into the music.

With shawm, cornet, and tambourine, we were doing loudly what the old minstrels would have done more quietly with pipe and tabor: laying down a heavy beat and playing and repeating, with maddening insistence, a deceptively simple eight-bar theme. The starting tempo we set deliberately at 74 to the minute, a shade quicker than the normal pulse-beat. The third time through, building up the pressure in my lungs and bronchial tree, then expelling air through my embouchure, I felt my own pulse begin to sing softly in accompaniment, *lub-dup! lub-dup!* Against my lips, the buzz of the double reed was teasing. As I warmed up, the crowing you get at first from the shawm gave way to its proper sound, an insinuating, oriental, oboe-ish wail. The magnificent acoustics threw back the sound in a triumphant snarl.

And out in front of the platform, against the texture of the music, Jackie and Ralph were moving through the steps, glides, and halts of the galiardo, enacting a ritual that seemed older than time itself.

They'd learned how to do the dance for a concert tour we'd never given, a tour of children's schools. Small children love to move to music. In our one trial performance, we'd found out how responsive they were. I never forgot the rapt faces, the squirming bodies, the mounting excitement, the longing to join in and the rapturous sense of release when the teacher let them follow the dancers around the room. The memory is what gave me the idea. Children are not the only rhythmical animals. If we could get this crowd in Markneukirchen excited enough with music and dance. . . .

It was time for Stage Two of the exercise.

David kept up the beat and Terry continued to drill out the theme on the cornet. We wanted no one to forget it, even for a moment. Over the music, I said into the microphone: "Ladies and gentlemen, we will now select two people from the audience to help us with the demonstration." I passed the mike to Norbert. While he was still translating, Jackie and Ralph were choosing partners.

Kranz and Fornova.

I could see Fornova shake her head in refusal, but it was no use; the nearby crowd wouldn't let her refuse; goodnaturedly, they pushed her into the ring. And anyway, Kranz was licking his lips in his eagerness to get out there with the sexy American *tschiki*. With a last look at Kobrand, who was standing stonily in place, Fornova allowed Kranz to pull her by the arm into the center of the ring. For a few seconds, there was a lull while Jackie explained the sequence of simple steps. Then, Jackie nodded to us and I picked up the shawm and began to play it like crazy.

There was a shout from the crowd. And Fornova and Kranz were doing it . . . they were dancing the galiardo, Kranz surprisingly nimbly, Fornova with a kind of wooden determination, like a puppet with a learning problem. As Ralph held her hand and paraded her around the ring, I saw her pale lips parted in an unwilling smile.

We picked up the beat. And what we'd planned on and hoped for started to happen. Spurred by the obsessive quality of the music, people in the crowd began to do the dance. First one brave couple, then another, then three or four more ducked under the rope barrier and joined the others in the ring.

Stage Three.

Still playing, I jumped up and, like a belly dancer's clarinetist looking for laughs, I did a little dance of my own around the bandstand. And while I was doing it, Terry slipped off the stand and plunged into the crowd. My movements masked his. Neither Fornova nor Kranz, now gyrating in the middle of a swirl of other dancers, could possibly have seen Terry make his way around the outside of the ring to catch at Kobrand's sleeve.

Kobrand could move fast. One instant, he was standing there listening to Terry. The next, he was gone, thrusting his way through the crowd, pausing to see if his bodyguards had noticed his departure, then dodging out of my line of sight in the direction of the vacant booth to the rear of our stage. I kept on playing, to cover Terry's reappearance. Just as we'd estimated back at Flachsmann's castle, the whole incident took about ten seconds. Below us in the ring area, people were still dancing. But as the pace caught up with them, a few couples were already slowing down and standing still to watch. In another moment or two, the stimulus of the music would begin to lose its sharpness and the excitement would die down, and then . . . it was time to go.

Quickly, I tossed the shawm to Terry. "I think we've done it," I gasped. He nodded. "Hold the fort." The music had to keep going: he was already lipping the reed. David, sweaty from what he'd been doing for five minutes to that poor tambourine, flashed me a farewell grin. I stepped off the bandstand on the side away from the dancers, glimpsing as I did so the startled face of Norbert the guide in the crowd off to my right.

I ran.

The lusty wailing of the shawm pursued me as I sprinted past the empty changing booth and down the narrow alley by the Mlocek & Sohne shop. *Good luck, Terry. Good luck, Jackie.* Panting, I brought myself up short at the corner of the building and peered up the cross street like a nine-year-old playing hide-and-go-seek. It was shockingly quiet after the tumult in the square.

> [The good accompanist] never forgets that he is
> an accompanist, not a soloist.
>
> K.P.E. BACH, p. 386.

CHAPTER SEVENTEEN

THE RED VAN was still parked where it should be. Twenty yards beyond it, also where it should be, was a shiny black BMW. Standing beside the BMW, as patiently as he'd stood behind the rope in the square, was Kobrand. Beside him on the pavement was a big, boxy instrument case: his cello. He must have had it in the shop.

By now, they'd be looking for Kobrand . . . the thought sent me into motion again, around the corner at a dead run and up the street to the BMW. Fighting to catch my breath, I fumbled in my pocket for the keys, dropped them, picked them up, and then found myself looking into Kobrand's impassive stare.

"*Genosse*, er, Mister French, would you be so kind to please open the boot?" The boot? Oh, the trunk. Good God! Any second now, I knew, an angry posse of East German secret policemen would be after us. . . . I didn't argue. I opened the trunk. Kobrand carefully put his cello inside. The trunk looked much less roomy that it was. I thought: If it weren't Kobrand, the thing would never fit. But it did fit, and I slammed down the trunk lid and grabbed the keys.

"*Genosse* French, *ihr Gürtel, bitte!*" The episode was beginning to feel like a comic nightmare. Here we were, trying to escape from East Germany. Surely, surely there was some reason for haste. But this unshakable enemy of the state was cautioning me to fasten my seatbelt as if we were going for a Sunday drive in the park. Naturally, the tongue of Kobrand's belt clipped smoothly into the buckle while mine was still refusing to uncoil. I was still struggling with the jammed, damned thing when, down the street, the shouting began. Without even swiveling around (something I couldn't do anyway because of that *bloody* seatbelt), I could see in the side mirror that several men had emerged from a house up the street. It was odds-on which house it was and who they were. I gave up the battle with the seatbelt, snapped on the ignition, and, to my relief, felt the BMW come alive. But before I could put the car into gear, Kobrand was leaning over me.

"Excuse," he said. I might have known. One gentle jiggle from him and my seatbelt unrolled docilely and locked snugly into place. My sense of inferiority deepened.

Our failure to get the car moving may have fooled the men who were trotting up the sidewalk to take us in the rear. Or more likely, the East German authorities weren't sure exactly what to do about Kobrand and me. Anyway, they weren't swarming after us waving pistols. And they weren't shooting at us. So, exactly as the driver's manual admonished, I took my time. Gently, I eased home the clutch, stepped on the accelerator, and brought the little car off the sidewalk and all the way into the street. Only as we began to gather speed did we hear another volley of shouts from our pursuers.

Fifty meters ahead was an intersection. A left turn, I knew, would bring us to the N283, the national route that ran down the *Hohestrasse*. Another left, and we would be on our way westward to Adorf and the border. The checkpoint was south of Adorf, just below Bad Brambach on the N92. The whole journey was about 20 kilometers, roughly 12 miles, and the scenery was supposed to be marvelous.

I turned right.

Aside from the national, only one other road led into or out of Markneukirchen. On the maps, it was a thread. What's more, if you were trying to go west, out from behind the Iron Curtain, it was the wrong thread to follow. It went due south, first up over a ridge, then down a river valley. And the next thing you knew, there you were in Communist Czechoslovakia. As a road, this alternative lacked appeal. As an escape route, it slipped us out of one prison cell into the one next door. I'd made these points to Flachsmann at the briefing. But he'd simply grinned. "You're absolutely right," he'd said in that damned disarming way of his. "You're absolutely right. But don't you miss that turnoff."

So I turned right, up a side street that seemed to be going nowhere, and I had the satisfaction of hearing Kobrand grunt with surprise. In less than a minute, we were out of town. The road climbed rapidly through groves of chestnut and pines into hilly pastureland. There were patches of dampness on the tarmac where the shadows of the trees kept the sun off the road. Incredibly, nothing was chasing us. I kept the BMW moving as fast as I could on the narrow, twisty road. Even when my hands began to shake on the wheel.

"*Essen Sie doch.*" Out of the corner of my eye, I saw Kobrand take something out of his jacket pocket. He broke off a corner and put the fragment on the map shelf where I could reach for it. It was a hunk of dark, rich chocolate, and it did miracles for my blood-sugar level. I was glad of the nourishment, because the road had started to hairpin its way up toward the crest of the ridge that lay between us and the border.

At the crest, they'd left an unpaved rest area. I pulled the BMW off the macadam and cut the ignition. Apart from the gurgle of a quick-running brook trapped in a culvert, all that broke the silence was the cooing of the wood doves in the pines to our right and, in a field somewhere below us, the sputter of a tractor.

I was still shaking.

Ahead, the road dropped away sharply, paralleling the brook that tumbled, through arable land just beginning to show green, straightaway into the valley. Where the road leveled out, no more than a couple of kilometers down the hill, was the border crossing point. It looked like nothing more than a masonry hut beside the road, with a red-and-white-striped pole to serve as barrier. The pole was upright. I longed to start the car, pick up speed, then coast down the hill. With my left foot down, I'd keep the motor noise from warning whoever was stationed in that hut. Painlessly, saving gasoline every inch of the way, we'd slip out of East Germany.

I knew better than to try.

"You have your papers?" Nothing, it seemed, could shake Kobrand's composure. Instead of answering, he reached into his inside pocket and produced a thick wad of documents held together by a heavy rubber band. From this packet he slid a well-thumbed booklet with Cyrillic type stamped in gold on its dark red cover: obviously a passport. I patted my own pocket to make sure my passport was there, along with the letter informing officialdom that Alan French, musician, was on an authorized trip across the border for sightseeing and also for the purpose of possibly obtaining samples of musical instrument manufacture for export from the People's Supreme Republic of Czechoslovakia to the United States.

"Everywhere else in the world, the dollar stinks," Flachsmann had said when he handed me the letter, "but not in Eastern Europe. If they think they can sell you something for dollars, you better watch it."

"Why?"

"Not only will they let you into the country, they may never let you out."

I started the car.

It was wise of me not to try to run for it. As we rolled down the hill toward the crossing point, the perspective changed. I could see, parked on the far side of the hut, the big gray official car. The sun glittered on the paintwork and on the whip of the long radio-telephone antenna that sprang from one rear fender and arched forward over the roof. There seemed to be nobody in the car, but I couldn't be sure. All I could do was brake tamely to a halt at the *Achtung!* sign by the striped barrier. For a long moment, nothing happened. On my forehead, under my arms, I could feel the sweat pop forth. Even Kobrand shifted nervously in his seat.

Then the door of the hut opened and a man emerged. He was enormously, grotesquely fat, so freakishly fat that I wanted to laugh. The man was dressed in a freshly pressed khaki uniform. As he waddled toward us, you could sense the straining of the fabric across his huge chest and his thighs. But there was nothing comic about the little eyes through which this elephant of an official surveyed his world. His eyes were slate gray, like the paint job on the official car, and they made you think of Sidney Greenstreet at his unfunniest.

"*Papier'n,*" Sidney grunted at us through the car window. My passport and Kobrand's disappeared into a vast, suety paw. The paw withdrew, then all of Sidney withdrew into the hut. Time passed. With the painful, exhausted clarity of the dreamer of a bad dream, I noticed that the red paint on the barber pole barrier needed refreshing. I'd just finished this job, cleaned the brush, and started on the next job, shining up the rustled bolts at the base of the barrier with emery paper, when the door of the hut reopened.

Sidney let us through.

The same immense fist that had engulfed our passports now held them out to me. Warily, I reached through the window to take them. The whey face even cracked at the rosebud lips in the semblance of a cordial smile. "*Willkommen,*" said the face. "*Willkommen im Tsechoslovakei.*" Perhaps the most appalling thing of all about the

man-mountain was his voice. It was mellow, suave, artfully mod-
ulated. It made this hill of flesh sound like an evening TV news analyst.
Was I wrong, or was there a shade of irony in the beautiful voice?
"*Danke!*" I suppressed a shudder. At any second, I expected to hear
the telephone ring inside the hut, or the roar of the engine as the gray car
shot forward to block our escape. But while I was trying to restart the
BMW, failing, trying again, and finally getting the engine to catch, the
fat man merely stood there. And when we began to roll ahead, the wave
of his flipper was positively affable.

Five minutes later, we were through the townlet of Luby and on our
way southward. In another fifteen minutes, we'd be at the Czech N6, a
major artery that runs east-west along the route of one of the old
Hapsburg postroads. To attempt the Eger/Cheb crossing directly into
West Germany, we'd have to turn right onto the N6.

If Flachsmann's plans were still holding up, we'd find no gray car
awaiting us at the intersection.

I glanced over at Kobrand. He'd located the lever that controlled the
rake of his seat, angled himself comfortably back, folded his hands
loosely in his lap, and closed his eyes. He could have been asleep. I
wasn't too surprised that he could make himself relax even in this
situation. Musicians do develop the knack. Besides, without the self-
discipline that enabled him to will himself into passivity, Kobrand
could never have become Kobrand in the first place.

With my passenger quiet, there was nothing for me to do except keep
the little car moving at speed. Luckily, the traffic was light. A few
trucks, a farm wagon or two, and an occasional passenger car were the
only vehicles I saw on the road. I had plenty of time to wonder what had
happened to Jackie and the others. If they'd been able to do what the
plan called for, probably nothing. At least, I hoped so. And I was
beginning to think so. Nobody witnessed the contact with Kobrand.
Fornova and Kranz might be frantic, but they knew nothing. In fact,
Fornova and Kranz and the East German authorities might be operating
on the theory that Kobrand had forced *me* to get him away. Anyway,
I'd have loved to see the face of the desk sergeant at local headquarters
when the Antiqua Players descended upon him. Undoubtedly, the East
Germans would have some questions to ask. But they wouldn't want to
be too rough with official guests, and surely nothing bad would have
happened before Flachsmann's "fixer" arrived.

Please God.

I swung the BMW around the first of a series of curves. Its tires sang hollowly on the roadway of a bridge across a pretty little river: the Eger. Halfway through the next curve, I spotted the warning sign: Junction Ahead. I braked, slowed in anticipation of the *Halt!* Behind us, no sinister gray car loomed suddenly larger, then very large in the sunlight. Ahead, no gray car was parked to block our way. I glanced left and right along the N6. Nothing either side, not even a farm cart. I shoved the gear-shift into first and let the BMW pick up momentum. Crossing the N6, we followed the road we were on, the road that led southward according to plan.

Calmly, Kobrand opened his eyes and levered his seat upright. "Do you wish me to drive the car?" he asked in precise, accented English.

"No, thank you," I said.

"Very well. But if you should become fatigued, be good enough to let me know at once. This is a good car and I am an excellent driver. I see no reason to take unnecessary risk." I had no intention of letting Kobrand drive, but it was nice to know that in an emergency he could take over. Nor did his arrogance surprise me. Like the ability to relax in trying circumstances, a hyperdeveloped ego is not uncommon among concert musicians. No doubt Kobrand did drive well. Anybody with *his* eye-hand coordination would be superb behind the wheel.

"Also," Kobrand was speaking again, "if you will tell me where you plan to cross the border, I will select for us a safe route. I know this sector of Bohemia very well from my student days before the Liberation War."

"You are very kind," I said. His manner was getting under my skin. I decided to volunteer no information.

"I understand," Kobrand said. "If we are pursued and captured, you wish to be the only one who knows. That is proper." He leaned back in his seat, stretched his shoulders and yawned. Matter-of-factly, he added: "There will, I think, be no pursuit."

"I hope you're right," I said.

"I am right." What he meant was, I am always right. "Still, it is better not to speak where we cross, even to me."

"Yes," I said.

"Your little scheme was most ingenious, Mister French. Those two who were with me, my 'companions' they called themselves, they will be *agitato*, eh?" He chuckled at the thought. "*Molto, molto agitato.*"

I was curious. "What will happen to them?"

"To them? Oh, they will be under suspicion in People's Court for having helped a defector. Probably they will go to prison for quite a few years. Maybe they will be shot."

"Shot?"

"You would favor hanging? Ah! But we are not barbarians like you Westerners!" Kobrand, I could tell, liked having his little joke. "Anyway, *nichevo*! Those two, the Kranz and the Fornova, were state hirelings, creatures of our absurd bureaucracy. Forget them." Out of the corner of my eye, I saw him make a flicking-away motion with his right hand.

"Your friends, too, will be *agitato*," Kobrand went on. "Not a bad tactic, either, that ensemble of yours. Fresh young people playing so musically on the amusing old instruments. Charming! Who would associate such naive music with a political rescue? Quite clever, really. I must tell Hugo! But, oh! How tedious must have been your rehearsals!" Then and there, I started not caring very much for the celebrated Itzaak Kobrand.

"Don't you play Renaissance music in Russia?"

"Of course! We play every kind of music in Russia! I myself play Bach all the time. My Bach is famous. But your little dances! In Russia, student groups perform them in the parks for worker audiences." I made no comment, and for a few kilometers Kobrand too was silent. Then he said: "I have never had time for such slight things."

"You ought to try them," I said.

"Perhaps," Kobrand said indulgently. "Perhaps in the West I shall have time. Maybe some day I will come play sarabands with my rescuers, eh? But I do not think so.

"God gave me the talent, Mister French," he added. "God gave it to me and I must use it properly or die."

"I suppose you must," I said.

"*Goskonsert* was always trying to tell me, not what to play but what to think. Bureaucrats, always bureaucrats! Then, they tried also to tell me what to play. And where and when and even how. I am a good Russian citizen, I assure you, Mister French. But rather than die professionally, I leave my homeland and come with you." He shook his head sadly. "I accept exile. But not to play simple songs and dances with music students. That, no."

"What *will* you do?" I asked him.

"I am not certain," he said, still a little heavily. "All this must be arranged. First, there must be a tour, a *big* tour, to take advantage of the publicity about my escape. I must play in New York and London and Paris. Also Tokyo. I am *fantastic* in Japan. I will invite you to a concert, Mister French, *and* your young friends. I will see that you are sent tickets.

"People will want to know: Is Kobrand still Kobrand? They must be shown! I must rerecord immediately the Bach suites, the Liszt, the Saint-Saëns."

He went on cataloguing the interviews he'd have to grant, the concerts he would play, the records he would make. On one aspect of his exile from Mother Russia, he became positively cheerful. "My fees," he said with extreme satisfaction, "my fees will be very large." So they would be. A Kobrand, rescued from the Soviets and actively performing, would earn more money in one year than I could earn in twenty.

"My fees will be enormous," Kobrand was repeating happily. "And there will be none of the old nonsense about paying the money directly to *Goskonsert*. *Nyet!* Now, I shall receive all of the money directly into my own hand!" The idea of receiving money directly into his own hand brought to Kobrand's wintry face a broad smile, the first I'd seen there.

From making money, Kobrand went on to the question of where to live and what to do with his money. For a good Russian citizen, he knew quite a surprising amount about the stock market and the price of real estate on Fifth Avenue ("I have a friend who says she will sell me her flat very, very cheap because I am so gifted artist") and in Cap d'Antibes.

Only when the turnoff for Marienbad flashed past on our left did Kobrand interrupt himself. With grim gusto, he described a concert he'd given at Marienbad during the Occupation, for some high Soviet officials. "I was playing brilliantly. But the General in charge of the zonal defenses was so drunk he slid off his chair in the middle of the Haydn and rolled on the floor with his mistress! Eh, Mister French, you have no idea what they were like, those *akulturny* jackals of Stalinists! Try dissenting with *them* and see where you ended up. And do you know, my friend, there are still plenty like that, even today!"

Uncivilized or not, his countrymen had known plenty about zonal defense. Starting just south of the small city of Chodova Plana, they'd built about 30 miles of splendid military-access road through the dark

Czech forest, running 10 miles behind, and parallel to, the West German frontier. At a fork in our road, this highway stretched away temptingly to the right. But just short of its smooth surface, the fork had another tine, a narrow secondary road that angled off still further to the right to lose itself in the thick woods.

I made the sharp turn that put us onto this road.

In the middle of another anecdote, Kobrand interrupted himself again. "My friend, you are absolutely certain that this is the correct route?" I nodded. He shrugged. "To me, it looks like the path to the woodcutter's hut." I wasn't sure whether he meant *Hans Und Gretl* or some other, even gloomier Slavic tale. But I understood how he felt. The road twisted, turned, and looped back on itself amid armies of heavy-branched, shadowy trees. Although I knew the route by heart, there was something about that damned Teutonic forest that made the hair bristle along the back of my neck. Luckily for my nerves, after five miles or so the trees suddenly began to thin out. Within a minute, we were driving in bright sunlight through open meadowland. "Not this time, old man," I jauntily assured the startled Kobrand. "The wicked witch of the woods won't get us this time." Kobrand smiled, but I wondered if he believed me.

A stubby, green-painted wooden spire popped into sight to remind me that we were entering Tachov, the first of a couple of farm villages on our route. Kobrand sat quietly while I navigated the BMW through the empty, quiet streets and around the market square. The road into Tachov continues southward into the gorge of the Naab river, eventually joining another bit of the Soviet-built military road system. If we had in fact been racing for the border, that road would have been the quickest, most direct one to follow.

Instead, Flachsmann's plan angled us back toward the northwest, into a range of uplands along a quieter sector of the frontier.

A side road even narrower than the road we'd been on slipped us past a cluster of deserted-looking storage sheds into the countryside. Almost at once, the trees again closed in, cutting off the sun. On that crooked byway, any speed faster than 20 miles an hour would have been reckless. I wanted to go faster. But I kept us moving at 20. So I could listen as well as watch for whatever might be coming, I cranked down the window. But there was nothing to see except the empty, shadowy road; nothing to hear except birdsong and the remote rattle of an airborne engine. Probably a helicopter.

Just outside Obvra, the unpronounceable next dot on the map, the road began its climb. Obvra was even smaller than Tachov; its main street even quieter. Within minutes, we were cruising along a ridge above the village, on the last lap of the run to the West German border. The crossing point came into view abruptly. To stop in time, I had to brake sharply at the head of a curve. I pulled up to the striped barrier and switched off the ignition. But, oddly, the engine noise failed to stop. Another engine took up the tune.

On the far side of the customs hut, a military helicopter with Red Star markings was just settling mothlike to the ground. Its pilot never cut his engine. Even when the opening cabin door flipped back against the fuselage, the rotors kept up their lazy turning.

Down the cabin steps, his tread heavy enough to set the helicopter rocking on its skids, came Sidney. His uniform was as creaseless as it had been two hours earlier, when he'd welcomed us into the country. The flesh of his jowls was as pink and smooth as a baby's. Shouldering aside the anxious-faced officials who had ventured out of the hut, Sidney lumbered over to the BMW.

"Papier'n." Once again, the breathy grunt. Once again, the enormous hand gobbled up our passports. But this time, Sidney made no pretense of looking them over. He glanced at them, then thrust them back at me. "You had a pleasant journey?" He asked the question in unaccented English. I was so startled I simply stared at him. In his careful announcer's voice, he repeated the question.

"Yes, thank you, we did." It was Kobrand who had the presence of mind to reply.

"Splendid. As you leave our quiet country and enter the Federal Republic, please remember to drive carefully. Goodbye." Sidney waved a paw at the underling with the anxious expression, who stood timidly in the doorway of the hut like a gopher by the entrance to his mound. The gopher pressed a button and the vehicle gate shot skyward. Before the pole was all the way up, I stepped on the gas and rammed us through the Iron Curtain. A few meters farther on, a quiet man in a brown uniform stamped our papers and admitted us to West Germany. We never even heard the lift-off of Sidney's helicopter. Obviously, Flachsmann's influence had turned up a gracious host.

We'd done it.

I felt like kissing the rocky soil of the Böhmerwald. Even Kobrand seemed gratified. "Mister French, if I remember rightly, there is a small village down this road. Let us stop there for some refreshment."

The best cafe in Bärnau featured very dark pine paneling, chamois antlers, and local plum brandy. Kobrand drained his at a gulp. As usual, he could cope much better than I could. He ordered a second *slivovitz* to keep me company as I struggled with my first. Finally, between tiny sips of the sweet, fiery stuff, I was able to get out the inevitable question. "Does it feel different to be—here?" Kobrand looked amused.

"My dear Mister French, I see that you, like so many Americans, are an idealist." He held up his glass and eyed me through the rose-colored, 188-proof liqueur. "What a pity. I will not be saying this in a few hours to the press, but, no, it feels no different. Why should it? Here or there—" he jerked his chin in the general direction of the border "—it is the same. I have a commodity to trade, my talent. Where the price is highest, this is where I prefer to sell. Right now, the best price is in the West."

"But—"

"Besides, they say, do they not, that music is international, an art which knows no boundaries." He gave a sardonic bark of laughter. "Good! Then I am serving the cause of music." I wanted to say that a cynicism so practiced couldn't be real, but Kobrand overrode me again. "Listen, Mister French! You will say, in the West there is freedom! But I have seen New York, London, Paris—and Chicago and Leeds and Lyons. They are dirty places, these Western cities of yours, and in them fine musicians are working in factories and music shops. Or giving lessons to the daughters of the bourgeoisie and flattering their mamas. You call this freedom?

"No . . . listen, Mister French! You have a very pleasant talent. But I think that in New York—you come from New York, *da*?— you cannot be so very successful. Or else you would not be driving a defector over the Czech border for money.

"In the Motherland, Mister French, by now you would be director of Youth Symphony in Kiev or Kharkov. Maybe also head of chamber orchestra in Moscow itself. You would be earning good wages. You would receive the best medical care, free. A guaranteed old-age pension, also free. You would be respected, esteemed. How much better are you in your 'free' New York?"

I stopped choking on my *slivovitz* long enough to say: "Then maybe you'll be good enough to drive me back over the border." Kobrand laughed again.

"Not for me, Mister French. Not any longer. But maybe *you* should go."

Instead, I paid for the drinks. We got back into the BMW and headed it westward.

A kilometer and a half beyond Bärnau, the road suddenly swings south, away from the Naab, and the 950-meter bulk of the Entenbühl drifts into view almost dead ahead. The sharpness of this first turn forces you to brake hard, which is as well, because you can see that down the road another jog, a hard right, puts you back on course to the west. I did see this, but that's not what made me keep my foot on the brake pedal.

Drawn up in the shade of a huge roadside elm was a car, a big tan Oldsmobile. Beside it stood two men in civilian clothes. I recognized both of them. One was Carroll, the American cultural attaché and CIA boss in Geneva. The other was the Swiss journalist, Bauer.

Alongside the Olds was another vehicle. It looked something like an outsized Jeep. Its occupants wore military uniforms and carried rifles. Mounted on a frame behind the driver's seat was a firearm bigger than a rifle. It could have been meant for a pursuing tank. But no tank was rumbling after us down the road from Bärnau. Besides, the big gun was trained squarely on the silver and blue "BMW" we wore on our radiator.

> If the accompanist has an inept leader
> who precedes him with inept . . . variations,
> he must choose the safest way out.

K.P.E. BACH, p. 405.

CHAPTER EIGHTEEN

AUTOMATICALLY, I PUMPED THE BRAKE, my lips framing a word or two of salutation to the welcoming committee by the Olds. But I never got the chance to make the speech. As soon as we came to a stop, perhaps even sooner, Kobrand embarked on a solo of his own.

For one astonishing second, his big square left hand clawed at my right forearm, his lightish brown eyes blazed into mine. Staring at me, his face contorted with rage, he spat out an expletive. I have no idea what he said or even what language he was speaking. I was stunned. But I remember thinking to myself as you do think in words when you're under sudden stress, *Alan, this time you're really afraid.* And it was true. Kobrand's sudden tigerish move, his furious face had nothing to do with the game we'd been playing so far, with Flachsmann's game. This was a deeper part of the jungle. It frightened me.

That may be what made me freeze. For what seemed like whole minutes, I sat like a startled rabbit while Kobrand unclipped his safety belt, reached out for the handle of his door, and got the door open. Then, with another curse, this one almost a sob, he was gone, sliding out the door and scuttling half-bent around toward the rear of the BMW.

For another long moment, incredibly, nothing happened. But then, almost simultaneously, there came a yell from one of the men by the Olds—Bauer, I think—and a thump from the back of our car. I tried to spin around, but my own seatbelt and the contour of the BMW's cushions made it a struggle. As I fumbled with the belt latch, I sensed rather than saw that Kobrand was opening the trunk of the car. *Why does he want his cello?* I mumbled to myself idiotically, *You can't run very fast with a cello in your arms.*

By this time, it was my turn to half-step, half-dive from the BMW. As the door on my side swung open, it blocked my view to the rear. But I could see clearly what was going on over by the Oldsmobile. Carroll, in a tan gabardine suit the exact color of the Olds, was reaching frantically into the attaché case he had propped open on the shiny hood. From it, he was taking a gun. The moment I saw it, I instinctively dodged away, mimicking Kobrand in a quick scuttle around the nose of the BMW to what felt like the safety of the far side.

I nearly fell over Kobrand. Like some bulky predator, he was crouched over his locked cello case, his mouth tight in a grin of rage, his hands busy with lock and key. Momentarily, the lock jammed. Then he wrenched open the case. It held a cello and a fine Torte bow: I saw the sun gleam on the silky surface of the cello's body. But there was extra room in the case, room enough for the large black pistol Kobrand was grabbing with one hand and for the greasy clips of spare shells he was stuffing into his jacket pocket with the other.

When I blundered into him, he grunted and raised the pistol. Thinking he was about to shoot, I flung up an arm to fend off the bullet. But Kobrand, of course, detested waste. He immobilized me the economical way, by ramming the muzzle of his gun briskly into my unguarded solar plexus. Gasping, I went down, with just enough strength left to roll partway under the BMW for refuge against the next disaster.

From there, I watched dazedly as Kobrand slammed shut the cello case, glanced quickly around, and, gun in hand, began to back carefully away from the BMW, keeping low, using the car for cover. His awkward posture, the exaggerated cautiousness of his movements, were clichés from all the war and gangster movies I'd ever seen. Even the cello case, lying on the ground like a midget's coffin, seemed to belong in the picture.

"French!" It was Carroll's voice. "You and your buddy there stop the bullshit and *freeze!*" Another cliché.

At the sound, Kobrand stooped a little lower, almost squatting, duckwalking backward away from the BMW, the hand with the gun thrust out mechanically for balance. A few meters away, off the mown verge of the road, beyond the shallow, dry drainage ditch, a thicket of dusty shrubbery marked the beginning of the forest. Even with a regiment, Carroll would find Kobrand hard to extract from a lair in those woods.

I didn't think Kobrand wanted to shoot me. I hoped he didn't. I wriggled farther under the BMW. Then, I called out to Carroll: "It's Kobrand, the cellist! Don't shoot! He wants to escape!" At least, that's what I think I said. Nobody heard me, because as soon as I started to shout Kobrand pulled the trigger. There was a roar and a clang of metal as the bullet ricocheted off some solid part of the BMW's frame near me. I got my head all the way under the car and lay still. I decided never to move again.

When I dared to open my eyes and peer out, Kobrand was still duckwalking grotesquely away from me. Quite a surprising amount of smoke was trickling from the muzzle of his gun. I kept quiet. For a long moment in the cheery sunlight of the May afternoon, all I heard were the slight scuffling sounds of Kobrand's feet. Then, from behind me, I heard the sudden thudding of heavy shoes or boots on the road and felt the impact as somebody slammed up against the other side of the BMW.

When the shot took him, Kobrand was just starting to inch his way down the slight gradient from the edge of the road into the dry ditch. The force of the bullet shoved him backward into the ditch. His heels caught. He sat down abruptly on the far bank, spine straight, knees spread as if to accept his cello for one more encore. The hand clutching the gun first rose stiffly in an upbeat, then dropped down limply. The gun slid from the fingers to the ground. Kobrand's head sagged forward, the sun shining on his close-cropped hair. Finally, his whole body, breaking the rhythm, somersaulted forward into the dirt. Nothing alive would have landed so bonelessly.

I got to all fours, out of the stink of road tar, rubber, gasoline, and dust, then climbed wearily to my feet. Even before the nausea overcame me, I was one hundred years old.

"Better let him get it over with," said a voice.

"Suppose so. Neater." The second voice belonged to Carroll.

"Why . . . Why . . ." croaked a third voice. It took me at least a second to recognize that the third voice was my own.

"Why what?" We were standing in the hot sun and the sweat was pouring off me. But still I felt shivery. Carroll's face with its silly moustache swam in front of me like a mirage.

"Why what, French?" Carroll repeated.

"Why . . . You shot . . . Kobrand."

"What are you talking about?" The waves of sickness were receding. I could focus on Carroll more clearly as he leaned, facing me, against the passenger door of the faithful BMW. Kobrand's door. "What makes you think *we* shot anybody?" The lilt of emphasis in Carroll's voice should have warned me. It didn't.

"Saw you do it." In the background, a couple of the khaki-clad figures from the gun-carrier were at work. Already, Kobrand's body had been lifted onto a stretcher. A canvas cover had been put in place. Only his feet in their dusty black oxfords bore witness to what was underneath. Watching them load Kobrand's body in to the back of the gun-carrier, I missed the next few words. "Say that again, will you Carroll?"

"Sure thing, good buddy. We heard there was going to be a breakout here. We came to bring help. And I'll admit we wanted to meet your friend and maybe ask him a few questions. I guess he just . . . overreacted. It's a darn shame."

I stared at him in bewilderment. "But how did you know?" Carroll gave his good-ol'-boy smirk.

"Maybe a little birdie told us. But we knew, now didn't we? And when we got here, we found your car by the side of the road and you with a gun. And Kobrand was dead."

"And you're trying to frame me?"

"Now, now, Mr. French." Bauer edged his way between Carroll and me and spoke soothingly. "Nobody is trying to, as you say, frame anybody. But you must appreciate the situation. A week ago, we are talking, you and I, in Geneva. You say that you are here to play music. Only that and nothing more. The next time we meet, you are hundreds of kilometers from Geneva, in an obscure corner of German territory on the Czech frontier. Are you playing music? No. Instead, you are in a car with a leading so-called dissident Soviet artist. There is an exchange of gunfire and your illustrious passenger, unfortunately, becomes a casualty.

"Many inquiries will be made concerning this incident, Mr. French." Sadly, Bauer shook his head. "We only want to make sure, you understand, that the answers to all questions are the right answers."

"That's it, French," Carroll said. "After all, a lot of wild accusations on your part won't bring what'shisname, Kobrand, back to life. So why not be sensible?"

I felt the anger and the fear bubbling away inside me. I fought to keep my head clear. "Who are you people?" I asked.

"Now, that's one of those matters we'd like you to be sensible *about*," Carroll said. "Let's just say that we're not the U.S. Department of Wildlife and Fisheries."

"Are you CIA?" It was a stupid question, and Carroll snickered.

"Sure," he said. I longed to smash a fist into the middle of his wiseguy moustache.

"Mr. French!" Once again, Bauer stepped into the role of peacemaker. "We cannot possibly discuss with you our affiliations. Or anything else. But if your conscience is really troubling you, be reassured. Your friend Kobrand was not at all the noble figure he claimed to be. A great artist, yes, but a self-serving, evil man."

"Yessir*ee*," Carroll chimed in in his endearing style. "A real bad-ass character."

I looked from one of them to the other. Sincere, moustached Carroll, foxy-suave Bauer. Which one had made the sprint over to the BMW to pick off the retreating Kobrand? And why? I had no idea. Neither of them looked the part of a professional gunman. Besides, what actual difference did it make? Carroll was right. Kobrand was dead. No heroics on my part would ever bring him back.

"All right," I said dully. "What do you want me to do?"

To my surprise, Carroll shrugged. "That's your business," he said. "Go back to Geneva, go home, do anything. As long as you stay sensible—" he gave the word a certain delicate emphasis "—we won't care."

"What about Kobrand's death?"

"A tragedy!" Bauer exclaimed. "When this great artist was only a few steps from absolute freedom, a Communist bullet cut him down."

"Yep," Carroll said mournfully. "Sure was too doggone bad."

"And what about my friends?" I said.

"Mr. French," said Bauer, "I am of the opinion that if you return to Geneva, you will very soon obtain word of your friends. Your patron *Herr* Flachsmann—do you know, by the way, that he is a KGB finance officer?—will be able to assist you. I should go back there, Mr. French."

"He's right, French," Carroll said. "Go there. Go now." He put a hand on Bauer's shoulder to urge him away. The two of them turned and walked together toward the Oldsmobile. I watched while they climbed inside. The big American engine roared into life and the tan car swung onto the road. Like a satellite larger than its planet, the gun-carrier followed at once. In a few seconds, both had disappeared around the sharp bend in the road back to Bärnau. All that was left of the whole bloody scene, I saw numbly, was Kobrand's cello in its case. I couldn't imagine what it was doing there. But rather than leave it, I retrieved it and loaded it back into the trunk of the BMW. Then I stood for a while listening to the silence.

A correct performance will be ample compensation
for the lack of sonority.

K.P.E. BACH, p. 106.

CHAPTER NINETEEN

ONCE I STARTED UP, I kept the BMW moving, first down the narrow
forest roads from the border to Neustadt, then on the busier routes that
led from Neustadt to Weiden to Nuremberg, then finally on the *Auto-
bahnen* southward through Munich and beyond. Somewhere south of
Munich, I stopped for gasoline and a meal. The restaurant concession,
grotesquely, was in the hands of Howard Johnson's. I remember the
greasy white tile on the walls and the greasy lentil soup I spooned up in
place of clam chowder.

The Germans will some day finish the extension of the F8 westward
to Lindau on the Bodensee. But some day is not now, and so it took
hours of driving on back roads through villages to negotiate the 90
kilometers to the Swiss border. I was just in time for the four o'clock car
ferry. Nobody stopped me. Nobody even looked inside my passport. I
drove the BMW across the creaking gangway onto the ferry, jammed it
into the lineup of happy tourist cars, locked it, and went up on deck.
The diesel horn blew hoarsely. I leaned on the rail and watched the
surface of the water heave as we lurched out of the slip.

Nothing made any sense. Even allowing for the greatest possible
duplicity—even if Flachsmann, Kobrand, the Russians, and Carroll
were all lying their heads off—the whole episode was still insane. I
took it from the top: if the KGB had really *wanted* to rid the motherland
of this malcontent, why hadn't it arranged for Kobrand to go to London
or Paris or New York on a tour and simply defect? And if Kobrand the
malcontent had really had to make his run via the Antiqua Players'
Border-to-Border Taxi Service, why had Bauer and Carroll killed him?

Why not exploit the escape as another great Western victory in the unceasing war for artistic freedom?

I tried it from as many other angles as I could think of. "What if Kobrand wasn't Kobrand?" I wondered. A plump, jolly-faced German holiday maker glanced at me uneasily and edged away along the rail. I'd actually been mumbling my words out loud. I smiled what I hoped was a reassuring smile. Don't worry, *Wahnfried*, I'm not *auswitten*. But by the time the ferry nosed its cheerful way into the wharf at Romanshorn on the Swiss shore, I wasn't altogether sure I *wasn't* crazy.

The BMW and I were well on our way to Winterthur when the thought struck me: *Dummy, what's in the cello case?* Before the question was fully formed in my mind, I was swinging off the road onto the dusty shoulder.

I already knew there was a cello in the cello case. I picked it out of its velvet-lined resting place and plucked a string or two. It was a fine instrument, possibly even a Guarneri or a Strad, but I offered no clue whatever to the mystery of its late master, Itzaak Kobrand.

In the head of the case was a lidded compartment to hold spare strings, rosin, and whatever other small oddments the cellist felt he ought to have along. I tilted up the lid. Sure enough, inside was a set of strings and a cake of rosin. But there also, neatly wrapped in a piece of chamois and taking up almost no room, was a second gun. This one was sleek, flat, and, in proportion to its size, surprisingly heavy. Since my cap-pistol days, I'd never even fingered a gun. But I must say I wasn't sorry to see this one. I put it carefully on the front passenger seat. When I'd closed up the cello case and the trunk of the BMW, I got in behind the wheel and gave the gun as thorough a going-over as an ignoramus about firearms could give it. The trigger, unmistakably, was the trigger. The various levers, catches, and protuberances soon sorted themselves out. One catch popped a plastic magazine out of the butt of the gun. The magazine held seven shiny, menacing cartridges, its full load. Gingerly, I clicked it back in place. A metal stud by the trigger guard turned out to be the safety. I flicked it to "ZU," then half-ashamedly dropped the gun into my inside jacket pocket before pulling back onto the road.

After four more hours of driving, the gun's weight was no longer any kind of comfort. As I shifted gears to begin a long climb up a steep, stony street, the gun bumped distractingly against my chest. I was in Montricher. The BMW, its wipers beating softly back and forth across the windshield against a splashy spring rain, was taking me somewhere I didn't particularly want to go: back to Flachsmann's castle. Geneva, I knew, would be safer. But in Geneva, there were too many questions and too few answers, about Kobrand, about Flachsmann, and most of all, about Jackie and the others. As I began watching the roadside for the big gates and the narrow drive up through the pines, the gun bumped me again. I swore at it. But I also felt that somehow the gun had sent me here.

The BMW took the drive smartly. Nothing was coming down the hill, luckily, and the second set of gates was wide open. I spun the little car around the vacant courtyard and parked it facing back the way I'd come. The absurd drawbridge was down. In the rain, the inner courtyard looked deserted and forlorn, like a college quadrangle during vacation time. The huge wooden front door was shut, but to the right of the door a carved wooden pull invited the hand. I was about to give it a tug when Kobrand's gun, thumping me once more in the ribs, reminded me that I wasn't exactly calling as a guest.

When I pushed gently, the door swung noiselessly open. I stepped inside. The reception hall was unlit and gloomy, the corridor to the drawing room lighted only by one small wall sconce. Nobody was around. I kept on moving, down the corridor, across the drawing room, and through the big dining room toward the terrace at the back. I felt foolish and furtive and excited, like a child in a closed museum or a first-time burglar.

"Who's there?" The question hung, sharp and shrill, in the rain-damp afternoon air. At the far end of the terrace, the lights were on. Against the yellow glow, Anne De Soto was silhouetted. She spotted me as I emerged through the French windows. She called again, her voice anxious. I didn't answer.

"Mr. French. It's Mr. French," she repeated nervously as I approached her through the drizzle. Over her bony shoulders was draped a mouse-colored sweater, as if she'd just taken a moment from her duties to step outdoors for some air. "I'm afraid we're busy right now," she intoned. "We won't be able to see you." Her hands were clasped at her waist, the thin fingers worrying and tense. "You can't go in," she said. When I stepped to one side to pass around her, she moved with me, blocking the door to the office wing. "You can't go in," she said again. I didn't want to touch her. Finally, I just started forward, my bulk forcing her back and to one side. Her breath was so malodorous I almost choked on it. Then I was through the door and walking down the hall toward Flachsmann's office. I dimly sensed the noise of De Soto's flat heels scuffing hurriedly away across the terrace flagstones. "Alan!" Flachsmann was seated behind his baronial desk. A blue cashmere blazer hung on the leather back of his tilted chair. His collar was open, his cuffs turned back to reveal his bronzed forearms. When he smiled at me, his teeth were very, very white. The cordiality of his greeting was as sincere as a cancer surgeon's handshake. "How did everything go?" he asked. His eyes gave away that he knew.

"Everything went fine," I lied. "Kobrand's over the border." I watched Flachsmann's face as he assimilated what I was saying. He knew what had happened, all right. "You bastard," I said. "Where are my friends?"

"I thought you said everything went fine." Flachsmann put his hands together on the elaborate silver-edged blotter holder in front of him. The thumb of his left hand began to rub restlessly over the knuckles of his right hand. He looked into my eyes and smiled his dynamic salesman's smile. "If everything went fine, your friends should be back in Geneva in about—" he consulted the heavy gold watch on his left wrist "—in about fifty-six minutes from now, our time. Why don't you have a drink while you're waiting?"

"No drink," I said. "As you probably know damn well, everything didn't go so fine." Flachsmann's amiable expression changed slightly. He was trying to look pleasantly quizzical, an executive consulting a subordinate about a minor business mishap. "Kobrand's dead," I said.

"Yes," Flachsmann said. The friendliness drained from his face. He picked up a slip of paper. "Itzaak Kobrand, musician, was shot dead late this morning near the Czech-West German border, on the road just beyond the German town of Bärnau. Kobrand was attempting to cross the border illegally in a car, a dark BMW. Czech and East German police authorities have asked the West Germans to cooperate in the search for the driver of the car, who escaped. The driver is believed to be an accomplice, one of a gang of hooligans who helped Kobrand elude custody in Markneukirchen a few hours earlier. However, the possibility exists that the driver was coerced by the defecting Kobrand." Flachsmann's mouth twisted in an ugly grimace. "Is that what you want to tell me, Alan?"

"Not exactly," I said.

"Sure, sure." Flachsmann raised one hand and made a flicking gesture with the fingers. "It may not have happened exactly like that. It may not have happened *anything* like that. But still, it happened." He brought his palm down smartly on the blotter holder. "Kobrand is as dead as week-old tuna. I was supposed to get him out *alive*. Dig?" He wiggled his fingers on the blotter in mimicry of something that was alive. "So now, I've got a problem. You were supposed to *help* him get out alive. Instead of which, he got a bullet in the belly.

"Jesus Christ Almighty!" he said anxiously, "surely you understand!" He said it as if his own understanding were just coming into contact with events. His left thumb gnawed the back of his right hand. "*My* friends, they're the problem, not your friends." Flachsmann sensed what his hands were doing in front of a stranger, but he had to work to get them to stop. He smiled embarrassedly. "My friends can be difficult people," he said. He glanced hastily around the office, as though some difficult people were already lurking in the shadows thrown by the polished tables and bulky club chairs.

"I'm going to have a drink," he said. He rose, shoving back his own chair. When it thudded lightly against the wall, he flinched a little. At the bar, he rattled ice and crystal and poured Scotch. "Sure you won't have one?" While I was still shaking my head, he drained his glass and reached out for another installment. The liquor helped him. After the second drink, he no longer tiptoed across the carpet. He moved briskly back to the desk and sat down. "If you don't want a drink, I'm going to ask you to take a break," he said bravely. "I've got a lot to do."

"Wait a minute," I began.

"Listen, Alan," Flachsmann said. "Your friends are still in Markneukirchen. They're being held there for interrogation by the East German security police. I have no relationship with the East Germans." He made the statement with the dignity of a banker announcing that the person whose check you hold has no account with the institution. "I want to help you," Flachsmann continued sincerely, "but there's very little I can do."

"What do you suggest?" I wondered if Flachsmann could hear as clearly as I could the note of despair in my voice.

"I'm afraid we'll just have to wait," he said smoothly. The tone of his own voice had changed. He'd forgotten to be scared. He was working something out in his head: I could almost see the wheels going around. "Don't worry, Alan," he added, "everything's going to be just fine."

My own wheels were humming, too, and I didn't much like the tune. Kobrand, it said, was dead, dead, dead. If somebody slipped the East Germans the idea that Jackie and Ralph and the others were responsible, then Hugo would be off the hook. But Hugo wouldn't do a thing like that, would he?

It was my turn to be scared. If Hugo hadn't simply *sat* there, his automatic salesman's smile beginning to come back to his face, I might never have had the nerve to do what I did next.

"Hugo," I said in my best Humphrey Bogart voice, "pick up that phone."

Flachsmann sat astonished. For a second, I was afraid he was going to laugh out loud. But he didn't. It must have been years since anyone had given him a direct order, and his adrenals took over. His hand darted out for the telephone. "Karl-Heinz!" he snapped, "*Kommen Sie im Bureau! Schnell!*" Glaring at me furiously, he slammed down the receiver. As I spun around to look, the office door opened. Sure enough, in the doorway stood Karl-Heinz Schnittemann, formerly of the Bavarian Police. He looked very big and wide and very tough.

"What the hell are you doing here?" I asked stupidly.

"I work for the *Herr* Flachsmann now."

"Karl-Heinz," Flachsmann rasped in German, "escort *Herr* French out to his automobile. *Herr* French is a little excitable. Be sure to soothe him on the way."

Oh-oh, I thought. But seconds went by and nothing happened, or at least so it seemed. Karl-Heinz simply kept on standing in the doorway. I had plenty of time to reach into my jacket pocket and let the butt of Kobrand's pistol slip into my hand. I had plenty of time to pull out the gun. I had plenty of time, as I slipped it clear, to ease off the safety catch.

Still, nothing happened.

I remember being annoyed, as if I were standing onstage ready to take a bow and getting no response whatever from the audience. Irritably, I wagged the gun. At last, someone reacted. "Hey, Alan," Flachsmann said, "stop fooling around with that thing, will you?" He sounded exasperated but not at all frightened. I couldn't understand why.

Karl-Heinz was different. Karl-Heinz knew only too well what a nervous amateur like me could do with a gun. During the instant when I'd thought time had stopped, he had started after me, moving quickly for so bulky a man. But as soon as he saw what I had in my hand, an almost ludicrous expression of fright appeared on his beefy face. In midstride, he tried frantically to check himself.

To be honest, I enjoyed what the sight of the gun did to Karl-Heinz. But I wish he'd managed to stop in time; I really do. My finger never twitched. I have no memory at all of actually touching the trigger. All I remember is that Kobrand's gun bucked gently in my hand once, then again. Each time, it made a flat sound like a sudden handclap in a silent hall.

The next thing I knew, I was smelling gunpowder and watching Karl-Heinz smack back against the jamb of the door. With deliberation, he bent sharply over, as if to show that even a stocky ex-cop could still touch his toes. Only, Karl-Heinz missed his toes. He sagged to the carpet. "*Ach, Herr Je'*," he moaned, not loudly. On his knees, cradling his right arm against himself, he began to rock rhythmically back and forth like a worshipper in an Orthodox synagogue. He didn't look to me as if he was dying, but he didn't look too happy, either.

Flachsmann was sitting rigid in his chair, his face paper-white. It hadn't taken him long to master Karl-Heinz's lesson on amateurs with guns. When I turned the gun toward him, he cringed. "Don't," he said. "Please." A mistake. So appalled was I at what the gun had done to Karl-Heinz that a display of courage might have made me collapse. Instead, Flachsmann's panic fed my anger and stiffened my own backbone.

"Hugo," I said softly, "right now, your KGB friends are a long way off. They're not your problem, Hugo. I am." He nodded quickly. I could see the sweat on his forehead. "Okay. The first thing you're going to do is pick up that telephone. And this time, you're going to call whoever you have to call and say whatever you have to say to get *my* friends out of trouble. That't the first thing."

"I can't," Hugo said.

"That's too bad," I said. I made a tiny movement with the gun, and his hand, which had started to move, stopped dead. "I've had a hard day," I said patiently. "Lots of terrible things have happened. If anything else terrible happens, or even looks like it might happen, like Jackie and Ralph and the others don't show up in Switzerland tonight," I needed a deep breath for the finale, "well, Hugo, I am going to shoot you straight in the face with this gun. *Versteh'*, Hugo, baby?"

He understood.

"Okay. Go ahead and make your call."

"What about—?" he flapped his hand at Karl-Heinz, who by this time had slumped sideways to the floor.

"First, make your call. *And be careful.*" In all, it took three calls. The first was to Moscow, in Russian. After the first one, we had to wait while somebody in Moscow did some telephoning of his own. I pulled up an armchair next to Flachsmann's desk and sank into it, my knees like putty. But a few moments later, Flachsmann was dialing East Berlin and Karl-Marx-Stadt and grunting out orders in rapid German, and it was over. The whole process took less than fifteen minutes.

"The release order is going through," Flachsmann said. "A military helicopter will pick them up and fly them to Prague. I've arranged for a private jet from Prague to Geneva. They should arrive about ten o'clock tonight." He put his head down on his folded arms as if he wanted to shut out the whole interfering world. Then he raised it again. "Goddammit," he demanded, "why does this have to happen to me?"

I couldn't think of an appropriate answer. "Better get somebody in here to take care of your boy," I said. Dutifully, Flachsmann rang for assistance. While A. De Soto and a Japanese houseboy in a white tunic were gathering up Karl-Heinz, I kept the gun aimed carefully at Flachsmann. I also kept well out of the way. Now was no time to let anybody jump me, and the Japanese was probably a karate expert who could shatter steel bars with the edge of his hand.

After Karl-Heinz, still mothering his shattered arm, had been led from the room, I sat back down in the armchair. The office, I noticed, had a tendency to sway slightly. The gun felt heavy in my hand. A few more episodes like those that had so far enlivened the day, and A. De Soto could do without the houseboy. She could mop up my remnants all by herself.

Flachsmann had gone into a melancholy trance. I had to rap sharply with the gun barrel on the edge of his desk to arouse him. "Coffee," I said.

"What?"

"Hugo," I said, "we're not in good shape, you and I. We both need some stimulation, and I could use some food in my belly. Be a good host, will you, and ring up for a platter of sandwiches and a great big pot of coffee."

"What the hell do you think this is, a hotel?"

"I like your spirit," I said, showing him the gun. "Tell them to leave the tray outside the door and knock three times. Then, *you* go over and bring in the tray. We've had enough company for a while.''

When the knock came, Flachsmann looked sourly at me. He glowered again when I appointed him official taster of the contents of the tray. But neither he nor his retinue tried anything odd, and I was too hungry to let his petulance annoy me. The sandwiches tasted like buttery manna. And one advantage of being rich is that you never have to put up with bad coffee, even when a pistol-wielding desperado has forced you to order it and pour it. What coffee! Whoever brewed it struck a potent blow for the arts that night.

With my flagging metabolism revived, I felt momentarily as elated as if this were a concert and I'd just picked my way brilliantly and at sight through ninety-six treacherous bars of sixteenth-notes. But in a concert, you're not worrying about how to get away alive as soon as the last encore is over. What really drained away the elation was the feeling that fairly soon my fatigue was going to catch all the way up with me. When that happened, Flachsmann's castle was the last place I wanted to be.

By the time the last of that wonderful coffee was cooling in my cup, I'd thought of three or four escape schemes, all subtle and all more or less unworkable. The hell with it, I thought. What would Humphrey Bogart do?

"Hugo."

"What now?" His eyes flickered at me hostilely.

"Order your helicopter. Have it stand by to take the two of us into Geneva."

"Suppose I say no?"

His truculence was forced; he wasn't going to say no. But I gave him the answer he wanted. "I'll use the gun on you."

On Flachsmann's face there suddenly appeared the pallid ghost of his old charming Ivy League grin. "Maybe I should let you. When Moscow Center figures out what's been going on here. . . ." He left the thought unfinished and reached out again for the telephone.

Twenty minutes later, we were clattering through the rain-washed Swiss skies over Lake Geneva.

Pupils must learn the figures with dispatch.

K.P.E. BACH, p. 180.

CHAPTER TWENTY

"SOONER OR LATER, you're going to be sorry. Sooner or later." Above the chatter of the engines and the mindless outbursts, part speech, part static, of the radio, Flachsmann had to shout his litany. He'd docilely issued the instructions that had garaged the BMW and turned out the helicopter's crew. Giving the orders had made him feel happier. The short walk through the pines to where the helicopter was waiting had eased more of his tensions. Flachsmann was recovering, and he was planning to wait me out.

The radio squalled again, insanely. Like a diner with a mouthful of good *poulet chausseur*, I grinned foolishly at Flachsmann and made a waving motion with the gun to signal that I'd answer him later.

Strapped into the seat behind me was the third passenger on our flight. Thick-necked, with sloping shoulders, the third passenger looked disconcertingly like Karl-Heinz. Only, it wasn't Karl-Heinz. It was Kobrand's cello in its case. Carrying the bulky thing from the BMW to the aircraft had given Flachsmann something to do with his hands. But I had other reasons as well for wanting the cello as a traveling companion.

The helicopter lurched down lightly on the rain-dampened roof of the International. Even over the fumes of the aviation gasoline, I could smell the tarry concrete. Below, the lights along the lakefront shone fuzzily through a glaze of fog. I wriggled out of my seat and through the exit door. I made Flachsmann edge backward out of the hatch and down the ladder with the cello in his arms. He was none too fond of being a porter. By the time we found the *descenseur* and made our way down to my room, he was puffing a bit.

173

Through the room door, I thought I could hear the ringing of the telephone.

"Open up." I tossed Flachsmann the key and had him enter the room first, still lugging the cello. If the phone had been ringing, it had stopped. I looked at my watch. It was ten minutes to ten. The room was stuffy. I made Flachsmann get the air conditioning going. Then I sat him in an armchair on the far side of the room, the cello in front of him to block his way, while I perched on a bench within reach of the telephone. I'd been holding the gun for so long that my fingers were aching, but I didn't put it down, even when the phone did ring.

Watching Flachsmann, I picked up the receiver carefully.

"Alan! Is it really you?"

"More or less," I said. "Ralph, where are you?"

"Thank God! You're intact?"

"Um," I said. "Where *are* you?"

"Milan, dear heart, in a dreary little room at the Milan airport."

"What the hell are you doing in Milan?"

"Fog and rotten weather everywhere, so they said. The best they could do for us was Milan. Listen, Alan, it could have been Moscow."

"I know. Is everybody—"

"Jackie's absolutely fine. David, Terry, and I ditto. But absolutely *exhausted*. Dead, I was about to say, but that's not a terribly *appropriate* idiom, is it?"

"Not really," I said. I wondered who else was listening to this conversation.

"Then it's true what the people here are saying? That man *died* on the trip?"

"It's a long story," I said. "Very long."

"Ah!" Ralph was consoling. "I understand. Now, listen, Alan. The people here say they can't possibly fly us to Geneva before late tomorrow morning. What should we do?"

"Don't argue with them," I said. "Kiss them goodbye. Then, get yourselves into a friendly cab and go to a nice, quiet hotel. In the morning, take another cab to the railroad station and catch a train. I hear the trains are wonderful. Very fast and very, very safe. Call me here in the morning and I'll meet you at the Geneva station."

"Sounds good. Actually, we were thinking of the train."

"Fine," I said. "Great minds."

"Jackie's sound asleep. She sends love."

"Send her mine." I couldn't think of anything else to say. "Ralph?"

"Yes?"

"You're sure you're in Milan?"

"We must be. The porters and customs men were all yelling in German."

"Great," I said. "*Vive la liberté.* Be careful."

"Will do. You, too. 'Bye." I let the receiver drop in the cradle and refocused on Flachsmann. He looked amused. "They're out?" he asked.

"O-U-T spells *out.*" Relief was making me lightheaded. But not lightheaded enough to overlook essentials. "There's another thing," I said.

"What's that?"

"A hundred thousand dollars." For one second, Flachsmann looked truly murderous. I think he thought *I'd* forgotten about the money. When he found I hadn't, *he* nearly forgot about the gun. He smiled a tight, angry smile. "If you—"

"I could make you pay us the whole hundred grand," I overrode his opening. "After all, the caper turned out to be a lot more dangerous than you said it would be. But I want to be fair. We only got Kobrand halfway out. So, we'll settle for half. Fifty thousand."

"Fifteen! That's what we said, and it's fifteen more than you deserve!" Watching Flachsmann fight for his money was teaching me the one lesson about the rich everybody else needs to learn.

"Fifty, Hugo, and let's quit haggling."

"Bastard. *Bastard.*" Snatch away a tiger's prey and the tiger gets angry, even if he's got a freezer full of prey back at the lair.

"Write it down, Hugo, so your bank manager and my bank manager will stay friends." I didn't think I needed anything in writing, but I couldn't be sure. So Flachsmann wrote a note on International Plaza stationery. It said that Alan French or his agents could draw immediately against the one hundred thousand dollars at Flachsmann's bank, up to fifty thousand dollars. Flachsmann dated the note, signed it, and practically threw it at me.

"Now, now," I said, tucking the note in my wallet.

"Sooner or later, you're going to be sorry." Flachsmann returned to his favorite theme.

"You could be so right," I said.

"I *am* right."

"Well, Hugo," I said, "there's just one more thing, and then as far as I'm concerned you can walk out of here as free as a bird."

"What one more thing?" The prospect of freedom was giving back still more of Flachsmann's confidence. "Jesus, you're a tough kid," he said. "You've kidnapped me, blown my business relationships wide open, and extorted a small fortune from me. *What* one more thing?"

"You can answer my question. Why wasn't Carroll waiting at the border with a busload of reporters and a medal? Why would the CIA want to murder the leading dissident Soviet artist?"

"French, you musical thug, did you really mean it that I could go?" I nodded. Immediately, Flachsmann stood up and began patting his pockets. He was like the nervous man sitting next to you on the bus, the one who's always checking his wallet and reaching for his keys before the driver taps the brake. Flachsmann carefully propped Kobrand's cello against his own chair. He ran a hand through his short hair and shrugged the wrinkles out of his cashmere blazer. "I'm not going to pretend that this has been an evening of sheer pleasure," he said, "or that our acquaintanceship has brought me the benefits the ads say we should look for in a friend. But it's been interesting." He began to edge past me to get to the door.

"You haven't answered," I said, raising the gun from my lap.

"Oh, I don't think you're going to use that thing now," said Flachsmann. "Why not put it away? As for your answer, just remember what Louis Armstrong once said about jazz critics."

"What was that?"

" 'There's some folks that, if they don't know, you just can't tell 'em.' " I nodded again. It was a good exit line, and Flachsmann used it well.

Clarity is attained through rests.

K.P.E. BACH, p. 326.

CHAPTER TWENTY-ONE

"IT'S BEEN A LONG DAY, *Tovarisch*," I said to Kobrand's cello. The weight of Kobrand's gun in my lap was another reminder. I had to haul myself to my feet and talk myself into the long trek across the room to the door. As quietly as I could, I opened the door and peered outside. The corridor was deserted. I let the door close, then snapped the lock and latched the steel security chain. Like a wary old widow living at 104th Street and West End Avenue, I padded cautiously through sitting room, bedroom, and bath, locking windows and checking closets. The air conditioning was chilling, so I slipped on a sweater. It's not easy to slide a gun through a sweater sleeve. Finally, I hunched back on the bench by the telephone for the one more chore I had to perform. "Please," I said to the hotel operator, "get me the American Consulate."

The night operator at the consulate was less than pleased to get a call at ten o'clock P.M. Nor was she happy with my request. It took me several minutes of persuasion. But in the end, I got the number I wanted. "Is this Mister Robert Carroll, the cultural attaché?" I could hear party noises in the background.

"Who's this?" Carroll's voice sounded blurry, as if he were tired or a little bit drunk.

"Hi, Bob. This is Alan French."

"Well, well," Carroll was smoothly sardonic. "Did you follow our advice?"

"Yes," I said, "I'm back in Geneva. Say, Bob, you know what?"

"What's that, good buddy?"

"You guys kind of left something behind this afternoon."

There was a silence at the other end. "What sort of something?" Carroll asked carefully.

"The sort of something that makes beautiful music," I said. "That is, if you know how to play it. You left it in the trunk."

Another silence. "Well, that was careless of us, I admit. But I don't see that it matters."

"Maybe not," I said. "But you're going to be telling one story about our late friend. I know another. It's much funnier. Ordinarily, nobody would listen to my story. Why should they? A kook musician smearing the memory of a martyr to the cause of freedom. But with this piece of equipment I've, uh, *inherited* from our friend, maybe some people will listen. The people at *Time* and *Newsweek*, for instance. Or *Der Spiegel*."

.This time, Carroll stretched out the silence for six or eight slow beats, long enough to make the skin prickle at the base of my scalp. "How embarrassing," he finally said. "All right, French." His voice was the voice of the cop who was just itching to belt you with his nightstick but who didn't dare because the lieutenant was watching. "All right. What is it you want?"

"Not much," I said. "Just to make sure you people leave us alone. All of us."

"All of you? The guy with the fancy castle, too?"

"Him, too," I said. I wasn't quite sure why I said it, but I said it anyway.

"I don't think I can guarantee that," Carroll said.

"Gee, Bob, that's too bad, because I don't think I can *guarantee* this equipment will stay secret too much longer."

"Where is it now?" Carroll asked. I laughed.

"You so-and-so-and-so," Carroll said.

"Just so we understand each other," I said.

"Okay," Carroll said. "We'll leave you alone. We'll even see that nobody else bothers you. But if we do, don't you get smart. No *Time*, no *Spiegel*. Not even a teensy-weensy paragraph in *Musical America*."

"Of course," I said.

"Because if there ever is a leak," Carroll said, "We'll know *exactly* whose valve needs fixing."

"I promise," I said. "Girl Scouts' honor."

"One more thing, old buddy."

"What's that?"

"*Our* Kobrand story is going to break tomorrow. I'd personally feel a lot better if you made the decision to get out of Switzerland fairly soon. Say, by tomorrow night." Carroll clicked down his receiver gently enough. But it felt like a gunshot in my ear.

I put down my own receiver. Then I picked it up again and dialed the hotel desk. "This is Mr. French in Twenty-One-Eleven."

"Yes, Mr. French."

"I have just come into possession of an extremely valuable musical instrument," I said pompously. I winked at the cello. "For tonight, this instrument will be lodged here in my room."

"I regret, sir, but we cannot be responsible—"

"Naturally not," I said. "But you can notify your security staff to keep an eye open."

"Our security officers are always alert," the man at the desk said placidly. "However, they will of course be notified."

"Thank you," I said and meant it.

After such a day, it felt grotesque to brush the teeth, scrub the nails, and leave the shoes in the little cupboard for the night hall porter to shine. But that's just what I did. And then, I did something even odder. I took out my flute and, without actually playing aloud to the International Plaza's clientele, I ran through the finger exercises that were part of my practice routine. Seeking refuge in the familiar: that's what the psychiatrists would say. But I had another motive. Getting my fingers back into music, I felt, would somehow clean off the smell of the gun. Not to mention the blood in which they'd been dabbling all day long.

Later, in bed, I tried to add up the results of that unbelievable day. For us, fifty thousand dollars, plus the possibility that both sides would leave us alone. For Carroll and Company, one martyr to beatify and one discredited enemy. For Flachsmann, if only he could explain things to Moscow, his life. Even Karl-Heinz got away alive. The only permanent loser, it seemed, was Kobrand himself.

I switched off the light. For one moment, I was back at the wheel of the BMW with all of East Germany whipping at me. Then, nothing.

Galant notation is so replete with new expressions and twists that it is seldom possible
even to comprehend it immediately.
    K.P.E. BACH, p. 165.

CHAPTER TWENTY-TWO

IN MY DREAM, I became Kobrand. His right arm swept back for an
upbow and the muscles of my fingers, wrist, arm, and back bunched
and tensed in anticipation. His left hand performed an extension, and
my own extended inside his. Then, he—we—rose to bow to the
orchestra. But the conductor's baton blossomed flame and the muddy
bottom of the ditch drew us irresistibly downward. In the mud, a single
fly buzzed frantically on and on.

Miserably, drenched with sweat, I dragged myself up out of the ditch
into daylight. Never had a nightmare frightened me so much. On the
bedside table, the telephone was buzzing with vehemence. "Room
Service, sir," it said when I fumbled the receiver to my ear. "Your
breakfast will arrive in one minute."

When the discreet tap sounded on the room door, I picked up
Kobrand's gun. Holding it out of sight by my side, I unlocked the door.
It hadn't taken me long, I thought, to acquire some of the reflexes of the
professional thug.

Through the gap the burglar chain allowed, I could see a room-
service cart in the corridor and smell the coffee in the big pot under the
white linen napkin. Only the white-coated waiter, his back to me, was
visible. The waiter mumbled something like, *Vous permettez, M'sieu*,"
and I eased the chain off its catch and let the door open wide.

The waiter quickly rolled the squeaking, rattling trolley inside.
While the delicious aroma of the coffee was filling the air and I was
struggling to hide the gun in the folds of my bathrobe, another figure
appeared in the doorway.

"Mr. French, Mr. French, Mr. French." As Colonel Jerzy grumbled my name, the waiter picked up two crystal champagne flutes, flicked each with his towel, and set them upright on the trolley. "Please putting away your ridiculous automatic pistol," the Colonel said to me. "You are not needing here."

The waiter, stone-deaf it seemed, turned his attention to the dark green bottle nestled snugly in the silver ice bucket. He spun the bottle twice, plucked it out of the bucket, and dexterously untwisted the wire that netted the cork in place. A momentary pressure of the thumbs on either side of the cork and he was filling the two glasses with the chilled wine.

"Thank you, my friend," said Colonel Jerzy, handing him a folded bill. Without a word, the waiter left the check, bowed, and departed. I put Kobrand's gun on the table by the bed.

Colonel Jerzy shot his cuffs gently, centered his tie, and reached for his champagne. "*Prosit!*" he said. I drank with him. The champagne tasted wonderful.

"My dear Mr. French, I am very, very cross with you. Yes, very cross." He sat down smartly in the same chair Flachsmann had occupied the night before. "Why, *why*, when you are having your so much trouble at the border, why you do not call me at number I am giving you?" The Colonel leaned back in the chair, crossed his ankles in their dark blue silk socks, and looked sad. I started to say something and he sat quickly upright. "No, no, no," he said. "You do not need to explaining. You are thinking, if I call this Colonel Jerzy, the mouse will be let out of the bag."

"The cat," I said automatically, then swore silently at myself for playing the Colonel's little word-game.

"*Of* course. Also, you are thinking, the Colonel Jerzy is the employer of the terrible Karl-Heinz. From such a one, maybe you wonder what helping you get, *hein?*" When the Colonel smiled, his almond eyes narrowed and his trim moustache bristled slightly, making him look like a dapper tiger.

"Colonel," I said, "this is very nice of you. But why have you come here?"

"But my dear boy!" he exclaimed. "I must come! In our brief acquaintancehood—"

"—ship," I supplied.

"—*ship*, thank you. In our brief time of knowing, I am become very fond of you. You are artist, good. And your charming young lady, too, is *artiste*. Exquisite! You are very lucky!'' He sprang to his feet, loped elegantly to the trolley, and poured each of us more champagne. Not a drop was spilled, not a bubble wasted. *''Prosit!* To your happiness!

''I am so much liking, when I learn you are again coming from border, I say to myself, Aha! This boy will be tired, frighted—''

''How right you are,'' I said.

''Con-*fussed.''* I didn't correct him. ''First he will sleep, then he will try to understand all things that happen. *Then*, I say to myself, *then*, Jerzy, you go to your good young friend. You will say him things, maybe he will say you things. And so! Here am I !'' Having said me no things at all, he sipped exuberantly at his champagne.

''There are things I don't understand,'' I admitted.

''Of course! Of course! You must not worry! Listen: I tell you story, very little one, from time just after German war. I am in London, in Polish Squadron of RAF, that is Royal Air Force.'' I nodded. ''So. One night in pub man in raincoat offer me money—oh, four, five hundred pounds—for writings from my cousin.

''My cousin is aide to military attaché, Polish government in exile. Man in raincoat say my cousin committing treacheries for Red Russians. This man, he counterintelligence for British, that is M.I.5., also for Poles. He say he want writings for prove on my cousin. Then they can hang him.'' Colonel Jerzy made another raid on the champagne. I'd finished the orange juice and begun on the brioches and coffee, but I let the Colonel fill my glass again.

''Then what?'' I asked.

''At this time, I have the many debits.'' Debits? The Colonel explained patiently: ''You see, from the cards, the roulette, the shops—''

''Oh. Debts.''

''Sure.'' The Colonel lit one of his tan cigars. ''Besides, I know my cousin.'' He shrugged gracefully. ''What man in raincoat say could be true. So, I ask for much money.''

''And?''

''And I go to my cousin and I say, is it true you are making treacheries for the Communist dogs? And he laugh and I laugh. And I give him some money and we make writings for prove my cousin is no treasoner—''

''Traitor.''

"—and I bring back to man in raincoat and he say good, and he give me more money, little bit more, to be quiet, and he goes away.

"Just then, war is over and we going back to Warsaw, and I learning man in raincoat is Number One resident intelligence officer in UK, that is United Kingdom, for Red Russian Army. What he want really from my cousin is military plans of English and Americans."

"And your cousin?" Colonel Jerzy smiled his tiger's smile.

"Oh, now he is colonel like me. He is MLO, that is military liaison officer, Baltic Sector, between Polish High Command and Red Army. Very important man. Very amusing. In war, he is many times giving secrets to Russians. Only, he has own network, not use resident."

For a moment, I sat in silence, thinking about the Colonel and his amusing cousin. Maybe whole families went into the espionage business, the way some families take up law or engineering. Or music. Then, even though my stomach was already cringing with apprehension, I asked the question Colonel Jerzy wanted me to ask. "That's a wild story, Colonel. But what does it have to do with me?"

In his turn, Colonel Jerzy surveyed me silently. Then, gently, he asked: "Mr. French, what is Itzaak Kobrand?"

"What do you mean?"

"Kobrand is great cellist, not?"

"That, certainly."

"Very good. Kobrand is also dissonant." It took me a few seconds to figure out that one.

"Dissident." Colonel Jerzy gave a nod.

"Good. Kobrand is artist, also dis . . . what you are saying. And also other thing."

"What other thing?"

"Informant."

"I don't understand." The Colonel closed his eyes to try to think of a way to make me understand.

"Sometimes, Kobrand protesting. Sometimes, Kobrand going to police, saying this one, that one speaking against the regime, against the Ministry of Culture, against Holy Mother Russia, for Israel, worst of all, against the Party. Then—*tscheek*!" To make sure I really did grasp his meaning, Colonel Jerzy drew a beautifully manicured forefinger across his perfectly shaved throat.

"You're trying to tell me that Kobrand—*Kobrand?—was a fink?* An informer?"

"Inform-*er!*" The Colonel snapped his fingers. "Always, I am forgetting the speak of this word! But yes! Of course!"

"But . . . why?"

"Exactly, Mr. French. Why?" The Colonel shook his head slowly from side to side. "Is mystery. We *think* Kobrand make this arrangement with KGB to get rid of Ministry of Culture control. Also for money. Kobrand *loved* money. But maybe not. Who knows why any men does thing?"

I thought it over. God knows the man in the BMW with me did love money and did hate authority. But, still.

"I'm not sure I understand," I said. "Why did Carroll, the CIA, have to *kill* Kobrand?"

Colonel Jerzy looked at me thoughtfully, pursing his lips as if he were considering how much he should tell me of a long, convoluted story. Finally, he said: "You know, man like this have no friend. Informer like poison snake. What I think is, Kobrand offend someone in URSS, that is Soviet Union. Someone *big.*" The Colonel's gesture shaped a giant in the air. "Maybe someone with lady friend, boyfriend, who knows? Kobrand gives to KGB. And maybe this someone big in Russia knows someone big in America. It happens, it happens. And so, the debit is paid."

I thought some more. About the very first time I'd seen Kobrand, that time years ago when he'd borrowed my rosin for his bow. I remembered the perfection of his playing. And I remembered the enormously powerful, utterly self-assured man I had driven over the border. Could this man possibly have betrayed his fellow artists? "There's no way to prove any of this, is there?" I asked.

"No proves at all," the Colonel agreed cheerfully. "You permit?" He kindled another cigar.

I smiled like a good host, but what I really wanted was for Colonel Jerzy to go away. I needed time alone to sort out my impressions of Kobrand. I needed time to figure out why, although my brain was still puzzling over the Colonel's story, my belly was accepting it.

As if he'd been reading my mind, the Colonel abruptly sprang out of his chair. He paused to extinguish with a delicate gesture his half-smoked cigar. The check on the trolley-top caught his attention. "Aha!" he said, "you are leaving our friend the waiter no *teep*. Bad! very bad!" Hastily, I scrawled a generous addition to the bill. After all, Flachsmann would pay. "Better," the Colonel said, "much better."

He turned toward the door. "My dear young friend, thank you for having patience with old fool who tells tiresome stories. Remember," he wagged a finger, "no proves! But I will tell you this. *I* was one who brought message from man in Moscow in big fur hat to American man in Vienna! So now, goodbye."

With a wave of his hand, the Colonel departed. Generous as always, he did leave behind half a bottle of beautiful champagne.

There are many excellent musicians, but only
a few of whom it can be said truthfully that
. . . they end a piece as they began it.

K.P.E. BACH, p. 161.

CHAPTER TWENTY-THREE

THE GENEVA MUNICIPAL RAILWAY TERMINAL at eleven-thirty in the morning is probably the sanest environment in Europe. Under the watchful eyes of the ranked ticketsellers, porters, baggage masters, tour leaders, and other assorted functionaries, nothing wrong would *dare* to happen. Without incident or irregularity, the Antiqua Players held their reunion at the gate of the *rapido* morning service from Milan.

Jackie was wearing the same dress she'd worn the day before, the century before, at Markneukirchen. Her face was pale against the frame of her dark hair. When I saw her, my heart literally missed a beat and a half. I held out my arms, and for a moment we embraced. I could feel the electricity between us, as they say, but the others were standing there and our private concerns had to wait.

"I'd better tell you how it happened," I said to the circle of tired faces around the table in the International Plaza teashop. I gave them a quick summary of the events on the road from East Germany. When I came to the end, I made it as impersonal as I could. But it still shocked everybody. Hell, it still shocked *me*. Jackie's eyes were enormous.

"Why did they do it?" she asked wonderingly.

"Yes, Alan, have you any idea at all?" Ralph echoed.

"Well," I drew a deep, deep breath. "I can only quote you the theory advanced a couple of hours ago by that master of psychology, Colonel Jerzy."

"You saw Colonel Jerzy?" Ralph was incredulous.

I described the Colonel's visit to my room.

187

"What does the old creep say?" David wanted to know.

"The old creep, as you call him, thinks Kobrand was a stool pigeon. He thinks Kobrand was turning in other artists to the Soviet secret police in exchange for his own freedom and maybe money."

"No kidding," said Terry, interested. "So what happened, did the guys he was ratting on get wise and put out a contract?"

"Something like that," I said.

"Far out! And you say it was that character Carroll who actually did the hit?"

"Terry, I had my head so far under the car, I couldn't see anything. But it could have been Carroll, sure."

"Out of sight! Wow! And I had Carroll figured for the Mayor of Squaresville, U. S. A."

"We'll probably never know for sure who did do it," I said, "or why it was done. But it was a mess. Now, do me a favor, catch me up on what happened to you."

In fact, after the wild first few minutes, things in Markneukirchen had gone pretty much according to plan. Just after I ducked out, the reed of Terry's shawm snapped. This brought the music and the dancing to an abrupt halt. Kranz parted from Jackie with leering politeness. But Fornova was made of harsher stuff. "She sank her claws into my arm," Ralph said with a shudder. "When she couldn't find dear Kobrand after the hoedown, I really thought she was going to rend my flesh."

Jackie found her way back to David and Terry, and the three of them managed to pack up all the instruments and gear. But as they were finishing, Fornova got going in earnest. "There she was, the bitch," Ralph said vindictively, "clutching me in a death grip and screaming at the top of her lungs in German. I couldn't understand a word. But I guess she was saying that the American cryptofascist jackals were kidnapping a People's Artist or something. It was quite funny, actually, and what made it even funnier was that nobody in the crowd paid any attention. As soon as I saw that, I decided to fix her."

I was enthralled. "What did you do?"

Ralph smiled broadly. "I let her drag me up to a policeman. Then I demanded that he arrest her for assaulting an honored guest of the German Democratic Republic."

"My God," I said.

"She let go of me right away, I'll tell you that. Then I told the cop—in English, of course—that my friends and I were driving straight to the police station to swear out a complaint, or whatever you have to do. And I asked him for his name and badge number.''

"Did you really?''

"I did. He was getting madder and madder, because obviously he didn't want to get involved. So he turned on Fornova and started to give her a very hard time. You know: 'Citizeness, are you not aware that it is a crime to assault someone?' Citizeness! Like something out of *A Tale of Two Cities*. I could see that in about another second Fornova was going to take that poor cop apart. So while they were arguing, I just left.''

Ralph slipped out of the *Platz* and found the others loading up the red van. "Poor Norbert. He was very upset. He was afraid *you* were going to get hurt and *he* was going to be in the soup, you know, for not looking after you.'' While Jackie and the others were calming him, the driver maneuvered the van, through streets suddenly rather crowded with official traffic, to the police station.

"What then?'' I asked.

"The Fornova was there already,'' Ralph said. "When we walked in the door she started in all over again, haranguing the CIA-financed lackeys of the subhuman American superstate, that sort of thing. For a while, I was little nervous.''

"We were terrified,'' Jackie said.

"Yeah,'' said David. "Yell at cops long enough and they start to want to fight back.''

"Anyway,'' Ralph went on, "just then, in walked Kranz. He went straight up to Jackie and said in English, 'My dear young lady, what on earth are you doing here?' Fornova began yelling about our being God knows what. But Kranz must have heard something from the Russians, because he said about three words in Russian to her and she shut up like a clam.''

Shortly after, Fornova and Kranz left together, and for the rest of the afternoon the four of them simply sat on the hard wooden benches of the police station. "Just like doing detention in high school,'' David said. The police made them give their names, addresses, and passport numbers. But they were clearly waiting for orders, and there was no further interrogation.

"They fed us,'' Jackie said. "Sausages and beer and delicious dried apricots. I think they felt sorry for us.'' It was raining and getting dark outside when they finally heard the clatter of a helicopter. Two of the policemen helped transfer the luggage and instruments from the van to the helicopter and they took off for Prague. "The last I saw, Norbert and the driver were just getting into the van. I think they were allowed to leave, too."

For a few moments, we all sat together, saying and doing nothing. Then, Jackie sniffed loudly. "I think I'm catching a cold," she said. "That damn drafty police station." We laughed.

"*Please* forgive me for being so mercenary," Ralph said, "but I'm *dying* to know . . . What about our little arrangement?"

"Hey, that's right," said Terry. "What about the dough?"

"We get half," I said.

"Shit," said Terry.

"No, actually that's not so bad," Ralph said. "It's really more than the contract calls for."

"That's right," I said.

"So we each get ten grand?" David asked.

"Plus the twenty-five hundred for the concerts, don't forget, plus all expenses, plus a great adventure," I said. "Better than Disney World."

"Alan, what about the rest of the tour?" Jackie asked. "What about the Shropshire Festival?"

"Good God," I said, and stopped. The question caught me completely by surprise. "I don't know. I haven't given it a thought." They all looked at me. "Well, I haven't. And I'm not going to, until later."

"No, you're quite right," Ralph said obligingly. "I don't know about the rest of you, but I'm *exhausted*. I'm going straight up to my room for a nap. We can decide all these things another time. At dinner." He got to his feet. "It's been lovely." A few minutes later, everybody else called it a morning.

"Alan." Jackie followed me straight to my room. "Lock the door."

I turned to her and saw in her face the tension she'd been controlling downstairs. And I saw something else as well, something that made my heart skip another beat or two. Then she was in my arms. For a moment, I held her at a distance so I could look at her. "No more maidenly bashfulness?" I asked.

"No more," she said gravely. I was the first one into the bed. As she stood naked to display herself to me, I remember being amazed at how small she was, how delicately fashioned. She made love as she made music, withholding nothing, giving everything, utterly unafraid.

Afterward, lying at peace in the curve of my arm, she asked: "What was he like, Alan?" I kissed her and tried to put off the question, but she wanted to talk. What the hell, I thought, maybe it will do us both good.

"I don't know," I said. "I've been asking myself the same thing. Was he a great man or a great rat? And I just don't know. His ego was huge, that I can tell you. But then, his *talent* was huge. I wish I *had* known him."

For a long time, Jackie was silent. I thought she might have fallen asleep. But then she said softly, "It was a game."

"What was, darling?"

"We were playing a game," Jackie said. "For money and for the adventure. The kicks. We were going to get Kobrand out and he was going to be a hero and we would be heroes, too. And he's dead. He was so great, and maybe he was rotten, and now he's . . . nothing."

"And so?"

She heaved a deep sigh. "I don't know, either." Then, suddenly, she propped herself up on one elbow to look down at me. "But there I was, sitting in that awful airport in Prague and thinking how horrible it was that Kobrand was dead and how it could have been *you*. Listen." She grabbed a handful of my hair and gave it a fierce yank. "No more of that cops-and-robbers stuff, you understand?"

"Ow," I said. "No, okay. Strictly Super Mouse from now on, that's me." Jackie laughed, and for a while there was no more talk.

"You are definitely not Super Mouse," she said eventually.

"Your endorsement is welcome," I said. Then:

"Alan?"

"What?"

"You like being James Bond-ish, don't you?"

"Curse you for being so perceptive. Part of me does, I must admit. But part of me very definitely does not. I'm a great one for firesides and snug armchairs while the storm rages outside." Like now, for instance. It was delicious to lie there in the shaded room with Jackie by my side and the noise of the afternoon and the death and destruction in the outside world far, far away.

"I'm glad," she said. "Because you're too good at it. The planning, the scheming, the excitement. It's like our rehearsals. When I had to undo my dress and get out there with that slimy Kranz, do you know what you were doing?''

"Trying to see down your dress," I said.

"No. You were *smiling*, the way you always do at the start of a concert."

"Pure nerves," I said.

"Like fish! You were *enjoying* yourself."

"If I was," I said, "I learned my lesson."

"I hope so. Maybe it's fun for you, playing James Bond. But not for me. I'm just plain ordinary Jackie Craine, and I like my sheltered life. And my music."

"Well, plain ordinary Jackie Craine, maybe that's the real adventure," I said, and we left it at that.

Much later, we got up, and lo and behold! It was dinnertime. We'd forgotten all about lunch. If the others wondered why we fell on our food like hungry savages, who cared? After dessert, there was a pause in the conversation. David put down his coffee cup. ''Alan, what about this Shropshire Festival?''

"I think we should cancel," I said.

"Why?" asked Terry.

"I don't know," I told him. I didn't know. "I just don't feel like going on to England and playing another gig. I guess I'm too tired."

Terry and David exchanged glances.

"We figured you might be feeling that way," David said. "We've been thinking, me and Terry. Maybe we could do the Shropshire thing without you. I've never been to England, and it's pretty good bread."

"What about you, Ralph," I asked.

"Well, if we're finished here, and very frankly I hope to Heaven I never *see* this place again, I was thinking of Paris. But I *could* go on from there and meet you all in England."

"Jackie?"

"Not me," she said firmly.

"Aw," Terry began, disappointed. I looked at Terry, David, and Ralph. Young, talented, and hungry, all three of them; and all three of them, after everything that had happened, ready to hop on a jet and go where the music was. I envied them.

"Listen," I said, "why don't the three of you go? It's a good idea. Bill yourselves as the Antiqua Trio. Do a split program, the first half dances, the second half trio sonatas."

"We could try the Bach lute and harpsichord sonatas," David said.

"We could *try* them," Ralph said, "but we'll never get them in time for Shropshire." The three of them started arguing about which music to rehearse. Jackie and I looked at each other.

"You guys work it out," I said. "Jackie and I have a couple of errands to run."

"Don't do anything I wouldn't do," Terry called after us as we left the restaurant. But he was a little late with his advice.

We strolled outside. After yesterday's rain, the weather had turned warmer. We could sit on a bench overlooking the lake without contracting frostbite. Somewhere, a nightingale was tuning up for his evening concert.

"What about us?" I asked.

Jackie eyed me anxiously. "You won't be mad?"

"About what?"

"Wunschler has asked me to stay on," Jackie said. "To give some master classes with him at the Music School."

"Oh," I said.

"You *are* mad."

"A little," I admitted. "I've got to go back to New York, don't forget, or our friend Carroll will be stir-frying me very slowly for his breakfast. I was sort of hoping you'd come along."

"It's only for a month. And then I'll be back, too."

"I'm not feeling too good about this."

"Darling, do you want me to say no?"

In spite of myself, I was charmed. "That's the first time you've ever called me that."

"Darling . . . darling Alan."

"Of course I want you to say no," I grumbled. "But you musn't." Ralph, Terry, and David, I was thinking, aren't the only ones who live for their music. Jackie certainly does. And whether I like it or not, I do, too.

Back at the hotel, I booked two seats, first class, on the ten A.M. Swissair flight to New York. Then, we went back up to my room.

"Feel *very* guilty," I commanded.

"I'll do my best," Jackie said.

The International Plaza's bus took me to the airport. I kept the gun in my pocket, but nobody even glanced in my direction. Just before flight time, I ducked into a quiet corner and tucked the pistol back inside

Kobrand's cello case. They opened the case, of course, at the security checkpoint, but they didn't look too hard at the interior. Maybe Carroll had had a word with the Swiss; I don't know. But they let me through, gun and all. I gave the cello the window seat.

> [The accompanist] need feel no anxiety over
> his being forgotten. . . . No! An understand-
> ing listener does not easily miss anything.
>
> K.P.E. BACH, p. 368.

CHAPTER TWENTY-FOUR

FOR THREE MORNINGS, Itzaak Kobrand's death made *The New York Times*. There was a front-page story on Kobrand himself and on his musical career. Hedrick Smith wrote a special article on "Kobrand, Apostle of Dissent." There was even a brief editorial on "the tragic event and its root causes, the oppressiveness of all totalitarianism everywhere." No mention was made of Hugo Flachsmann, the CIA, the KGB, the Soviet Ministry of Culture, Colonel Jerzy, or the Antiqua Players.

For the first time in ten years, the mangy gingko by the front entrance of my building is in bloom. I've seen a lot of the gingko, on my way out with armload after armload of junk. Springtime, remember, is cleanup time.

"Hey, man, whaddaya doin'? Gettin' the place ready for your old lady?" Apollo, you are so right. Like the little birds, I'm tidying up my nest.

This season, fiddlers seem to be in demand, so I've been practicing hard on the violin. For one friend of mine who wanted to get away to Fire Island, I did a three-night stand-in at a Broadway theater. Then, there's a Catholic church in the neighborhood that sponsors, of all things, a string quartet. Two nights before the season's last recital, the second violinist sprained his wrist playing paddle tennis. He gave me a call and I subbed for him, too.

Already, a rich coating of New York City grime has covered the case of Kobrand's cello where it leans against the studio wall. The pistol has gone into a bureau drawer, along with my passport, my International Driver's License, and the sheaf of letters and contracts from the Philomel Foundation. The ten thousand dollars—plus the twenty-five hundred for *playing*—has gone into my bank account. There it will stay until the next phone bill arrives. Then it will undoubtedly vanish, like fairy gifts fading away.

"We've got to do something about these phone calls," I said to Jackie on the eleventh night after I got back. But we never did.